DOLPHINS' WORLD

Danny DiVinci's Life on Sea

BY

SAM MELNER

Van Cortlandt
Press

Eugene, Oregon

Printed in Victoria, Canada

Cover art by Burt Von Roy
Book design by Lyle Mayer

National Library of Canada Cataloguing in Publication

```
Melner, Samuel
 Dolphins' world : Danny DiVinci's life on sea / Sam
Melner.
 ISBN 1-55369-553-4
 I. Title.
 PS3613.E45D64 2002        813'.6        C2002-902154-5
```

Published by:

Van Cortlandt Press
P.O. Box 2324
Eugene, OR 97402
USA

in association with:

TRAFFORD

This book was published *on-demand* in cooperation with Trafford Publishing.
On-demand publishing is a unique process and service of making a book available for retail sale to the public taking advantage of on-demand manufacturing and Internet marketing.
On-demand publishing includes promotions, retail sales, manufacturing, order fulfilment, accounting and collecting royalties on behalf of the author.

Suite 6E, 2333 Government St., Victoria, B.C. V8T 4P4, CANADA
Phone   250-383-6864   Toll-free   1-888-232-4444 (Canada & US)
Fax   250-383-6804   E-mail   sales@trafford.com
Web site   www.trafford.com   TRAFFORD PUBLISHING IS A DIVISION OF TRAFFORD HOLDINGS LTD.
Trafford Catalogue #02-0366   www.trafford.com/robots/02-0366.html

10   9   8   7   6   5   4   3   2

With much love to
Marjorie, Peter, and Rick
and to
Grenada, where the seed was planted
Chocolate Decadence, where it sprouted
and
Videra, where it came to fruition.

PROLOGUE

There I was, Daniel David DiVinci, known professionally to my small but devoted audiences as Danny DiVinci. Still trying to make it as a 39-year old stand-up comedian.

Maybe I should have listened to my Italian father and Jewish mother, finished college and become a doctor or lawyer, who in his free time cooked great food without recipes while singing Puccini arias or Bei Mir Bist du Schoen.

Was I unhappy? You bet.

Was I depressed? Damn right.

Olga had just jilted me for the twenty-three year old lead singer of a barely known Bay Area rock group called Whiplash and The Lawyers. He was 16 years younger than yours truly, and Olga was four years older than that unread, unwashed ring-in-the-nose, ear and who knows where else long haired no-talent with the diaper-rash voice.

They had first met on Valentine's Day evening. I was doing a gig at a singles bar in San Jose and he was on the program after me. Olga had come down from Berkeley where she worked in a book-store near the Cal campus. We exchanged Valentine's gifts back-stage just before I went on.

Because of our mutual interest in science fiction in general and the old Star Trek TV shows in particular, I had bought her a cus-tom made bracelet with a gold replica of the Starship Enterprise. On it I had had inscribed, "Because we boldly go where no couple has gone before."

She laughed when I gave it to her, gave me a big hug and kiss, and passed it around to show.

When it got to Whiplash, or "Lash" as he liked to be called (I never did find out his real name; nor did I care), he read the inscription aloud, roared "cool", gave Olga a long penetrating stare and what I assume was meant to be a sexy smile.

I ignored his reaction and opened Olga's gift to me. It was a handsome wood framed certificate from the Intergalactic Starmapping Society informing me that I was now a member and that a star had been named after me. It gave the exact location in astronomical terms, informed me that it would be listed in the next edition of the Intergalactic Encyclopedia and shown on the starmap of that sector of the Universe as "Star DiVinci".

At the bottom of the certificate in old English style gold letters was the sentence "You Now Have Your Place In The Universe", followed by the single word, "Congratulations". I had heard their commercials on the radio and seen them on television, thought they were humorous, and almost got Olga the same gift.

I smiled and passed it around for everyone to see. When it got to Lash he again said, "cool", looked longingly at Olga and said "Double cool, you are really something!"

"Cool down, pal", I said. "You're too young for her."

"Yeah", he answered, "and you're too old."

I guess he was right. That was the beginning of the end of my relationship with Olga…and a reason for my depression.

The second reason was that I was out of work without a booking in sight. My agent had suddenly quit show business to become a Talmudic Catholic Priest. I guess that's what you would call a priest with an overwhelming interest in the intricacies of the Hebrew Talmud that almost made him decide to become a rabbi instead of a priest. "God is the same," he said. "I just can't give up Jesus or my devoutly Catholic mother."

But worst of all… I bombed at my last gig, and the one before that, and the one before that. I could no longer make people laugh. My brand of humor was now obsolete —making jokes about the day's events with a newspaper as my only prop. September 11th took care of that.

Would I have to train myself for a whole new approach to comedy? Would I have to go out into the real world and get a real job? Was life still worth living for me?

If you recall, Sam, you were so upset by my depressed state that you took off work in the middle of the week and insisted we go sailing. I thought it was just the therapy I needed.

We left San Francisco in your 35-foot sailboat on that bright sunny May morning in an ideal 20-knot southeast wind that filled our sails beautifully, and sent us briskly under the Golden Gate Bridge out to sea.

You had checked the weather forecast before we left; it was almost perfect except for a storm front about 75 miles north that was moving away from where we were headed. But because you are a very safety-minded sailor you kept the radio tuned to the weather channel all the time. At about noon the station reported that the wind had unexpectedly shifted direction and that the storm was heading south toward us.

We immediately came about to try to make it back to San Francisco before it hit us. We had just sighted the Golden Gate Bridge when the squall smashed us with a combination of roaring winds, driving rain and huge nasty looking foam-topped waves.

Minutes before it arrived we had reefed the mainsail and released the jib halyard, which should have dropped that smaller forward sail to the deck in the bow. Much to our dismay it didn't.

A shackle had broken and tangled the sail about half way down so that it was still catching wind even though you had already started the motor and were trying to keep the bow pointed into the wind to avoid the jib catching a blast of wind from the side that could knock us over.

That didn't work though, because by that time the squall had already hit us and the high waves kept pushing the bow off the wind and causing the jib to fill. And every time that happened the boat heeled way over on its side.

This was a dangerous situation because if another wave were to hit us while we were heeled over it could easily knock us completely down on our side with the mast and sail in the water, and possibly turn us upside down. In that case we would be fish food. Since you were at the wheel and I was the crew it was obviously up to me to get the jib down.

I worked my way forward to the bow holding on to the lifelines and tried to pull the jib down. I got nowhere.

I tried climbing up the halyard to reach the point where the sail had tangled, but was unsuccessful.

My bulky lifejacket kept getting hung up on the lines that were whipping around me, so that almost all my movements were curtailed. I had to do something; so in a macho violation of boating safety rules I managed to wriggle out of it.

But I was still unable to climb the halyard. Then I got the bright idea that I like to think saved us — or at least saved you and your boat. I reached into my pocket, pulled out my trusty Swiss Army knife and began furiously slashing the sail. It worked. I made enough holes so that the wind passed through without filling the sail.

The boat immediately righted itself, and you were able to keep its nose pointed into the wind, so the motion was up and down from the front to the rear and the danger of capsizing was gone, as long as the waves didn't turn from merely huge to mountainous.

I completed shredding the sail with one hand holding on to the bow rail for balance to keep from going over, secured all the loose lines that had been flopping in the wind, crawled my way to the mast, and wrapped my arms around it.

Then I pulled myself up to a standing position facing the cockpit and smiled triumphantly at you. I was proud and very pleased with myself for the first time in many weeks.

You smiled back, gave me a thumbs up and motioned me to come back to the safety of the cockpit.

But I didn't want safety. I wanted exhilaration and the adrenalin high that went with it. That was a hell of a lot better than depression.

So I just stared back at him, duplicated his thumbs up, turned and crawled my way back to the bow. There I held on to each side of the bow rail and slowly stood up facing into the wind, the rain, and the waves.

For some ridiculous reason I thought about Whiplash and laughed aloud. Talk about "cool". Yeah, this was really cool. Double cool, triple cool, and so on.

It was also something I always liked to do on a boat long before the director of Titanic ever thought about it, and I did it with voluptuous women, too. But I had never done it facing such a high wind, driving rain and huge waves.

And the waves. Wow! I loved the sensation of riding those enormous sloping walls of water. As each wave crested it would carry the boat to the top and I would gaze down into the deep trough between it and the next one. It was almost hypnotic.

The boat would hesitate for a moment with its bow and me literally suspended in the air. Then whammo! A roller coaster plunge into the trough, a fast elevator in a tall building descending so swiftly that you feel you left your stomach behind. What a ride! Extraordinary!

We did this about a half dozen times. I guessed the waves from crest to bottom were at least thirty to forty feet. They say that waves run in sevens, with the seventh wave being the biggest.

I wasn't counting, but what most have been the seventh was so tall and the downward plunge into the trough so swift that it buried our bow and me in the bottom of the next wave. The wall of water hit me so fast and so hard that it tore my hands from what I thought was a secure grip on the rails and flung me back first against the mast, then the cabin, and into the churning water.

I must have hit my head on the cabin and bounced overboard because by the time I reached the water I was feeling woozy and ready to pass out. I tried to raise my arms to swim, but couldn't. The cold water failed to revive me and I felt myself losing consciousness. Then everything went black.

The next thing I knew I was floating peacefully in the air above the violent churning sea. I could see your boat with you at the wheel frantically searching for me, going up and down on the waves in ever widening circles, sometimes almost capsizing when a wave hit you broadside. While turning you threw everything that floated overboard — cushions, life jackets, rubber fenders, lines to trail in the water. Anything that I might be able to grab on to and that would keep me afloat.

But to no avail. I was nowhere in sight.

Then all of a sudden I saw my body come to the surface, my head hanging down in the water.

"There I am, Sam," I screamed silently. "Off to your left." You didn't hear me and continued your search.

Slowly my body drifted away from the boat until there was no way you could possibly see me. I resigned myself to what was really happening, or appeared to be happening.

I was dead, or nearly dead, and was having one of those out-of-body experiences I had read about.

"Wow!" I said to myself. "Maybe it's really true. What a way to go!"

Then all of a sudden I was in darkness, drifting through a long tunnel with a bright light at its end. As I got closer to the light I experienced a wonderful inner glow of peace and relaxation. There was an almost sensual tingling inside my body, and I had to force myself to stay alert and not give in to the exotic comfort. I was making mental notes for a possible future comedy routine, if I ever survived this.

Was this the final stage before actual death, or near death, or whatever? If so, I didn't want it to happen just yet. I was enjoying the high too much.

This little tussle between my brain and body continued until my drift reached the proverbial light at the end of the tunnel. I giggled to myself as I thought about the origin of the expression "light at the end of the tunnel."

Then all of a sudden I found myself in a standing position, standing on nothing. Ahead of me as if through a gauzy fog were two bright golden arches touching one another. I could hardly wait to see what would happen next.

This is, according to the accounts I had read, the time for my loved ones who had died to appear before me and urge me to go back to my shitty old life, assuming I wasn't completely dead.

But I didn't have any loved ones who had died. My mother, father, sister and brother were still alive, as were the cousins of my youth. I couldn't stand my dead aunts and uncles, and they certainly never loved me and vice versa, except maybe when I was a baby and unable to make individual decisions, other than to shit, piss, cry or throw up.

And my grandparents had all died before I was born. So what now? Groucho Marx maybe?

I peered through the golden arches. Why did they suddenly remind me of McDonald's? Had I arrived at the great McDonald's in the sky? Would I be able to eat as many Big Macs as I wanted without having to worry about saturated fat and cholesterol, not to mention putting on weight?

But I could see nothing, not even Ronald.

I waited, and waited, and waited. But even inner glows of peace and relaxation have their limits. I grew peacefully impatient.

"Hey out there," I whispered loudly in my best imitation of a mortician scolding his assistant and not wanting to disturb the dead. "Anybody home?"

After what seemed an eternity — no pun intended — there was the sound of a cough, as if someone were trying to get my attention.

Then there slowly emerged from one of the arches an intensely bright ball of white light, like the kind of energy mass seen in science fiction movies.

"Ahem," said a deep sonorous voice emanating from the ball of light. "It appears you lack for loved ones. Your dead aunts and uncles refuse to venture forth."

"Not a surprise," I said. "So what's next?"

There were a few moments of silence, another "ahem", and then another ball of light emerged from the other arch. I heard hushed whispers, and the whispers seemed to be arguing with one another.

This went on for what seemed like another eternity until the sources of the voices became visible. The balls of light faded away, revealing two robed but fuzzy figures.

They walked, or rather floated, to me and stopped. I could now see them clearly. They appeared to be two males, one obviously older than the other.

The older one had a large head of long white hair, a beard of almost the same hue and size, and was dressed in a long white flow-ing robe. He carried a stout walking staff and looked like Charlton Heston before he switched from a staff to guns.

The other was much younger and very thin. He had long dark hair and wore a tattered rough-hewn robe that barely covered his bony body. I could see a loincloth underneath.

Both of them had serious expressions on their faces, and a kind of "new age" spiritualism about them. Especially the younger one.

He spoke first. "Well, my son," he said. "It appears you lack for loved ones, dead ones anyway. Your dead aunts and uncles refuse to come forward."

I understand," I said. "Thank God."

"Thou shalt not take our father's name in vain," he said. He was obviously critical and irritated, but there was love in his voice.

"Sorry," I said. "I guess you guys aren't God."

"Heaven forbid," said the older one.

"Then I guess this isn't heaven either," I said.

"You should live so long," said the older one, and he laughed heartily.

"Not funny,'" said the younger one.

"That's your problem," said the older one. "Lighten up. You have no sense of humor. You take life too seriously."

"We're not talking about life," retorted the younger. "We are talking about death. And it is serious."

"Just trying to keep it light," said the older one. "This visitor is a comedian."

"Thank you," I said modestly. "I try. Did you hear the one about the farmers' daughter and the angel? One day —"

"Silence!" thundered the older one.

"But I was just trying to keep it light."

"That's not your job," said the younger.

"Correct," said the older. "If anyone is going to crack jokes around here, it will be us, or rather me."

"I don't think your jokes are very funny either," I said. "I've heard better."

"Silence," said the younger one. "You are supposed to be awed and thrilled being here."

"Consider me awed and thrilled then," I said. "Just who are you guys?"

"We are the Gatekeepers," said the older one. "And in your case the gate is closed. Locked. You're not dead. It's not your time yet, so you have to go back."

"I don't want to go back," I said. "My life sucks."

"Sucks?" said the younger one. "What does that mean?"

"It means it stinks," I said. "Lousy".

"Please speak English," said the older.

"Shitty," I answered.'

"Much better," he said. "I think we understand. You mean it's wasted, messy, and smells bad."

"Exactly."

"And you don't want to go back to that…uh…excremental situation," said the younger.

"Thou hast said it," I answered. "Not only do I not want to go, but I won't. I ain't going!"

"I'm afraid you have no choice," said the older. "We can send you anywhere we want. You simply have to go. It is not your time yet. You are still alive, and will be for many years to come."

I thought back to the life I was leading, the death of my performing life, the death of my love affair with Olga, the death of my enjoyment of life.

"I'm as good as dead," I muttered.

As a stand up comedian I was good at thinking on my feet, although I wasn't actually standing. So I pretended I was on stage being heckled by the audience for a joke about President Bush, thought quickly and came up with a response.

"Gatekeepers," I said loudly.

"Yes," they answered in unison.

"I have a plan, a cunning plan."

They raised their eyebrows in unison. "It will do you no good," said the older. "The only plans around here are made by us."

I ignored the comment. "Gentlemen, do you remember the exact position I — or rather my almost dead body — was in just before I began this…expedition to your gate?"

"No," said the younger. "No," agreed the older.

"Well," I continued, "I was lying face down in the water, apparently not quite dead. Do you remember now?"

"Yes," said the younger. The older nodded his head in agreement. "So what?" he said.

"Well here's so what," I continued.

"I don't doubt that you can send me back if you want to, but suppose when you do I refuse to turn over to breathe air. Suppose I just continue to lie there with my face in the water. As you probably know, we humans can't breathe water. I will surely die. Right?"

"We will make you turn over and breathe," said the younger.

I looked at them long and hard.

"You may have power here," I said. "Wherever here is, but I doubt you have power on Earth, or it wouldn't be the way it is. Right?"

They looked at one another.

"Don't bullshit me," I said. "It would be unworthy of your positions as gatekeepers."

A resigned look came upon their faces. "Right," said the younger, quietly in a downcast voice.

I looked at the older for confirmation. "You son of a —" I

interrupted him before he could finish what I was sure was blasphemy, considering where we were.

"Uh, uh," I said waving a finger. Since it's not my time yet, and I'm not going back, what are you going to do about it?"

The older one looked at me severely. "This has never happened before. You are disrupting the forces of nature."

"It's my job," I said modestly. "Frankly, I don't care what happens to me as long as I don't go back to my old life. What are my alternatives?"

They looked at each other. "Would you excuse us," said the younger, and they both turned. Suddenly the two balls of bright white light engulfed them and retracted back under the golden arches.

I floated there alone, smiling. "Hey," I called after them. "Bring me back a hamburger and French fries, would you please?"

I guess they didn't hear me because there was no acknowledgement. Just silence, and more silence, and more silence. I was beginning to get bored.

I tried to step back into the tunnel in order to get that high I had before, but I couldn't move. I just stood there — or rather floated, waiting.

Finally the light balls returned from the golden arches and the gatekeepers emerged from them, without the hamburger or even the fries.

The older one spoke first. "Well, Mr. DiVinci, we have a solution… ahem… assuming you are willing."

"I'm listening."

"As we informed you previously, we are the Gatekeepers."

"Yes."

"Of the Universe," said the younger.

"So," I said.

"That means, Mr. DiVinci," he continued, "that we can send you anywhere."

"So."

"Are you familiar with the Videra Galaxy?" said the older.

"No."

"Well, you should be," he said.

"Why?"

"Because," said the younger with a beatific smile, "that's where you are going."

"Assuming, of course, that you are willing to breathe," said the older.

"Now wait a minute. I don't —"

"You wait a minute," said the older, and he waved his arms with a flourish, like a magician about to pull a rabbit out of a hat. But instead of a rabbit, a scroll of what looked like rolled up paper or parchment appeared in his right hand.

Then another flourish with his left, and the scroll unfurled and hung motionlessly in the air, or ether, or whatever.

"Behold!" he said pointing to a sector slightly to the left of the middle. "The Videra Galaxy."

"Yes," I said, my adrenalin beginning to stir.

He looked me straight in the eyes, stroked his beard and smiled.

"Star DiVinci!" I shouted. "I'll go! It's my place in the universe. You could look it up in the Intergalactic Encyclopedia, if you have the new edition."

"Not quite your place," said the younger.

"What do you mean? That's my place in the universe. I said I would go. And I'll breathe, deep breaths and often. I'll go. I want to go."

"If we send you there," he continued, "you will burn to a crisp, quicker than even in Hades itself. Star DiVinci is a star, and a star is a sun, a giant ball of fire."

"You would be instant toast," said the older, grinning broadly. "However, we have a plan."

"Yes," I said. "I'm listening."

"There are planets orbiting Star DiVinci."

"Yes, yes."

"And one of them has an earthlike atmosphere."

"Yes, yes!"

"So technically it's still your place in the universe."

"Of course. I'm ready to go."

"Are you sure?" asked the younger.

"Send me, please, now."

"All right… Danny. But first we have to do something for you."

"Whatever you want. I'm ready."

And with that, the scroll disappeared and they both extended their right hands straight out. At that same moment a small silver disk about two inches across came floating down. They picked it out of the air together, each with a thumb and forefinger on one side, and drifted over directly in front of me. Then they placed it on my chest, and withdrew their hands.

The disk stuck to my skin for a moment, and I realized for the first time, that I was naked. I gazed at it and watched it slowly being absorbed into my body. I felt nothing.

When it was completely gone they stepped back and smiled benevolently.

"What was that?" I asked, feeling my chest, but feeling nothing.

"That," said the older, "is your Universal Translator."

"Wow!" I exclaimed. "Just like on Star Trek. Does this mean

that I'll be able to talk with the inhabitants on my planet — in perfect grammatical English, like on Star Trek?"

"As on Star Trek" said the younger. The more advanced ones anyway."

"Goodbye," I said. "Thanks for everything."

"Till we met again...."they said in unison, as I began to float away.

"Nice meeting you guys," I called as I receded further away from them, and they stepped back into their bright balls of light, and the balls receded into the Golden Arches.

"Say hello to Ronald for me," I called after them.

The Golden Arches shook as if they were shuddering, and disappeared.

Then everything went black.

CHAPTER 1

The next thing I knew I was in the water...again. Except it was not stormy; there were no waves, nor wind nor rain, and the water was warm. My body felt buoyant, so I tasted the water. It was salty. Unless this was my place in the Universe's equivalent of the Great Salt Lake I was in a tropical sea on a beautiful summer day.

"Thanks, Gatekeepers," I said to the blue sky and began leisurely swimming toward a little speck on the horizon I took to be land.

I was completely at ease with my new environment and looked forward to my new life, whatever it may bring.

I felt like a teenager again and began to frolic in the water, splashing around, alternating my strokes between the backstroke, the sidestroke, the breaststroke, and no stroke at all, just lying on my back and letting the sun shine on my smiling face. I was a happy man, a very happy man.

My happiness lasted all of about 10 minutes until I felt a hard bump against my right leg.

I looked down into the clear water and gasped in horror. Right below me was a huge gray fish that looked very much like a shark. I ducked my head under the water and opened my eyes. It was a shark.

I jerked my head back out of the water and after my eyes cleared looked around. There were fins cutting through the surface all around me, moving in slow circles. I tried to control myself, remembering all the television shows I had seen about how to behave in the water with sharks.

I ducked my head under the water again, opened my eyes and saw three or four more below the ones on the surface. They, too, were circling around me as if sizing me up for dinner.

I remembered that a good way to keep a shark from attacking was to hit him on the nose when he came close. So, with a great effort to control my fear I put up my fists like a prizefighter.

The biggest one stopped circling, swam right up to me, and looked me straight in the eye. He was about two feet away.

I drew back my right fist to punch him.

He opened his mouth and displayed row upon row of enormous teeth. He opened and closed it two more times with a noisy clattering of teeth on each closure.

By this time I was out of breath so I raised my head out of the water to breathe. By the time I finished my first breath, the shark's head was also out of the water right next to me. He opened his mouth wide and made a noise like a laugh.

At this point I lost all my composure and panicked.

"No!" I screamed. "I've only been here for a few minutes. This can't be happening to me. Help! This is my place in the Universe."

I closed my eyes and prepared to die… again. But this time for real, and horribly.

I waited. And waited. And waited. Nothing happened. Was I being spared?

I opened my eyes and looked around. Not a fin in sight. I dove down under the surface and opened my eyes to make sure they were gone. They were not. They were still circling around me.

Suddenly I heard a fuzzy voice. "What did he say?"

Another voice. "I think he said 'no', and 'help', and something else I couldn't understand."

"Impossible," said another. "We're the only ones who can speak our language. Let's eat him and get done with it. I've got dibs on the leg I bumped."

"I'll take an arm," said another.

Then the biggest one with the big teeth stopped circling, swam right in front of me and hovered there, his tail slowly swishing. He opened his huge mouth and I realized it was indeed the same one I had the experience with before.

"And I'll," he said, "take that little thing hanging down between his legs. Not very much to eat, but it looks tender and juicy. And I think I'll taste that little sac hanging behind it, too. Any objections?" He eyed my lower body lasciviously.

There was silence. By this time I was out of breath, so I raised my head into the air and took a deep breath. Again my comedian's ability to think quickly came to my aid. I realized several things: one, that I was still obviously naked; two that these creatures on this planet actually had language and could talk among themselves; and three, that with my Universal Translator I was able to understand them, and vice versa.

I overcame my fear and decided that coolness and calmness were what was needed. Perhaps if they were intelligent enough I could speak with them logically to see things my way. I ducked back down below the surface.

"Wait," I said, trying to keep the water out of my mouth and at the same time covering my penis and testicles with my hands. I smiled inwardly as I realized the uniqueness of this situation. Here I was, an intelligent civilized human being on a strange planet about to enter into an almost philosophical discussion, assuming they would listen, with a bunch of primitive small brained low-on-the-evolution-scale creatures that didn't even have backbones.

"Ladies and gentlemen," I said, "I'm not good to eat. Don't you know that humans taste terrible? Why do you think we almost always find the remains of victims of shark attacks? They are inevitably found with an arm or leg missing, or with chunks of flesh ripped out of them. Some of them even still alive.

"Don't you think, my friends, that if we tasted good you guys would eat the whole thing? Bad. Very bad. In addition to tasting terrible, humans give sharks indigestion, often with awful gas pains.

"It's a fact. You could look it up. Or ask my ichthyologist, if you don't believe me."

"What's an ichthyologist?" Big Teeth in front of me asked. He looked around at the others. "Anybody here know?" he said.

"What does he mean to 'look it up?" asked another shark.

"Let's not waste anymore time," said Big Teeth, looking back down at my groin. "I'm hungry."

"Wait," I screamed, coming down after going up for a quick breath, and feeling that I was losing my audience, not to mention my life. "An ichthyologist is a scientist who studies fish."

"What's a scientist? And what's a fish?" asked another.

"You're a fish," I blurted out. "You could look it up in any encyclopedia or biology book or in the archives of the New York Times. They print everything — even shit about asshole fishes like you!"

I had become irrational, and I had obviously lost them. There were snorts of "let's eat", and the sharks started circling rapidly — very rapidly around me.

I yanked my head out of the water. "Can't you guys read?" I shouted, "You ignorant savages. Help! Help!"

I had bombed again. This time in my own short-lived place in the universe. Final curtain. End of show. Good night, ladies and gentlemen. I really enjoyed my time with you. Yeah.

I waited, but nothing happened. I waited some more, and still nothing happened. Did I actually convince them that humans tasted bad to sharks? And how much like Earth sharks were these sharks? Could Earth's sharks talk, too? Or had these, because this was another planet, developed far in advance of Earth's, even though they didn't know what an ichthyologist was, let alone a fish?

And as far as encyclopedias and reading were concerned, well, what the hell? Why was I thinking those thoughts? Why was I thinking at all? Why was I still alive?

I looked around and with great relief saw that the fins were streaking away from me, as if in panic. I could hear fading voices calling to each other.

"Swim! Swim! Away! Away! The dolphins are coming! The dolphins are coming!"

"The dolphins?" I shouted. "Yeah, the dolphins are coming." So it's true. The old myths are true. Dolphins do save humans from sharks. I'm saved! I'm saved! Thank God I'm saved!

I thrust my body as high out of the water as I could and waved my arms wildly in the air.

"Here I am! Here I am!" I shouted gleefully.

In less than a minute I was surrounded by a group of smiling dolphin faces peering at me above the surface. I had heard that dolphins really didn't smile and that that facial expression was just a circumstance of anatomy. But they sure looked as if they were smiling.

I know I was.

"Well, well, what have we here?" said one of the dolphins, and I'd swear his smile got bigger. So dolphins could talk, too. I was delighted and thought of all the people on Earth who would have loved to talk with dolphins.

Just as I was completing that thought, and before I had a chance to reply, another voice said:

"Looks good enough to eat, although it's kind of pale and

doesn't look much like a fish."

"Wait!" I yelled.

"I'm not a fish and I'm not good to eat… and besides, dolphins don't eat humans. They befriend them, and love them, that's why you chased the sharks away."

The smiles on their faces vanished, and they looked at one another quizzically. I was immediately struck by two thoughts: one that the dolphins really didn't have smiley faces, at least here, and that two, they understood my language. Now all I had to do was convince them I wasn't a fish, or anything else they might like to eat.

"I am not a fish. Do I look like a fish?" I raised my arms in the air and waved them around. "See, I have arms. Does a fish have arms?"

I lay back and raised my legs out of the water and kicked my feet. "See legs and feet. Do fish have legs and feet?"

The one who had first spoken, and who appeared to be the leader came closer and peered into my face. And then I saw an astonishing thing. What I thought was a flipper extended out to touch my face, and I realized it was an arm, with a hand and five fingers at its end.

I looked to his other side to see if that flipper was also an arm. I didn't have to look closely because he held it up in the air. It's hand held about a five-foot spear with a needle-like point on the end. He inclined it slightly toward me in a semi-threatening position.

"So," he said, "you speak, and in our language, too. I never heard of a talking fish. Apparently you are not a fish."

"Of course not," I replied.

Before I had a chance to say any more he pulled his head away from my face, dropped his spear arm into the water and then his whole body back down a few feet. I looked down into the clear water and could see that he was observing my body. Realizing that I was naked I reflexively put my hands over my genitals. He pulled them away, stared at them briefly and came quickly back up to the surface.

At that moment I realized that dolphins could also laugh, because that is what he was doing. "Hey, everybody," he said, "go down and take a look at what I found, or almost didn't find."

They all sank down below the surface and I could see them staring at my genitals as the leader pointed to them. I figured there was no point in trying to cover them, so I just stayed in place treading water, while all the while knowing that on Earth when I went swimming my penis shrank considerably.

They all came back up smiling.

"Well," said the leader, "it looks like we've found ourselves a new species of mammal, and a pretty puny one at that."

"It gets bigger than that," I said defensively, "under the right circumstances."

"I should hope so," sniggered another dolphin in a high voice, which I took to be female.

There were laughs all around, and then the leader turned to the others and said, "I think we should terminate this patrol. Let's take this specimen home and see what we can learn about him. I guess it's a him. And Soria," he said to the dolphin with the high voice, "if you can take your eyes off his tinky, you and Ibi each take an arm and bring him along. I doubt if he can keep up with us without a tail."

They did as they were told and began swimming rapidly toward the speck of land I had seen earlier. So rapidly that my head went below the surface and I couldn't breathe anything but water.

I struggled to get my head out of the water and yelled, "I'm not a dolphin. I can't stay under water very long. I have to breathe."

They realized the situation immediately and waited while I regained my normal breathing.

"Thanks," I muttered. "I guess you don't know much about us humans, and our limitations."

Soria looked at me curiously. "What do you mean 'us humans'? You are certainly not one of us. I don't know what you are, but you are not human. You have no tail."

Ibi chimed in. "Unless it's as small as your tinky, and we can't see it," he laughed.

"Well I admit I'm not equipped for life in the sea. No, I don't have a tail and am certainly not a good swimmer compared to you folks. All I have are arms and hands and fingers, and legs and feet. These feet also are made for walking, on land."

"What do you think these are?" said Soria, raising her lower body out of the water and kicking her feet in the air. "These feet also are made for walking on land."

She dropped her legs down into the water. Her eyes drifted below the surface in the direction of my penis. "And that little tinky," she said, "does it always hang out like that instead of retracting into your body when it's not in use, like the males of our human species." She said these last few words with a trace of sarcasm in her voice.

"Yes," I said. "Always, but it does really get bigger, a lot bigger."

"Then you better be careful. Big or small it looks like prime fish bait. We've got fish in these waters that would love to grab on to that thing, and I don't mean for sex."

My hand immediately darted down to cover it.

"Don't worry," laughed Ibi. "We'll protect you. Let's get going again."

Both he and Soria grasped my arms and swam swiftly to catch up with the rest of the group — they with their heads just below the surface and me on my stomach sort of surfing with my head above the water, my "tinky" underwater, no doubt hanging down, I thought nervously, enticing every carnivorous fish for miles around.

CHAPTER 2

We slowed down when we reached the rest of the group, and the pace was leisurely towards that speck of land, which had now taken on the shape of an island amidst a vast sea. So my new home was going to be an island. I always had "a thing" about islands, often thinking of escaping to the Caribbean or South Seas to live on one.

By the time we were close enough for me to make out the physical features of the island the sun was beginning to set, but it was still light enough to get somewhat of a good look.

It was green and hilly, that much I could see. And there was a narrow opening to a harbor or bay that we were approaching. Then I saw that the opening was closed off with a gate that extended about 10 feet up in the air and down to what I assumed was the bottom of the water. There was a tower on the point at each end.

We stopped just outside the gate, and our leader waved to the dolphins on a tower with his spear. They waved back and the gate started sliding open from each side.

My two escorts let go of me and Ibi spoke. "Can you stay up without our support?" he asked with concern.

"Of course," I answered. "What did you guys think I was doing before you got there?" I thought for a moment. "I'm sorry, I shouldn't have answered like that. I am grateful you dolphins saved my life. But really, I do know how to swim, tail or no tail. What's going to happen now?"

"The tower guards are opening the gate, as you can see, to let us into the harbor," Ibi said.

"But why do you need a gate to close off the harbor?"

"To keep out the sharks," Soria answered.

"But I thought sharks were afraid of dolphins."

"Only when we have these," Ibi said, raising his spear in the air. "See that point on the end? It's tipped with a poison. We never venture out into the sea without our spears. That's why they are afraid of us."

"I see."

"See, but don't touch," said Soria with a smile, as the gate opened wide enough for us to go through. "Now" she continued, "your external tinky is about to become safe. At least from fish, but watch out for the crabs."

"She's just kidding," said Ibi, "the crabs are on the bottom, and I seriously doubt that it will get close enough to them, unless you want to dive down there for a look."

I was glad to see that these dolphins had a sense of humor; at least I hoped that they were joking.

As the gate opened wider it revealed a lovely sight that set my heart fluttering. It looked just like I expected my island escape paradise should.

The harbor was almost a complete circle, about a half mile across, with picturesque colorful houses and small buildings all around the water's edge. The land was flat for a short distance then began sloping up gradually toward low-lying hills that were a lush shade of tropical green.

My escorts took hold of my arms again and began swimming toward a building larger than the others at about the midpoint of the circle. My escorts were all smiles as we headed for it.

"You guys seem pretty happy now," I said. "Glad to be almost home?"

"Yes, of course," answered Ibi, " but its more than that. We're glad to be out of the range of the sharks, and not to have to be on guard all the time."

"But you said they were afraid of you when you have your spears."

"Yes, but they have been known to try to sneak up behind us. Especially if they divert us to look in one direction. Sometimes they can be pretty smart."

"I don't doubt that," I said, not at all. You know where I come from sharks are afraid of dolphins without spears. In fact our dolphins don't have spears."

"I don't know where you come from," said Soria, "but it's obviously far from here. I'll bet you don't have the kind of sharks we have around here either. Our sharks are big, ferocious, intelligent, and numerous. We can't even go out into the sea in our boats without an armed escort. They'll attack an unguarded boat, turn it over, and gobble up the poor people in it."

"Are you safe anywhere outside this harbor?"

"Fortunately, our coastline has numerous coral reefs just a few yards off shore. We post armed patrols at each opening in the reefs while the boats are crossing them, so it's safe to travel inside them."

This aspect of my place in the universe didn't sound like much fun. I was afraid of sharks long before I ever got here, and this afternoon's experience didn't help. But I was learning things already, and I hadn't even reached land yet.

"Are the spears the only weapons you have?" I asked.

"Yes, and knives of course, but they're not very useful against sharks. The poison tipped spears are what do the job."

"Where do you get the poison from?" I asked.

He looked at me as if wondering whether or not to disclose the information. "I guess there's no harm in telling you," he said. "It's distilled from especially poisonous sea urchins that grow on the windward side of Sea."

"Sea?" I said. "So this really is an island, and are you saying it's name is Sea?"

"Of course," he answered with a quizzical look on his dolphin face. Dolphins here certainly have expressive faces, I thought.

We were interrupted by the leader, who grabbed my arm while pushing Ibi aside.

"That will be enough conversation for now," he said gruffly. "Sea is the name of our world."

"World?" I thought this was an island.

"Enough for now. The council will decide your fate."

"Fate? Does that mean I'm in danger of not being allowed to stay here? Or in danger, period?"

He ignored my question and looked up at the darkening sky and said, "it's too late for them to see you today, so it will have to wait till morning."

"I don't mind. Do you have a good hotel here where I can spend the night?" I hoped that the council would pay for my room? "Or even a Motel Six? I'm not choosey."

He frowned at me and said, "Did anyone ever tell you that you talk too much? So please be quiet. You are going to be detained. You are not a guest here, or at least until the council says you are… if they do."

"I won't say another word." I said. And I didn't.

We swam the remaining short distance to shore in silence. When we reached there I saw that the quay was on two levels, the first just a little above the water line, and the other about five feet above that with the ladders all along the quay leading to the upper level.

There were small canoe-like boats moored along the lower level. The upper one, which appeared to be street level, was lined with dolphins peering down at us curiously.

The leader motioned for me to climb up the closest ladder, which I did, followed by the rest of the patrol.

After we emerged, the dolphins on the upper level began staring at me with broad smiles on their faces. Soria tapped me on the shoulder and said, "You had better cover up your fish bait."

I did that. The spectator smiles faded away and were replaced by inquisitive and perplexed expressions.

"Why are they still staring at me?" I asked Soria.

Now she looked at me inquisitively. "Has it occurred to you," she said not unkindly, "that you don't look like us, and that they have never seen anyone or anything like you before?"

Of course she was right. By now I was so used to looking at dolphin faces and bodies that it didn't register how different I was, what with a different face and color and even though we all had arms and legs, I definitely did not have a tail. I looked back up at them and smiled broadly with as much self-confidence as I could muster.

"Wait here," said the leader as he climbed up the steps to the second level and walked to the largest building, opened the door and stepped inside. One of the other patrol members accompanied him but waited outside the door.

I noticed that even though the dolphins had legs and feet they did not walk as steadily as humans. It almost seemed that they waddled, although they were sure footed enough.

"What building is that?" I asked Ibi and Soria, who were now holding me securely by the arms again.

"The Administrative Council Building," answered Ibi, "and please, you are not supposed to ask any more questions."

"I'll be a good boy," I said, peering at the building. It seemed to be made of pinkish coral blocks with openings cut into them.

The openings appeared to be windows made of glass or something similar, judging by the light passing through them from the inside as well as some of the reflections. The door seemed to be also made of coral, but of a brownish rather than pink color.

The patrol leader returned in a few minutes. "It looks like we will definitely have to hold you in detention until the morning, even though you do look harmless," he said apologetically.

"No problem," I said. "What is it gong to be like?"

"Well, I wouldn't call it luxurious, but it's the only kind of detention room we have, at least in this part of Sea. It does have a bed and sanitary facilities."

"So does a prison cell?"

"What's a prison cell?"

"Never mind, I'm ready," I said, and mentally rehearsed the karate moves I had learned in a class I had once taken in order to be able to deal with a drunken rowdy or belligerent hecklers. I was prepared to be thrown into a cell with hardened criminals. It turned out I needn't have worried.

I was led up the steps and over to the big building where Soria and Ibi turned me over to two other bigger dolphins with unsmiling tough expressions on their faces. I waved to my former escorts and said, "Thanks for your help."

They smiled at me waved their arms and then pointed the palms of their hands straight out. I had no idea what that meant and made a mental note to find out in the future, assuming I had a future.

My guards opened the door and led me through a hallway, down a set of stairs —was I on my way to a dungeon? — and through another hallway lighted by what appeared to be candles in holders attached to the wall. We came to a door where one of the guards pulled the long narrow piece of stone, which served as an outside bar and latch, opened the door, and motioned me into the room.

Then without even saying goodbye or smiling, they closed the door behind me. I heard them re-latch it.

I looked around the room. It was small, about 12 feet square, and relatively pleasant looking with the basic amenities the patrol leader had informed me about. It had no windows, but was lit by several candles set in clamshells on a table in the middle of the floor.

There were also two beds, one on each side of the room. One, presumably mine, was empty. The other contained a dolphin laying on his side staring at me incredulously.

"Hi," I said, "I'm Danny."

"Is that what kind of animal you are, or is that your name?"

"It's my name. What's yours?"

He stared at me. "Where's your tail? Is this a test? Are you disguised as an alien creature of some sort to try to scare me into submission to your murderous inhuman ways? Well, you can't, and I won't. I am what I am, and I'm right. And I am not a same-sex, so you can retract your tinky.

"You can do whatever you want to me and I won't change. And neither will others like me. So forget it."

"Forget what? I don't have the slightest idea what you're talking about. And I can't retract my tinky because it is un-retractable."

He sat up on his bed and I noticed that one of his arms was in a sling. "It looks like you're hurt," I said.

He glared down at the sling and patted it. "I like to think of it as a medal," he said. "The arm is hurt, but it was in the line of duty. I'm proud of it, even though it did cause me to get caught."

"Wait. Stop, please. Explain why you are here. Would you please start from the beginning. I'm new around here. And I'm certainly not disguised as an alien. I am an alien."

"From where?"

"From a planet called Earth."

"Never heard of it."

"I doubt if anybody here has. And since we're roommates, so to speak, I'd like us to be friends. Okay?"

"Do you eat fish?"

"What does that have to do with anything?"

"I'm a member of FROS, an active one. In fact, I'm the vice-councilor of our chapter."

"What does FROS mean?"

"You don't know?"

"I told you I was an alien."

He looked at me suspiciously. "Are you sure?"

"Absolutely."

"Then we have done a lousy job of publicizing our cause."

"Not necessarily. I've just arrived here. What does FROS mean?"

"It means Fish Rights Of Sea."

"What does FROS do?"

"We protect the rights of fish, or at least try to."

"And what rights are those?"

"Primarily, of course, the right not to be eaten. Dolphins should not murder fish just so they can eat them. There's plenty of nutritious food in the sea and on Sea for us to eat."

"In the sea there are all kinds of seaweed, kelp, tidal grasses and moss. And on Sea grass, vines, fruits and bushes, a veritable cornucopia of wonderful nutritious foods. So why should we have to kill other living things. Fish can think, too, you know, and feel pain, and they have feelings. Why do you think they struggle when hooked or caught, and why do you think they swim away when somebody or something is after them?"

"I see. And is your membership in FROS the reason you are here in detention?"

I hoped he would answer in the negative because I did not like the idea of my place in the universe being a repressive society.

"No, of course not," he answered much to my relief. "I'm here because I was caught opening the gate of the Northwest Fish Farm to let the fish escape out into the sea. We released thousands of fish before I was caught," he said proudly.

"And how did you hurt your arm?" Were you run over by the fish?"

"Of course not. They were very careful to avoid me, detouring around me and my companions. My arm got caught in the gate as we were closing it when our lookouts reported that the Fish Police were on their way.

"I pulled and jerked to free it, and I guess I severely sprained it. I had just barely managed to get it loose and start swimming away after my fellow FROSs when the Fish Police grabbed me. I just wasn't able to swim fast enough because of my arm to escape."

"Were they rough with you?"

"No, of course not. We are a non-violent people. That's why I don't understand why dolphins have to kill living things to eat. Why can't we treat other animals as we treat ourselves?"

"Maybe it's because Dolphins have been eating fish for probably millions of years to survive. Fish are full of protein and fats."

"And so are some plants; we have found that out in the last twenty years."

Before I had a chance to mention how difficult it was to change cultural habits and practices after thousands and millions of years there was a knock on the door.

"Come in," my FROS roomy said. And I realized I still didn't know his name.

I could hear the outside latch being raised. The door swung open and a guard came in holding two trays of food. He looked at me and said, "Sorry that we have to give you the same food as Tali. I'm sure you will enjoy it." He put the trays on the table.

He paused, gave me a smirk and a wink and continued, pointing at the table, "May I present... the culinary delights of FROSs everywhere... seaweed soup and that gustatory delight: kelp cutlets smothered in sea urchin sauce. And for desert... moss mousse. Enjoy, gentlemen."

He smiled at me again, turned, went out through the door and latched it behind him.

"All right!" Tali exclaimed. "Let's dig in." He picked up a spoon from his tray, scooped out a thick spoonful from the soup bowl and slurped it into his mouth. "Umm, good," he said.

"Just like your grandma used to make? So your name is Tali. Was that your grandfather's name, and is that a FROS nom de guerre?" I was stalling for time.

"I don't know what nom de guerre means, but this sure is good. Dig in."

I gently dipped my spoon into the soup and sipped. It was awful, very fishy; but I did my best to hide my feeling, lest I offend him. I didn't want to make an enemy my first day in my place in the universe.

"Very good," I lied. "But I'm not too hungry. I think I'll go directly to the kelp cutlet. It looks delicious."

Actually it did look very good, but I had learned that even on my ex-planet looks can be deceiving. It, too, was terrible tasting, although not quite as bad as the soup. It had more salt in it, which slightly covered up its fishy taste. Nevertheless, I managed to eat about two thirds of it before setting my fork down, and almost throwing up, as much as I would have liked to.

"Did you like that?" asked Tali.

"What's not to like? I can't recall ever having eaten anything quite like it."

He smiled broadly. "See, you don't have to sacrifice flavor to be FROS."

"It was hardly a sacrifice. Flavor is a thing that should never be sacrificed. And this food certainly has a sacrificial flavor."

"Uh… I'm not quite sure what you mean by that, but I'll take it as an agreement. So would you like to join FROS?"

"Uh… I don't know if I'm quite ready for that. After all, this is my first day on your planet. I'm too new on the block to make a commitment."

"I understand. We'll stay in touch after we get out of here."

"That sounds like a good idea." At that point I should have shut up and let it go. But my big mouth and argumentative nature got the better of me, even though I was beginning to like Tali.

"Tali," I said casually, "by the way, how do you feel about killing in self defense?"

"As long as it's not for food its okay."

"Suppose you were starving and were attacked by a big fish and killed it with one of the spears you guys carry whenever you go out into the sea. Would you eat it?"

"No."

"Suppose you were starving to death and if you didn't eat it you would die. What then?"

"I don't know."

"I won't press you, but did you know that plants are also alive, and when you eat them you are often eating ex-living things that were killed for food. Do you see anything wrong with that?" Of course there was an answer to that, that plants were not conscious beings. Or were they? I remember reading a book on Earth called "The Secret Life of Plants" which stated that plants respond to the way humans treat them. At any rate, he did not answer my question.

His eyes narrowed as if he could kill me, but not for food, of course.

"Where did you say you came from?"

"A planet called Earth. And we have people who believe as you do, too."

"Does everyone on Earth try to tear down other people's beliefs?"

"No, not everyone. Not even me. Hardly anyone." I was feeling bad; I should really have kept my mouth shut. I actually have a lot of empathy for vegetarians. They are invariably nice well-meaning people. Olga was a vegetarian who not only didn't eat meat, but also refused to consume dairy products of any kind. That bitch. I hope Lash eats meat three times a day, and for between meal snacks. And drowns himself in milk, sour milk, un-pasteurized. And the lawyers in his band have to bail him out or pay his hospital bills.

What was I doing? I resolved then and there to get over my bitterness. I was beginning a new life and it was time to forget the past. Olga was gone. Literally. She was millions perhaps even billions of miles away. And I was here, in my place in the universe.

I gave Tali a friendly smile. "Really, Tali, I was just arguing for the sake or arguing. I wasn't trying to tear down your beliefs. You are entitled to believe anything you want. And I respect you for it."

"You're damn right," he said, got up from the table and plopped himself down on his bed facing the wall with his back to me.

"Tali," I called.

No answer. I tried again, but there was no response. So I blew out the candles, made my way to my bed and went to sleep with a heavy heart, while at the same time thinking about not eating moss mousse... ever.

CHAPTER 3

I was awakened by the sound of the door being unlatched. I opened my eyes to see a guard coming through. He was a different one from the night before, bigger and not very friendly looking. Nor did he have a smile on his face.

He motioned for me to get up and stepped to the bed. He gruffly dragged me to my feet, hooked an arm around mine and together we went out the door.

"Goodbye Tali," I called as we left. "I hope I'll see you again." There was no answer. Just outside the door we were joined by another big unpleasant looking guard who grabbed my other arm. We proceeded down the same hall as yesterday and up the same stairs. I assumed it was morning because when we got upstairs there was natural light coming through the windows.

My escorts were not the slightest bit friendly and for the first time I felt like a real prisoner.

We turned and went through another hallway until we came to a huge double door guarded by two tall dolphins standing as straight and stiff as the guards outside of London's Buckingham Palace.

It was actually somewhat amusing, because instead of staring straight ahead with seriously bland facial expressions, their eyes followed me as we approached and their brows were furrowed in astonishment as they gazed at me.

"Hi, guys," I said. "Aren't you supposed to be looking bored and straight ahead?"

"That will be enough of that," said one of my escorts. "Open the doors, please." He said to the guards.

They immediately did so, never taking their eyes off me.

We stepped inside and I was greeted by the sight of more dolphins in one place then I had ever seen in my life or in films or on television. Moreover, they were not in the water where dolphins are supposed to be, but seated on chairs, their legs in front of them, their tails behind. We were in a large auditorium with row upon row of staring dolphins following me with their eyes as we made our way from the back of the auditorium down its center aisle to two raised platforms in the front.

One platform was small and low, about four feet above floor level, the other about four feet higher. On the upper one was a long table half facing the small platform and the audience. Seated behind the table were seven stern looking dolphins apparently trying their best to hide their surprise at seeing me.

When we reached the platforms the dolphin in the middle of the table spoke. "Put him on the display stand."

"Yes Mr. Administrator," said my escorts almost in unison, and they guided me up the steps to the smaller platform, or rather the "display stand", as the Administrator referred to it. I didn't like the word "display" and hoped it was a minor glitch in my universal translator.

My hope was in vain because as soon as I reached the top, with my back to the audience, he said to me, "Turn around slowly so that everyone can see you."

The stares of astonishment on the faces of the dolphins in the audience remained, but now were accompanied by dolphin smiles on many faces, and the sound of twitters among them. Their eyes focused not so much on my Earth-human face but rather on my groin with it's mass of dark hair, its shrunken non-retractable tinky, and my unshrunken testicles hanging behind it.

Because of my experiences so far on Sea I understood their amusement. But I was still embarrassed as hell, and I'm the type of person who when embarrassed gets belligerent.

I half turned to face the Administrator and his cohorts.

"All right," I said, summoning up as much toughness as I could muster. "Why am I on display, or am I on trial? I haven't done anything. I am an innocent man."

"You're not on display and you are not on trial," came the calm but firm voice of the Administrator. "Moreover, you are not a man. A man is an adult male of our species, and you obviously do not qualify, although you do seem to qualify as a male, at least somewhat."

"I resent that. I am a man of my species and altogether a man, although I am standing here before you in the altogether."

"Do you have a name?" asked the Administrator.

"Damn right I do. DiVinci. Daniel David DiVinci. Citizen of the U.S.A, Citizen of Earth. Any other questions?"

"Calm down, Daniel DiVinci", said the Administrator in a calm but firm voice. "You are not on trial, and this procedure is neither a display nor a trial. The reason you are appearing before us is that since you are obviously not a dolphin but are intelligent, and you can walk and talk our language, we are trying to determine if you are dangerous."

"First I'm not a man? Now I'm dangerous?" I replied. "Are you prejudiced because I am not gray, or because I don't have a tail, but do have a non-retractable tinky, as you call it? Could it be a case of penis envy? Some of us are hung and some of us aren't, you know."

"Are you quite finished?"

"Not really. Or is it that I'm not as good a swimmer as you people — and I use the word 'people' loosely. But I'll bet I can run a hell of a lot faster than all of you. The 100-yard dash, or the 440, or the mile. I could even whip your respective asses in the Boston Marathon!"

"Are; you quite finished, Daniel DiVinci? Because if you are not I will have one of the guards stuff a sea urchin in your mouth."

"Dead or alive?" I said.

"Alive, of course. We eat the dead ones."

"You do? I had them once in Trinidad. They're great fried in beer batter, a little pepper, a lot of garlic with a touch of ginger."

"Daniel DiVinci, if you don't stop blabbering, we really will stuff a live sea urchin in your mouth, and tape it shut."

I guess I believed they might really do that, so I stopped talking. "Yes sir," I said. I do talk a lot when I'm nervous, and I really was. As a matter of fact I was scared shitless that they might think I really was dangerous and do something about it. Like feed me to the sharks? They wouldn't do that, or would they?

I decided I'd better be on my best behavior, so I took a deep relaxing breath, tried to look calm and relaxed, and politely said, "Proceed with your questions, sir. I'd be happy to answer anything you may ask."

"That's much better, Daniel DiVinci. Now let us proceed in a civilized manner. First, please tell us what part of Sea you are from. You are obviously a land animal. We are not aware of any other land on Sea. We would also like to know why you are here, how long you plan to stay, what you expect from us, and what we can expect from you. We don't really think you are dangerous, but nevertheless please begin."

"Thank you for being so civilized." I said. "Where I come from we are also civilized, at least some of us. But one of the facts of our civilization is that we don't walk around naked."

"The word naked is not in our vocabulary. Kindly explain yourself."

"Kindly shmindly," I said. "Look — no don't look, listen. Although I am proud of my un-retractable tinky, I am very uncomfortable, not to mention embarrassed, standing here in public bare assed naked."

"You used that word 'naked' again. What is its meaning? And while you are at it please explain the expression 'bare assed'."

"Nude, unclothed. For God's sake, get me something to cover myself with!"

There were laughs throughout the audience, and smiles among the dolphins seated at the table with the Administrator.

"I think he wants to cover his dinky tinky," a voice from the audience shouted out."

"And I think," called another, "that the 'bare assed' refers to those pillow-like mounds below his back."

More smiles and nods of agreement among both the audience and those seated at the table.

Another voice shouted out, "Look, he's changing color, like an octopus. See how red his face is." Another wave of laughter.

"Or like an intertidal sand slug," said another. More laughter and smiles.

"Enough!" said the Administrator in a very serious voice. "This covering up what he calls 'naked' must be important where he comes from. Will someone please volunteer to lend him a dakti?"

One of the dolphins in the front row stood up and wiggled out of a garment that had been around his waist. He came up to my platform and handed it to me. "Here, put this on," he said. "Naked, huh?"

I took it from him, examined it briefly and stepped into it. It was like a woman's, an Earth woman's, I might add, short sheath skirt, except it had pockets, two in the front and two in the back. I tied it on with what looked like apron strings, except they were in front.

"Thank you," I said and turned back to the Administrator." I feel much more comfortable now. It is important to me to be covered. It's cultural. A custom of our species."

"And just what is your species?"

"Human," I said proudly, momentarily ignoring my conversation with Soria and Ibi about the word "human".

The loudest laughter yet swept through the crowd. Even the stern faced Administrator and his fellow council members flashed dolphin grins.

"Please do not try to deceive us, Daniel DiVinci," said the Administrator. "There is no possible way you can be one of us. The only thing we have in common is your obvious intelligence and you ability to speak and understand dolphinese, or as it sometimes referred to as 'humanese'."

"Humanese," I said. "So you really do think of yourselves as being human?"

The Administrator looked at me incredulously. "Of course we do. 'Human' is another name for dolphin. In fact it is used in everyday conversation as often as dolphin."

I looked at him long and hard. I could see there was no further point in pursuing my humanity. "All right," I said. "I am a Homo sapien," I continued as proudly as I could under the circumstances.

"'Excellent," he said. "Now we are getting somewhere. Let us continue. For the sake of brevity may we refer to you as a homo?"

I gulped. I am absolutely not homophobic — some of my best friends are homosexuals. Perhaps it was a hangover from the past, but it did bother me being called a 'homo'. I was disappointed in myself for feeling this way, but managed a cheerful smile.

"Certainly," I said. "An accurate brevity. I'm honored." I immediately imagined in my mind 72 beautiful naked women, not virgins, not dolphins either, just human women, writhing sexually, their arms extended toward me.

"Now, homo," said the Administrator, "We expect —"

"Please, Sir," I interrupted, " I would prefer that you call me by my name."

"All right, Daniel DiVinci, we expect honest answers to our questions. And please, no more trying to pass yourself off as one of us. Understood?"

"Understood."

"Now," the 'Administrator continued, "What part of Sea do you come from? We have never seen a creature like you before."

"Sea?" I asked. "Is that the name of this whole world?"

The administrator looked at me quizzically. "What do you call our world in your part of Sea? You speak our language but obviously my use of the world 'Sea' surprises you. Do you have another name for it?"

"Uh, not really," I said. I was speechless for a moment, and looked around at the sea (no pun intended) of attentive dolphin faces. I grinned inwardly, satisfaction and joy washing over me like a wave of melted chocolate. Sea, I said to myself. So that's the real name of my place in the universe, and its inhabitants are evolved dolphins. I wondered how far from Earth it was — I was — not that it mattered.

"Daniel DiVinci," said the Administrator, "please answer my question. What is your name for Sea?"

"Well," I answered. "We don't really have a name for Sea. As a matter of fact, we don't even know about its existence. Would you believe that there isn't a single person in the world I come from that even knows that Sea exists? They know your Sun exists, sort of, but not your world."

"What are you talking about, Daniel DiVinci?"

"You can call me Danny," I replied. "It's a long story, but I come from a different world, a planet called Earth."

"Another world!" Gasps traversed the crowd. All the dolphins gazed at me, and then at each other, then back to me, as if trying to decide whether I really was from outer space or just crazy.

"Daniel DiVinci — Danny — do you actually mean that you are from one of the stars in the sky?"

"Sort of," I replied. "What you call stars are actually suns like yours. My world is called a planet, and it revolves around our sun, just as Sea circles your sun. Sea is also a planet."

The Administrator looked at me disdainfully. "We know that," he said, "our scientists figured that out long ago. What we didn't know was that stars are actually other suns, not planets. Are you sure of that?"

"Yes, almost all of them. There may be a few more planets like Sea revolving around your sun, but all else are stars. I wouldn't lie to you."

"You already did," was his answer.

"Not really," I replied. "In my world we are called 'humans'. 'Homo sapien' is the scientific name for our species."

"Explanation accepted. Now please tell us how you came here."

"Well," I said, "it's a long story, but I'll tell it. There I was on a boat in a storm at sea —"

"Wait!" the Administrator interrupted. "'Sea' is the name of our world. And you said you are not from Sea, but rather a place called Earth."

"That's true, but —"

"But what? Are you lying again?"

"No, I am not. I said at sea, not on Sea. Sea is a large body of water —"

"We know what 'sea' is. Our world is almost all composed of sea. That is how we got our name. Now please continue. How did you get here?"

"That's a good question. Let's just say that I am a space traveler and that I chose your planet above all others because... uh... because it's here."

"At the risk of repeating myself, Mr. Homo sapien, how did you get to Sea? Certainly you did not swim and you don't look to me as if you are capable of flying."

"Uh... That's a good question. Suffice it to say that I did fly, sort of. Obviously, I didn't swim, although I am an excellent swimmer. Not as good as you folks of course. But considering my species, quite good. Especially with the backstroke. I'm also pretty good with the crawl — American of course — and with the sidestroke. I'm also excellent at swimming under wa —"

"Daniel DiVinci, are you evading my question?"

"No, of course not. Why would I want to do that?"

"Perhaps you really are from Sea, from a distant part that we don't know about that's inhabited by strange creatures such as yourself. But how does that explain why you speak our language? I don't understand."

"Exactly," I replied. "No, I am not from Sea, and yes, I am from a distant planet, called Earth. Uh...and as for how I got here..." I tried to think fast. I knew they wouldn't understand how I really got here. As a matter of fact neither did I, if I really and truly was here.

"I arrived in a spaceship," I lied. "One that flies through space to distant planets such as yours."

"And just where is your flying spaceship, Daniel DiVinci?"

"Uh...it sank to the bottom of the sea, you see the bottom of Sea's sea.

"Yes, I see. Hmm…and when our patrol found you, you were as you describe it, 'naked' in the water. Is it the custom of your planet to fly through the air or space as you put it, 'stark naked'?"

"Of course not," I replied. "The truth of the matter is…is that the impact of hitting the water, uh, partially tore my clothing off, and then… the sharks did it — yes, that's it! The sharks did it. They were going to eat me, but before doing so they ripped the rest of my clothes off. And then they spit them out. I guess sharks don't like the taste of Homo sapien clothing. And just after they finished spitting out the last remnants and before they could eat me, your dolphin patrol came along and scared them away.

"That was a really close call, and I appreciate it. It's a good thing the sharks were having a discussion about which one would get what part of my body. Otherwise I would have been shark food before you fellows got there."

"Discussion?" said the Administrator incredulously, and looked at the other members of the panel, and then out at the audience. "Do you mean that they were actually talking?"

"Of course, how could they have a discussion without talking?"

"Sharks talk? And you understood them? I didn't know they could talk, or that they were that advanced. What language did they speak?"

"The same as yours," I shot back, relieved that we were getting off the subject of how I got to Sea stark naked.

And then it struck me. It was my Universal Translator. The sharks didn't actually speak dolphinese, and the dolphins didn't know the sharks could talk at all, and of course, neither did I until yesterday.

As a matter of fact, how the hell did they evolve so far as to be able to speak real language? Sharks are primitive creatures with no backbones and minute brains for their size — at least on Earth.

What kind of a place is this? And what other animals or fish could talk? Was my detention-mate Tali a FROS because the fish complained to him about their mistreatment?

"Daniel DiVinci," asked the Administrator, "are you saying that the sharks speak dolphinese?"

"Not exactly," I tried to explain. "It's just that I can understand and converse with them in their language, just as I can with you in yours. It's a...a sort of gift I have."

"I see, or at least I think I see. If I understand you correctly, the sharks, which we assume to be primitive cruel killers, actually speak an intelligible language, and you can understand them."

"Yes, their language is definitely intelligible, and I was able to understand everything they said, although I must admit that their vocabulary was pretty much limited to eating various parts of my body."

"Incredible," said the Administrator, and his fellow council members and the audience nodded in agreement. "We never knew they could actually talk, that they had any language at all, other than some sort of sounds or symbols. They are so primitive and we are so advanced. Why they don't even breathe air...and they lay eggs!"

"True enough," I said. "But they do talk. I was not imagining it."

The administrator looked around at his fellow council members. They moved their chairs closer together and spoke briefly among themselves. Then they separated to their original positions and the administrator addressed me.

"Can you converse with any other animals, Daniel DiVinci?"

"I don't know, but I would like to try."

The administrator motioned to the side of the hall, and a dolphin who had been standing there came up to him. "Bring in a seal and a cat, please," he said.

I was pleased to hear that this planet had seals and cats because I really liked them and they liked me. I didn't expect them to be able to talk and really didn't care. I was looking forward to petting them and maybe getting a wet lick from the seal and a sandpaper one from the cat. I was curious to see if they would look the same as on Earth.

"We have seals and cats on Earth, too," I said while we were waiting for their arrival. "

"That's nice," said the Administrator and he and the council members began conversing among themselves, as did the members of the audience while I stood there awkwardly waiting.

After about five minutes the messenger arrived with a seal on a leash and carrying a cat in his arms. They did indeed look like a seal and cat. I got down off the platform and waited.

"The seal first," said the Administrator. The messenger handed the cat to a nearby dolphin and stepped toward me with the seal.

I smiled, put my hand out and stepped forward to pet him. The black eyes narrowed and darkened; he snarled, jerked on his leash as if trying to get at me and began barking and growling in a decidedly unfriendly manner, more like a dog than a seal.

"Hands off, sucker," he said in a menacing voice. "I may be a dolphin's best friend, but you're no dolphin and you sure as hell are no friend of mine. Get that hand any closer and I'll bite it off."

So they could talk. I knew seals could bark, but growling and biting were new to me. I was shocked at his attitude, but tried not to show it.

"Well," said the Administrator, "can he talk?"

"Oh yes," I answered, faking a smile.

"What did he say?"

I thought quickly. "Well, he said he's a little afraid of me because I don't look like a dolphin, that he is a dolphin's best friend, and that he'd rather I didn't pet him because he's used to being petted by dolphins."

"And what did you say to him?"

"I haven't said anything yet, but I will now." I leaned forward toward the dolphin's best friend, being careful to stay beyond the length of the leash.

"So, sealie," I said soothingly. "You obviously don't like me, but you could learn to. I'm really a good guy and love animals, especially seals"

"Would you scratch me behind the ears?

"Whenever you would like."

"And feed me good food."

"Of course."

"And take me for swims whenever I was in the mood."

"You know I would."

His eyes turned warm and opened wide. He looked up at me adoringly, the way a dog can do.

"So can we be friends?" I said. "I really and truly do love animals. We can become best friends."

"Not a chance."

"Why not?"

"I'd like to, but you're obviously not a dolphin."

"What does that have to do with it? I love animals, and animals on Earth love me."

"So go back to Earth, wherever or whatever that is. You ain't no dolphin and I ain't going to be your friend. It would be a sign of disloyalty. And as a seal I can never, ever be thought of as disloyal. So bug off and leave me alone."

He backed away from me, bared his teeth, growled and snapped his jaws.

"Well fuck you, too," I said. I couldn't believe I was actually saying this to a seal… and a talking one at that.

I was disconsolate. Was this going to be the way I would be treated on Sea? Was I going to be discriminated against because I wasn't a dolphin?

Was I going to have to sit in the back of the bus, if they had busses?

"What did he say this time?" asked the Administrator. "Neither of you look very happy."

This time I made no attempt to hide my feelings. "He said he will be forever loyal to his master and other dolphins and that he considered you to be his best friends, and," I continued, "he doesn't want to be friends with me because I am not a dolphin."

"I am sorry he feels that way," said the Administrator. "If you decide you want to stay here, and we decide we will accept you I promise we will not discriminate against you. Dolphins are not like that. And remember, even though he can talk, seals are still more primitive than dolphins and certainly not as enlightened."

He motioned to one of the guards. "Take him back to his master, please. And tell his master to be careful what he says or does around the house."

He turned back to me. "Very interesting, Mr. Daniel DiVinci. Now let's see if cats can talk, too. And let's hope that if they can they don't have such closed minds." He motioned to the guard holding the cat. "Put him, or her, down please."

The guard did as he was asked, and I stepped forward. I noticed that the cat's tail was like that of an ordinary Earth cat, not flattened like the dolphins or seal. He didn't look like his or her ancestors had ever lived in the sea. Just a yellowish tan tabby. Were Sea cats land survivors?

I approached it gingerly. "Hi, kitty," I said sweetly.

"Hi, yourself," came back a soft cooing voice. So Sea cats could talk, too. This place may have the same atmosphere as Earth, but it sure as hell is different.

"Want to pet me?" it said. "My name is Millie. What's yours?"

"Danny," I replied, reaching out and patting her head.

"That's nice," she said. "Now under my chin."

I did that, too, and she purred even louder. I was delighted. "I'm pleased to be pleasing you, kitty," I said.

"You can call me Millie. I like you, Danny. Ah yes, that's wonderful." Then she rolled over on her back. "A little bit on my chest, please."

Again I complied.

"Oh, yes. Now my stomach, please."

I rubbed her stomach. "Oh, yes, you do know how to please."

"What is it saying," asked the Administrator.

"It's a she," I replied. "Her name is Millie, and she's just giving me instructions, and telling me what a good job I'm doing.

"She does appear to be enjoying it."

"What did he say?" Millie asked.

"He said you do appear to be enjoying me?"

"Oh, I am," she cooed.

"Then will you be my friend?"

"Of course. You will pet me whenever I want it, won't you?"

"Is this a test?"

"I don't know what a test is."

"If I say I'll pet you only when I want to?"

"Then I'll let you, of course, but you really won't be my friend any more than the other dolphins who pet me whenever they feel like it."

"That's good enough for me. But no less either?"

"No."

"Thank you," I said.

"Hey, no problem. You pat my back I'll pat yours."

"It's a deal," I said.

I turned back to the Administrator. "We just made a nondiscriminatory arrangement. Millie will be my friend and treat me like any other dolphin. Or should I say 'use me' like any other dolphin."

The administrator smiled, turned to the other council members, and had a brief discussion with them. Then he turned back to me.

"We seem to agree that it appears that you may well be able to talk with other creatures. And you do not appear to be dangerous. Would you excuse us for a few minutes?"

He got up from the table, motioned to the other dolphins seated there, and they all got up and retreated out a small door in the wall behind their table.

I stood awkwardly waiting, not knowing what to do. Should I try talking with the other dolphins, or should I tell jokes? Instead I just grinned and nodded my head at those who looked and smiled directly at me.

I didn't have long to wait. Within five minutes the Administrator and council members filed back in and took their seats. I knew it would be good news because they all had big dolphin smiles on their faces. The Administrator addressed me.

"Daniel DiVinci, Danny," he said. "We would be most honored if you would be our guest for as long as you would like to stay."

"Thank you, Sir. I am equally honored, and I would like to stay." Oh yeah, I thought, I sure as hell would like to stay — not that I had any choice. This was, indeed, my place in the universe and I was welcome.

The administrator motioned to a guard, and spoke with him briefly. The guard turned, left the hall and was back in less than a minute with two other dolphins.

"Danny," said the Administrator, "these are your escorts. They will take you to our best hotel. No charge, of course. Not that you could pay anyway." He smiled again.

I smiled back at him and at all the other council members. "Put the charge on my bill," I said. "The check is in the mail." They laughed.

I was beginning to feel at home, as strange a place as this was. Talking, walking dolphins, talking sharks, seals and cats. What other surprises await me? What adventures await me on this dolphins' world I now call home.

As Captain Jean-Luc Picard would say: "Engage...."

CHAPTER 4

My escorts led me out of the building through a side door and out onto a narrow walk at the water's edge. Except this wasn't the harbor, it was a canal. I looked ahead and saw other canals intersecting it. No streets; only canals, like Venice.

I looked down into the water. It was clear, not like Venice. I hoped it was clean, too, because one of my escorts said, "I wasn't here when you arrived. You do swim, don't you?"

"Certainly," I said mustering some bravado, "like a fish, my mother used to tell me. But not like a dolphin," I added. I take it we're going there by water.'" I eyed the walk along the canal, but decided not to push it.

"By the way, I said, "my name is Danny. In case I need help along the way and have to call you, you do have names, don't you? And are you males or females?" They glanced at each other and looked at me curiously.

"I'm Aba," said the taller one. "And I'm Daba," said the shorter. "We're both men of course. Can't you tell?"

"No, I can't. As you know I'm new here."

"I'm sorry," said the taller. "How impolite of us. Let me explain."

"Please."

"It's simple. The women are usually not as tall as men, have wider hips and shorter tails. They also have smaller flatter faces. Makes them easier to kiss, you know." He laughed

"The wider hips help, too," added Daba with a lecherous grin. "And, of course, their voices are usually a little higher."

"Sounds like Earth, gentlemen, except for the lack of breasts and booties."

"Breasts? Booties? What are they," said Aba.

"Nothing you would understand. Shall we proceed? By the way, if you want to go faster than I can swim, just each take an arm and pull me. But please make sure you keep my head above water. I can't hold my breath as long as you guys can."

They looked at me disappointingly. "You mean you want us to swim on top of the water?" said Aba.

"Not underwater?" said Daba.

"Please remember, guys, I am of a different species. We are land animals and never lived in the sea, at least not for many billions of years, and I don't believe we ever had tails.

"How far are we going?"

"Just down the canal a little ways; then we turn right at the first intersection, and a left at the next one. Not far," said Aba.

"Any signal lights or stop signs?"

"What?" they said in unison.

"Never mind," I said. "Well, here goes nothing." I jumped in and began to swim toward the right, going as fast as I could using the American crawl. That wasn't very bright because it is the most tiring swimming stroke, emphasizing speed over stamina.

Soon my arms grew tired and I switched to a sidestroke, which was naturally a lot slower. Aba and Daba swam one on each side of me just under the surface. They poked their heads out of the water as soon as I switched to the sidestroke.

"I told you I was a good swimmer," I said.

"As good as any sea snail fighting a head wind," said Daba as he motioned to Aba.

I immediately felt myself being grabbed by the arms and pulled through the water at a speed easily many times my American Crawl pace. Maybe that's why they call it a 'crawl'.

I tried to keep my head above the water, but because of our speed it kept getting into my eyes, mouth, and up my nose.

"Stop!" I shouted until they heard me.

When we finally stopped, I coughed up and spit out as much water as I could, rubbed and linked my eyes until I could see at least semi clearly and spoke.

"Let's do this a little more scientifically. Here's my plan. You probably don't know it, but most human Homo sapiens on my planet can only hold their breath for about 30 seconds on the average. Since I play racquetball three times a week and I'm in better shape than most Homo sapiens, I can hold mine about 45 seconds. With ease, I might add."

"So," I continued, "I'll take a deep breath and close my eyes. Then you can pull me underwater at your regular speed for about 45 seconds; then we come back to the surface, I inhale a deep one, and then you pull me along under the water for about another 45 seconds, and so on. How does that sound?"

"What's racquetball?" asked Aba.

"And what's 45 seconds?" asked Daba.

"Do you not keep time here on Sea?" I asked. I decided to ignore the racquetball question.

"Of course we do," said Daba, "but we don't have what you said. Was it 'seconds'?"

"Yes."

"No. We don't have that. If that's a shorter amount of time than a minute you aliens must certainly be in a hurry."

He was right, of course. We, at least in America, did often seem to be in a hurry. Another thought went through my mind. Was there such a thing as a 'second' in the tens of thousands of years of human history before the invention of the modern clock? Was there even a minute?

"All right, then. How about this…" I continued. "You can hear sounds underwater, right?"

"Of course," they replied together.

"Good. Let's do this. You pull me along underwater and I'll yell — more like an 'eee!' a little before I run out of breath. Then you quickly bring me up to the surface. Okay?"

"Okay."

So that's what they did and it worked. I counted the repetitions, and after the twelfth we came to the surface and stopped. There in front of me was a raised walk wide enough for two people to walk side by side. Behind that was a series of windows and doors that ran the length of a long pinkish building. Several dolphins sat in chairs watching our arrival.

"There's your new home," said Aba, sweeping his arm along its length. One of those rooms with doors will be yours. Let's go."

He and Daba leapt out of the water and on to the walk, which was about two feet above the waterline. They reached down to help me up.

"Wait!" I shouted. "I can do it myself." I was determined not to show any more Homo sapien weakness. So, remembering my days in swimming pools in my California youth, I extended my arms; put both hands on the edge of the walk and cleanly vaulted my body up on to the pathway, gracefully landing on my butt with not too much of a thud, but with plenty of pain because the walk was made of gravel or something akin to it.

I faked a smile and casually put my hands flat on the walk pushed my body up and around and sprung to my feet with more agility than I thought I had. Not bad for a thirty nine year old washed up stand-up-comedian, well former stand-up comedian.

All the dolphins were looking at me; a few were even smiling.

I smiled back. "So what's new?" I said. "You are," said one of the seated dolphins.

"That was fairly well done," said another. We heard about how uncoordinated you are; that you are from a world called Earth. Can all Earthers do that move?"

"Only a select few," I said modestly. "But he's a lousy swimmer," said Aba. "You can say that again," said Daba.

"Do not say that again," I said. "I've heard enough about my swimming. Can I go to my room?"

We turned to the left and walked along the pathway for about 50 feet until we came to a door larger than the others, which was obviously the entrance. I looked toward the water just before we entered the building and saw there were steps coming out it leading up to the walk.

"How come we didn't stop there and use the steps?" I asked my escorts.

They looked a little embarrassed. "I guess we just wanted to see how you would get out of the water," said Daba. "Not bad."

"Better than I expected, said Aba. "Thanks," I said sarcastically. "Now let's go inside."

We went through the door into what looked very much like the lobby of a hotel on Earth.

"Please wait here," said Daba.

He walked to a high table at one end of the lobby, had a conversation with the dolphin behind it and came back smiling.

"Room 23," he said. "A room with a view."

We went down a long hallway and through a door with an undecipherable symbol on it.

It certainly was a nice room. There was a large comfortable looking bed with a depression in the foot end of the mattress, which I assume was for a dolphin's tail if he wanted to sleep on his back. There was a table next to it, which held an unlit candle in what looked like a clamshell, and another table next to a wall with a wash basin on it and with a single drawer underneath.

And it definitely was a room with a view. I could see the walkway and canal through a large picture window. There was also a door right next to it leading outside. I started to walk toward it and stopped.

I had a sudden disturbing revelation. The symbol on the outside of the entrance door to my room was obviously a number or some other form of room designation, and I was not able to decipher it. My Universal Translator had a flaw! It could translate all speech, including my own, but it could not read symbols.

Then another revelation hit me. The dolphins may also have a written language.

I walked over to the door and checked the inside. Sure enough there was a plaque there with more symbols I could not read. Probably things like checkout times and other information you find on the backs of hotel and motel doors on Earth. The dolphins most certainly did have a written language, and I was an illiterate bumpkin who could neither read nor write.

"Uh, guys," I said as casually as I could, pointing at the sign. "Do you think the information on the back of the door is grammatically correct? And is it spelled and punctuated correctly?"

They looked at me questioningly. Aba spoke. "Are you a teacher?"

"Uh, no," I answered. "But I have studied grammar. Just curious. And speaking of curiosity, who are the other people staying in the hotel?"

"Visitors from some of the small outlying islands," said Daba, "and some down from the hills and from other towns on Sea. Most are here on business of some sort."

"What kind of business?" I was determined to learn as much as I could about Sea.

"Selling things mostly, like fruits and vegetables they grow, and shell fish they harvest, furniture they make, and so fourth. And of course buying things."

Before I could ask any more questions there was a knock on the door. I walked to it and opened it.

There standing before me was a dolphin with a shape that could only be described as pure classic dolphin. Streamlined, elegant, perfectly proportioned, a warm shade of gray, standing at about my height, and with an especially wide smile on its face.

"Hi," it said. "I'm Alia. I'm to be your guide and instructor while you are here."

"Hello," I answered. "I'm Danny, and I'm very happy to meet you."

"Thank you," it said, walking in while I was trying to determine from the clues my escorts gave me if our visitor was male or female.

"Hello, Aba; hello, Daba."

"Hi, Alia," they said together.

I noticed that the assurance and flipness with which they acted before had evaporated. They now seemed shy and self-conscious.

Aba looked at me with what appeared to be envy. "You're a lucky man Danny," he said.

"Why do you say that?"

"Because you have Alia as your guide."

"Why thank you, Aba. I hope Daniel DiVinci agrees," said Alia.

"Danny," I answered. "I'm sure I will."

"Well," said Daba, "I think it's time for us to go." He turned to Aba. "Shall we swim or walk?"

"Swim, of course," was the answer.

And with that they went to the door leading out to the water and turned to me. "Goodbye, Danny. Have fun!"

"I always try. Wait a moment and I'll walk you to the water."

"Goodbye, Alia," they both said. "And take good care of Danny," said Daba. "He's a lousy swimmer, but otherwise okay." Alia smiled.

"But a hell of a good vaulter out of the water," I added, as we walked to the canal. "Why did you say I was lucky?"

"Because she's one of the most beautiful women in Sea," he said.

"And a very smart and nice person, too. You'll really like her," said Aba.

Then they both smiled, shook my hand, and dove gracefully into the water with barely a splash. "Her! She!" I called after them. But they were gone. "It" is a "her," a "she", a female dolphin, a woman? A beautiful woman?

I turned around and walked slowly back into my room. "A beautiful woman", I said to myself. She looks more like a sleek well-formed dolphin who happens to have arms and legs to me. I still didn't really know how to tell a male from a female. And what makes her beautiful?

"Well, they're gone," I said awkwardly. "Can I ask you a question?"

"Certainly."

I was going to ask her about the differences, other than biological, between male and female dolphins, and about maleness and femaleness, but decided to wait for a more appropriate time.

"So," I said. "What happens now?"

She looked at me with her smiling face and asked, "what would you like to do? My job is to orient you to Sea, to answer your questions, to show you around, to explain our way of life, and so forth. We don't know how long you are going to be here since we don't know if you have any way of leaving. You don't do you?"

"No."

"Do you want to leave?"

"No."

"Than you might as well enjoy your time here. And the best way I can think of to do that is to learn or way of life and live it, if that is what you want to do. Do you?"

"Yes, Alia, I do. Very much."

"Good. Since I've never done this before, I don't know where to begin. How about questions?"

"Sounds good to me."

"Okay, what's your first question?"

"Well, let's see… I've got it. The first thing I would like to ask is do you folks have a sense of humor? The Administrator and the Council were pretty serious."

"That was their job."

"And neither did my FROS detention-mate last night."

"You shared a room with a member of FROS?"

"Yes."

"No wonder you ask that question. FROS people are very nice, but not typical. They are very, very serious. But believe me, most of us do have a sense of humor, and I have more than most."

"Really. All right then, why did the chicken cross the road?"

"What's a chicken? And what's a road?"

"Sorry. Uh…. Why did the eel swim to the other side of the canal?"

"To get to the other side of course. That's a childish joke."

"Okay, then. Take my wife…"

"Wife? What's a wife?"

"Uh.. Mate. I'll start over again. This man is telling someone else about his family life and says for example, take my mate...."

"Please."

"You have that joke, too. Remarkable."

"Do you know a lot of jokes?"

"Yes. On Earth I was a stand-up comedian."

"Did you have to stand up to be funny? You couldn't do it sitting down? Or lying down? Or Swimming?"

"Very funny," I said. If she were a human woman I could be attracted to her with that smart-alecky personality.

"I think I like you," I said. "I'm going to enjoy having you as my guide."

"Why?"

"Well, I like your sense of humor and quickness of mind."

"That's nice of you to say so. Most men are attracted to my looks. Do you think I'm pretty?"

I gulped. I didn't have the slightest idea whether she was pretty or not. I couldn't even tell for certain that she was a she. But I didn't want to hurt her feelings.

"I think you're lovely," I lied. "Do you think I'm attractive?" I asked, to see what her reaction would be.

"What kind of question is that to ask? I don't even know what to compare you with. I've never seen a homo before."

"Homo sapien!" I snapped. There I did it again. Surely I was brainwashed as a youth.

"Homo sapien," she retorted. "You don't have to get upset about it. For a stand-up comedian you certainly are touchy. I was just trying to be funny. I was at the meeting when you were brought in."

"Sorry," I said. "And what did you think of that little episode?"

"Hardly a little episode. That was the biggest thing to happen on Sea in years. I found it very educational. You Homo sapiens certainly are an interesting species. I'd like to learn more about you."

"And I you... uh... dolphins."

"That's why I'm here. We began with a question. Do you have another?"

"Lots, but is it possible to get something to eat first? I haven't had a bite since last night, and even then I didn't eat much."

"Oh, I'm sorry. I should have thought of that. There's a restaurant here in the hotel. Or better, still, how would you like to go to one of my favorite little places? It's not far from here."

"Do we have to swim to get there? I'm not really in the mood for swimming. My dakti is still a little wet, and I'd like to dry it off completely."

She looked at me and smiled. "I can understand that," she said. "You Homo sapiens don't seem to be built for swimming. Not having a tail can be a real handicap, and so is having that little tinky that hangs down to attract fish instead of retracting into your body.

"But I'll bet you can really walk, and climb, too. And I guess the tinky actually functions, after a fashion. Though I can see why you like to cover it up."

I stared at her, embarrassed, attempting to find out if she was trying to be funny.

She wasn't.

"Yes, the tinky does function, quite well in my case, I might add," I said modestly. "And we cover it up where I come from because that is the custom, not because we're afraid of fish."

"Why is it the custom? Are you ashamed of it?"

"Certainly not."

"Then let me see it... please. I was sitting pretty far back in the audience, so I've never really seen a Homo sapien tinky before, let alone a Homo sapien, before you, of course."

"I don't suppose you have," I said, trying to think of how to answer her. I certainly didn't want to show my penis to a strange animal, especially since it was soft and shrunken. Even if that strange animal acted quite human, and was supposed to be a beautiful woman.

Suppose I were to get an erection in front of her. I couldn't even tell by her looks that this animal was beautiful, let alone a female. What would that make me? A closet sodomist?

She was staring down at my crotch, as if trying to see through my covering.

"Well," she said, "are you or are you not going to let me see it? You're on Sea, and on Sea it's nothing to be ashamed of."

I looked straight into her eyes. My God, I was starting to get an erection! What to do? She kept staring as it pushed against my dakti, causing the garment to bulge out.

"No, " I said firmly. I can't... I won't."

"Gosh," she said. "I believe it's growing. Please let me see it."

"Absolutely not!" I said emphatically as it kept getting bigger and more erect. "It would be unseemly."

"Unseemly? What does that mean?"

"Not the right thing to do," I answered quickly.

She laughed. "You really are funny. Are all Homo sapiens like you?"

"Are all dolphins like you?"

"Oh yes, we're all curious, at least the intelligent ones. And we are certainly not ashamed of our bodies."

"Can we eat now?"

She sighed. "I guess. And by the way, if we wanted to we couldn't swim to get there. It's up the hill a little way."

"Good, let's go."

"Well, all right." She took one last look at my crotch, smiled and said, "well it stopped growing. As a matter of fact, it seems to have shrunk a little."

"You're quite right," I said with relief. At least I think it was relief.

And we left.

We went out a side door of the hotel, turned right and about 50 yards later started up a slight incline on a walkway wide enough for four people. I noticed for the first time that when Alia was walking she took rather small steps. I attributed it to the relative shortness of her legs compared to the length of her body, as well as the fact that her tail was trailing behind her.

There were other dolphins on the walkway going in both directions, and I noticed they walked about the same way. They, too, had short legs for the length of their bodies, and carried their tails about a foot off the ground.

We walked in silence for a while so I had time to think about where I really was and about the inhabitants of this strange and not so strange planet.

Was I really and truly on another planet, or was it a dream or an hallucination resulting from my hit on the head and prolonged immersion in the water?

I didn't have too long to think because Alia turned her head to me and said. "We're almost there. You're very quiet."

"I've just been thinking. You're quiet yourself."

"I've also been thinking," she said. "I should have realized you were a different species from a different place and not embarrassed you."

"I wasn't embarrassed."

"Oh yes you were."

"Maybe a little," I smiled. "But give me time. I'll get used to the way things are here on Sea."

"I'm sure you will. Oh look, there it is," she said pointing to the only building in sight on our left. Well it wasn't really a building, but rather a one-story storefront that seemed to be made of pinkish brick-like material, like most of the structures I had seen so far.

There was a sign hanging down in front of it, which I couldn't read, a defect which I resolved to do something about. However, I was able to understand one thing on it, a picture of a snake or eel, with teeth.

"Uh, Alia," I said as we pushed open the door and went in. "What kind of restaurant is this?"

"Why an Eeelaria, of course. I guess you didn't notice the sign. Best tasting eels on Sea. They raise their own and feed them sea slugs so they always taste good. No unsavory smell. I'm sure you'll love the food."

"I'm sure I will," I said, looking around nonchalantly. Then a horrible thought hit me. On Earth dolphins eat live fish, or dead ones in captivity. Do they cook their food in this restaurant, or was I going to have to eat raw eel, already dead, I hoped? Would it have a half digested sea slug in its intestine?

I felt like throwing up but instead decided to look around. There were about a dozen tables, all full or nearly full of chattering dolphins sitting at them. I tried to see if the food on their plates was alive or squirming, but we were too far away to tell.

There was also a small bar just inside the door we came in, with bar stools and low bar tables off to the side. Just like on Earth, I thought. Alia took me by the hand and we went up to the end of the bar where she gave her name to the dolphin staring at me. He wrote it down without taking his eyes off me. "It won't be long," he said, "just about ten minutes."

"Good," she said turning to me. "How about a drink?"

I looked around and saw that everyone in the place was staring at me. The chatter had stopped and I could hear whispers.

Alia noticed and squeezed my hand. "Try not to be uncomfortable," she said, "They'll get used to you."

"I hope so," I said, trying not to look as uncomfortable as I felt. "Do you think they know about me?"

"I'm sure most of them do. Word gets around pretty quickly here. Tomorrow it will be in the newspaper, but now it's all word of mouth. And the council helped spread the word by sending out messengers."

"Do you think they will attack me?"

"Of course not. We are a very non-violent people."

"I believe you. But do you think maybe you should make an announcement of some kind, let everybody know who and what I am."

"Good idea." She turned to the bartender, "Could you please get them quiet so I can say something?"

"That will be easy," he answered, "since you already have everybody's attention." Then he reached under the bar, withdrew what looked like a large conch shell, and blew into it. The noise was the same as blowing into a conch shell on Earth. I liked the familiarity.

The place immediately became completely silent. Even chewing stopped. Alia spoke. "Ladies and gentlemen. Most of you have already heard of the arrival of our guest." She moved her hand and pointed at me.

"You may have noticed that he doesn't look quite like us." Laughter. "He says the name of his species is Homo sapien and that where he is from all of the Homo sapiens look more or less like him. He says he is from another world, a planet called Earth. But he does speak our language."

"Where is this Earth planet?" asked one of the bar patrons. I didn't know how to answer him, if it was a him who asked.

"In the sky," I said, hoping that would suffice.

"Where in the sky?" asked another.

Before I could even think of an answer, Alia broke in.

"Ladies and gentlemen," she said, "there will be a complete report in the newspaper tomorrow. For now, I think it would be very dolphinese to just accept the fact that he is here and to welcome him. His name is Danny, Danny DiVinci."

"Hello, Danny," several of them said. "Welcome to Sea," a few others chimed in.

"Yeah, welcome," said a dolphin at the bar, obviously inebriated. "Your story as I heard it sounds fishy to me. So you just flew through the heavens in what you call a spaceship, and that spaceship landed you here and mysteriously sank to the bottom, leaving you miraculously alive as if God ordained that you be here."

"Perhaps," I answered, "I just don't know how it happened." I did a double take. "Did you say God?"

"Yes."

"Interesting theory," I replied. "I sort of was in heaven, I think. I wonder if —"

"I did say God. But surely you know that God is not in heaven. It lives in the sea."

"Oh," I said. "So God lives in the sea, in the sea on Sea, I suppose."

"Of course," was the reply. "Where else would it live?"

"Sea, shmee," said a voice from one of the tables. You're assuming that there is a God. "There were murmurs of both dissent and affirmation throughout the restaurant. I was dismayed to think I started an argument. It was only my second day in Sea.

Soon there was shouting back and forth across the room. My

dismay had turned to amusement. I really enjoy a good argument, and this reminded me of my former home, especially bars in San Francisco.

When things quieted down a little one of the patrons called out to me.

"Hey, Danny, did you mean to imply that on your planet God lives in the sky?"

"Sort of," I answered. "Heaven is beyond the sky, in a realm of itself."

"Do you believe in all that whale shit?" said one of the dissenters.

"Well," I said "sometimes, yes and sometimes no. Lately, especially in the last few days, more yes than no."

"And what does this yes and no God of yours look like?" asked another skeptic.

"Well," I answered, "nobody really knows for sure, but people picture him as an man with a beard, sort of like me except a lot older. And his beard is white."

There was laughter throughout.

"Danny," said one of the believers. "I certainly believe in God, but are you trying to tell us that God is a he and that he looks like a Homo sapien?"

"Yes," I said tentatively, "Or more accurately, Homo sapiens look like God. We are made in his image."

The laughter turned into snickers. And then it struck me! On Earth we believe man was made in the image of God. But here on Sea....

"What do you think God looks like?" I said.

"Why like us, of course," came an answer.

"Do you mean," I said, "that God is a dolphin?"

"Of course," came the answer, and there were nods and murmurs of agreement all through the restaurant. We certainly had everybody's attention. "Aren't we made in the image of God?"

"Hey", said the most vocal of the non-believers at the bar, "since he or it lives in the sea, why can't he or it look like a whale?" He laughed loudly and waved his arm around pointing to the tables. "Or," he said through his laughter, "maybe he or she or it looks like an eel. You guys might be eating God!"

"That's disgusting," said another one of the bar patrons. A few dolphins laughed, but most shook their heads and frowned. Some looked as if they could throw up, a few looked extremely angry, got up from their tables, threw what I took to be money on them and left the premises.

Alia squeezed my hand tighter and looked directly at me. "Is this what you call stand-up comedy on Earth?" she said.

"Not funny," I replied. "I think things got a little out of control."

"I would say so. At least we don't have to wait so long to get a table."

As we waited for someone to clear a table for us, the bartender put out his hand for me to shake and said, "that's the liveliest it's been in here for a while. Welcome to Sea. May you live long and prosper."

I looked at his face. Were his ears a little pointy, or was I just imagining things?

"Your table is ready, folks, please follow me," said a server, and she, he led us toward a table in the rear.

While we were walking I checked out the food on the tables we passed to see if there were any live eels on the dishes. I breathed a sight of relief when I saw that not only were they not alive, but they had been cooked, some with sauces on them. I thought I actually saw some spaghetti on one of the plates. A big plus for dolphin civilization. But then again, maybe they were baby eels.

We were seated at a nice table next to the back wall where there was a small window with a lovely view down the hill to the canal and the harbor in the background. There was a candle burning in a beautiful reflective oyster shell next to a vase that seemed to be made of cut glass containing red and pink flowers.

It was a very romantic setting. The only problem was that I was here with a female dolphin rather than a female human. I thought fleetingly of Olga, but that didn't last long. Olga was in the past. That was in another country, and besides, the wench was dead. At least to me.

I came back to the present. "So," I said to Alia. "Nice place, nice table. Isn't this romantic? Do you have that word?"

"Yes, we do, and it is. The view is lovely. She smiled at me. If I hadn't known better I would have thought her smile had sexual connotations. I dismissed that thought when she said, "so is the food."

"Eels?"

"Oh yes, they are truly a delicacy. We consider them food for lovers."

I gulped. Maybe her smile was what it seemed to be. "So," I said, "what do you think of all that fuss back there?" I looked over at the bar area. There was still a lot of agitated conversation going on, with occasional glances in our direction.

Alia looked, too, and shook her head. "I think it's a subject we can talk about in the future. For now let's order. I'm famished."

"I thought I was the one supposed to be hungry."

"We are very empathetic people." She motioned to a server who came over and gave us each a menu. I had the same sinking feeling as at the hotel. I couldn't read the damn thing.

All I could understand were the pictures of eels in various positions on the cover and along the margins on the inside. The pictures did not show the slime that every eel I ever touched had on its skin.

I remembered my father taking me fishing when I was a little boy and being disgusted every time we accidentally caught one. We never took them off the hook because they had such sharp teeth. We merely cut the line, but because they usually squirmed so much we often had to grab their slimy bodies in order to hold them still enough to cut.

No, eels were not my idea of a food for lovers. I tried to keep the distasteful expression off my face and looked at Alia. Her face was full of eager anticipation.

"Everything sounds delicious," I said. "Especially for eel lovers."

"I thought you would like this place."

"I do, I do," I said, afraid I was overdoing my enthusiasm.

"Good. What would you like? Since you don't have any money yet, I'm paying, or rather the council is."

I smiled knowingly. "How about some eel? Some extra special romantic eel."

"Very funny."

"Just kidding. Why don't you pick your favorite? You know the restaurant better than I."

"Not a chance," she said. "You are the honored guest, so it's your pick."

"Okay." I said, "being from a different planet, I'm not really familiar with your local cuisine, your herbs and spices and sauces. I'd just as soon you make the choice. I can't make up my mind."

"Oh well," she said seriously and with disappointment in her voice. "I think I'll order for you the live baby eels on a bed of dead pickled sea slugs with a side of comatose jelly fish. Doesn't that sound delicious?"

"Scrumptious," I said, forcing a smile, hoping she didn't notice how forced it was. "On second thought, maybe I will pick my own dish. How about this?" I said, pointing to an item at random.

"You don't like my choice?"

"It's not that I don't like it — it sounds delicious — it's just that I'm in the mood for something else."

"You've hurt my feelings, Danny."

"I'm sorry; please don't be hurt. I didn't mean to do that."

"I understand," she said petulantly. "Just go ahead and order what you want."

"Please don't be hurt."

"I'm not really just hurt," she said. "I'm simply devastated. I may never laugh or smile again. You've broken the cardinal rule of dolphin hospitality. And I'm responsible. How can I explain this to the council?"

"You don't have to explain anything," I said. "I'm just an alien, a stranger in a strange land. I'm not familiar with your rules of hospitality. I don't want to hurt you. I like you. You're very nice person."

"Woman," she said. A slow smile gradually crept across her face, and suddenly turned into a big grin. She looked at me mischievously.

"You can't read, can you?"

I stared into her eyes and began to smile myself. "How long have you known?"

"I began to suspect in the hotel," she answered. "I was just outside the door when you tried to read the notice on the back of it. I could hear everything. Your charade with this grammatically correct menu confirmed it."

"And the live baby eels on a bed of picked sea slugs with a side of comatose jelly fish?"

"I like to think of myself as a creative person," she said. "It did sound pretty repulsive, didn't it?"

"Well, maybe I'll just ask the chef if he can make that dish. Perhaps it will take my mind off God being a dolphin."

"Perhaps I can take your mind off God being a dolphin." There was that same sexual connotation smile again, not that I knew the real meaning of a dolphin smile. But it sure looked that way.

And why did I insist on thinking of them as dolphins. They certainly acted like real humans. They had arms and legs, and they definitely liked to talk and argue.

What did I expect intelligent life on another planet to look like? They surely wouldn't look similar to humans, Star Trek to the contrary, or should I say, "Earth humans?"

And even though atmospheric conditions seem to be the same as Earth – I could breathe, the sky was blue, the sun was warm – these inhabitants obviously evolved differently. Perhaps there were never any dinosaurs or ape-like creatures here.

Besides, who is to say that Earth dolphins aren't actually more intelligent than humans? Their brain size is approximately the same, sometimes larger, than humans' compared to body size. They just live in a totally different environment. They don't need arms and hands and legs and feet in the sea. And how do we know they can't talk to each other? We do know that they can communicate.

And if they are actually as or more intelligent, why couldn't God be a dolphin? Are we so species biased that we think God looks like us, or us like God? And why should God have a sex? Why should such an incalculable force that no one has ever seen look like anything? Why shouldn't its presence just be there?"

"Danny, Hello. Are you there?"

It was Alia. I was so preoccupied with my thoughts that she

must have been talking to me and I didn't hear her. "Yes, I'm still here. Just thinking about something."

"An oyster shell for your thoughts."

I found myself looking at her in a different way than before. "Well, I said, "I was just thinking about the differences between Earth and Sea, and the non-differences…"

"What conclusions have you come to?"

"I'm still working on it. In the meanwhile let's order our dinner. I'm starved. I haven't eaten good food for millions and millions, probably billions of miles. Order something and surprise me. But no slugs or jelly fish please."

She motioned to the server, placed her order by its number on the menu and looked into my eyes.

"Tell me about yourself," she said.

"Ladies first," I replied. "You first."

"Okay. For one thing I ordered broiled eel with lobster sauce."

Although I love lobster and was delighted to hear they had them on Sea, I said, "It sounds excellent, but that's not what I had in mind."

"I know, well for one thing, I'm 33 years old. I —"

"Wait. Stop. I've got to put that in context. What's the average life span here?"

"About 75-85 years."

"Hum, about the same as our on Earth. Go on."

"I was born in Cali, which is a little town about 20 miles down the coast. My parents still live there."

"How long is the coast? I realized I knew very little about the geography of Sea, except that it appeared that there was a hell of a lot of water.

"About 35 miles south from here in the direction I come from, and about 40 miles north."

"Then this really is an island. I thought so."

"I'm sorry, I thought you knew."

"All I know is what I've seen so far and what you just told me."

"Then I'll explain in detail, as much as I can. Our planet is almost entirely sea, as far as we know. Our island is by far the largest. There are a few outlying islands close by at each end. It's about 75 miles long and about 15 miles at its widest point. Do you know how much a mile is?"

"I know what an Earth mile is: 5280 feet."

"Ours is very close to that. I'll continue. There are high hills in the interior, which I'm sure you saw when you came in, that build up gradually from close to the sea's edge. There are beaches, reefs, cliffs, coves, and harbors of which ours is by far the largest."

"What about the population?"

"There are a little more than 100,000 of us, mostly between the hills and the sea. And the majority of those live in and around Sea, which is the capital and only real city. There are about 60,000 people living here and in the surrounding area."

"What about the other islands?"

"There are seven where dolphins live. The largest is about eight miles long and one and a half miles wide. A few hundred people live there. There are also several tiny unpopulated miles which aren't much more than outcroppings of the ocean bottom."

"And oh, yes, I forgot to mention. Although the climate here around Sea is warm, dry and comfortable, the temperature as you go higher in the hills gets increasingly cooler, and once you get to their other side there is a lot of wind and rain. The hills set as a shield to protect us from them."

"Very interesting, but I'm a little confused about names. The name of the planet is Sea, and the land where we now sit is also called Sea, and the city we are now in is called Sea. Do I have it right?"

"Yes."

"Not very original for a creative people, is it?"

"I'm afraid not. Dolphins are very creative, but we are also conservative about some things, like names that pass on through the legends, for example, and then into history."

I'd like to hear about them."

"The most ancient of our legends tell of our world at one time being all water, all sea. Than as the sea gradually receded, this island was exposed, and because it came from the sea our ancestors who came back from the sea called it Sea. Does that make sense to you."

"Yes."

"And they originally came here where we are because of the protected harbor. It was easier to defend against the ferocious sharks and killer whales, which used to like to eat us. They called it Sea, too."

"Killer whales! You have orcas here, too?"

"I don't know. I'm not familiar with the word orca."

"What do they look like?"

"They're mostly black and white, not quite as big as other whales, but still huge. They hunt in packs. And they're very intelligent."

"I'll be damned. Orcas here, too."

"You have them on Earth?"

"Oh yes. It's remarkable how similar our worlds are. Uh.. I don't suppose the killer whales here have arms, hands, legs, and feet, as you do. Do they?"

"Of course not, silly. They spend all their time in the sea. Why should they?"

"Just curious." I replied.

"That's a curious question," she said.

"I have another one. Can they by any chance talk?"

"We don't know. But they certainly seem intelligent enough, much more than the sharks, seal and cat you spoke with. We think they probably do, in another language, of course. They certainly do communicate. They used to eat us, but we're pretty friendly with them now. Perhaps you would be able to converse with them."

"I'd love to try. But before we continue talking about them I'd like to go back to what you told me about he history of Sea."

"Go, please continue."

"When you were telling me about the legends you said that when the sea receded and this island was exposed that your for-bearers came back to land?"

"Yes, I did say that."

"Does your use of the word back mean that before your world was all water, that there was land and that what is now this island was dry land then?"

"That's what the most ancient of the legends say. But of course we don't know for sure."

"Then is it possible that in those ancient times dolphins were land dwelling beings, and just moved into the sea as the water gradually rose and covered the land, and that your forebearers adapted to the water world by developing a tail in addition to arms and legs and so forth, and that in the distant past you looked more like Homo sapiens than dolphins?"

"I suppose that's possible."

I continued my train of thought. "And that the reason you never became more fish-like is that the period of water covering the planet was not long enough for that evolutionary step to complete itself before your forbearers came back to land and once again made use of their arms, legs, hands, and feet."

"That sounds plausible. I never really thought about it that way. And they don't teach anything like that in school. I think that after you get settled in I should take you to visit Abu Abu."

"Who's he?"

"He's a retired professor from the university. Well not really retired. Rumor has it that he was forced out because of his radical ways and ideas. He is now some sort of practicing shaman up in the hills."

"He was a friend of my father's and I've known him since I was a child. I really like him. He used to call me his little papu."

"What's a papu?"

"I don't know. It's not a dolphinese word."

"I think I'd like to meet this Abu Abu."

"I understand he lives in a cave, which I have never been to."

"I think I like him already," I said. "I'm considered to be a kind of radical myself. At least my parents and sister think so."

"I would love to see him again. It's been a while. We can visit him once you get settled in."

"Excellent," I said. "But now tell more about the orcas, I mean killer whales."

"You're getting very serious for a sit down comedian."

"Stand-up!"

"I know, silly. I'm just trying to get you to smile again."

I smiled. "You're right. I was getting a little serious. But on Earth most comedians are serious people. They're funny because if they weren't, they would be sad, and often unhappy."

She looked at me intently, her dolphin smile not so smiley. "And you?" she said.

"Did you ever hear the joke about the salesman and the farmer's daughter?"

"No, and I don't want to. You haven't answered my question."

"Maybe I don't want to."

"Please, pretty please with seaweed on it."

"Is that a joke?"

"Yes, who would want to eat seaweed?"

"Slug-fed baby eels?"

"Who else. You don't want to talk about yourself, do you?"

"No."

"Why not?"

"Because I was unhappy before I got here, if I am, indeed, here."

"What is that supposed to mean? Of course you are here. We are both here."

"And so is our dinner," I said, eyeing the server approaching our table. "I love lobster sauce," I said. "As a matter of fact I love lobster. It is my very favorite of all foods, assuming Sea lobster is the same as Earth lobster. I don't know about the eel yet."

Alia was silent and pensive as the server put the plates in front of us.

"Well, let's eat," I said, and began to dig in. The food really was delicious and I said so. And the lobster sauce did taste like Earth lobster.

"I'm glad you like it," Alia said, and began to eat. "Would you like some beer with your food? They brew their own here, and you can cry into it. Improves the flavor, you know."

"I'll bet it makes it taste funny," I said. "Or sad… all right. Yes, I was sad and unhappy before I came here. Very sad, and very unhappy. Are your satisfied?"

"Do you want to tell me why?"

"No. Another time. Let's finish eating. And I would like some beer."

"All right." She motioned to the waiter who came back in a few minutes with some beer. It went very well with the eel with lobster sauce.

I never thought I would enjoy eel so much. Because of my slimey childhood fishing experience I had always refused to eat it, although I knew a lot of people did.

We talked as we ate. About the décor of the restaurant, the clientele, which by now had quieted down, although we still got many polite and furtive looks, about other restaurants in Sea, and the weather warm and dry on this side, lush and green and rainy on the other. I surmised that the island of Sea was not too far from the equator, assuming Sea had one, and had a climate pretty much like our Caribbean islands.

We finished dinner and Alia ordered a beverage which tasted very much like coffee, informed me it was made from a bean which grew on bushes on the windward wet side of the island.

It was a good in its own way as the beer, which Alia informed me was made from several varieties of plants that grow on this side of the island.

Sea was beginning to feel like a slice of paradise. Did I really die and was actually in heaven or something akin to it? I didn't really think so. Everything was so real.

"Alia," I said.

"Yes."

"I am not sad or unhappy now. As a matter of fact I'm really enjoying myself here on Sea, and I'm especially enjoying this time with you."

"Well that's a very un-comedic statement to make," she said. "It must be the eel, or the sea slugs they have eaten. I like you, too."

"I'll bet you tell that to all the aliens you meet."

"Only to the ones from Earth," she replied. "And especially the ones with external non-retractable tinkys."

Even though Alia certainly didn't look like a woman, I was beginning to think of her as one... and a desirable one at that. Was there something wrong with me? Was I truly a closet sodomist? How could a creature with a pointy face and a tail and no hair be sexually attractive? And no breasts either.

True, the male dolphins consider her to be especially beautiful and she has the kind of personality I like in a woman. But no breasts! The only things "earthly" feminine about her were her eyes, her personality and the way she talked. But I could feel very definite feminine vibrations coming from her.

And speaking of the way she talked, although her voice sounded like a woman's, I had to realize that I truly wasn't hearing it. I was actually hearing what the Universal Translator was turning it into. For all I knew she might have been "talking" in squeaks and squawks and whistles that Earth dolphins use. Not very sexy. Yuk.

"So," I said as nonchalantly as I could. "Where do we go from here, Madame Guide?"

"Where would you like to go?"

"I don't know. Where would you like to go?"

"Why are you changing the subject?" she said.

"What subject?"

"The subject of you especially enjoying your time with me and me liking you, too."

She gazed into my eyes with as sexy a look as I have ever seen outside of the movies or television. Extraordinary! I couldn't believe she was actually getting to me. I knew from my reading on Earth that dolphins are what we would call promiscuous, but which they obviously considered to be natural, assuming they ever considered it at all. But this was not Earth and Alia was obviously not an Earth dolphin. She was hardly a dolphin at all. She was another human being from another planet with all the attributes of Homo sapiens except for her physical looks.

"So," I said. "Do you think the rain will hurt the rhubarb? You do have rhubarb here, don't you?"

"Rhubarb, shmubarb, whatever that is. I really am attracted to you. Do you find me desirable, too?"

"Alia, cut it out! We just met a few hours ago. I don't even know you," I said, feeling the beginning of an erection. My god, what was wrong with me?

"I know you," she said.

"Not a chance," I answered. "I don't even know me. I don't even know if this place is real or I am real, or you are real. This might be a dream or an hallucination."

"What's an hallucination?"

"It's a psychological term that means you are imagining something that seems completely real."

"Well, I don't know what psychological means, but I assure you I am very real, and I am not imagining anything."

"I'm not talking about you. I'm talking about me."

"Well I assure you that you are real, too. Put out your hand."

Before I had a chance to react she reached out, grabbed my right hand and dug her fingernails into it, hard. "Does this feel real?" she said.

"Ouch!" I said, and quickly pulled it away. Then she grabbed my other hand and did the same thing. It hurt, too. "All right," I said. "Enough. I believe you."

She reached for the candle on the table and picked it up by its oyster shell. "Would you like to put your hand over this?" she said, pointing to the flame.

"I said I believe you. Enough is enough. I'm convinced... more or less.... Pain in an hallucinatory situation can feel real, too," I said weakly.

She stared into my eyes. This time it wasn't a sensual stare at all. It was a look of surprise, and then sadness.

"Let's go," she said abruptly and started to get up.

I didn't know what to do. I really did like her as a person, and damn it, I was physically attracted to her. What to do?

"Alia," I said, "I hardly know you and you hardly know me. Do you really want to hear all the bloody details?"

"Bloody? Did you kill someone? Or are you intending to shed my blood?"

"No, mine," I said. "In the British sense."

"What's British? What does that mean?"

"Well, British is what on Earth we call people from England, or rather Great Britain, which is now the preferred name. It's one of their expressions. It means something like damn."

"Do you mean a dam holding back a lake...of blood? Do the British have so much blood that they need a dam to hold it back?"

I looked intently at her. "Are you putting me on?" I said.

"I don't know what "putting you on" means but if it's the same as "are you kidding me?" the answer is yes."

She flashed a big grin, and I gave it right back to her.

"I give up," I said. "I'll tell you the whole story. And I did, leaving out a few details I knew she wouldn't understand, such as the September 11th attacks, and Olga.

I started with my childhood, loving parents who fought constantly and wanted me to be something I didn't want to be, namely a doctor; to my at first semi-successful career as a stand-up comedian, and then its downslide; Sam's sailboat, the storm, my being knocked into the water, then floating through the dark tunnel, the bright light at the end, the Golden Arches (I didn't mention McDonalds); the meeting with the two gatekeepers, my refusal to go back to my old Earth-life, and their ultimate decision to send me to "my place in the universe" with the Universal Translator imbedded in my body; and finally my naked landing in the water and my experience with the sharks.

She sat enraptured throughout the whole story. When I finished she looked at me long and compassionately, and took both my hands into hers. It felt good, and I felt immensely relieved.

"So," she said, "what else is new?"

"It's not funny," I said, and began to laugh.

"I know. Just trying to lighten things up a little."

"I appreciate that. So… what do you think?"

She was quiet for a long moment. "I think," she said, "that in a previous life you were a dolphin and were reincarnated as a Homo sapien; but were unhappy in that life form; and that you were such a pain in the tail for disobeying the gatekeepers demand to go back to your old life that they sent you here just to get rid of you."

I laughed. "I guess that's as good an explanation as any. I didn't know dolphins believed in reincarnation."

"Most of us don't. It's hard for me to believe that I may have once been an eel or a sea slug."

"I don't believe in it either," I said. "But let's assume that your theory is true, and let's go on from there. Okay?"

"Okay. So what would you like to know about me?"

"Well, for one thing, are you now or have you ever been married?"

"What's married?"

"You mean dolphins here don't get married?"

"I guess not. What does the word mean?"

"Well… it's a ceremony that a man and woman go through where they make a commitment to live together as partners in life, supposedly till one of them dies. Not always honored of course, but that's what being married is supposed to mean."

"Oh, you're asking if I have ever had a lifemate. No, I just haven't found the right man I would want to spend the rest of my life with. And you?"

"No, not me either. I came close a few times, but it never happened. I guess that when you are a stand-up comedian or in other forms of show business you travel a lot and don't really get to know women well enough — or don't want to. At least I never did."

"You used the word women. Is that what females are also called on Earth?"

"Yes."

"What do these women on Earth look like? Do they look like you? I'm sure they don't have non-retractable tinkys," she said with what I swear was a leering grin.

"Don't be smart," I said. Of course they don't have non-retractable tinkys. Surprise! They don't have tinkys at all. They have vaginas, which are internal as, I'm sure, is yours. However, they do have breasts, and they are non-retractable.

"Really? What's a breast?"

"Yes, really. And a breast is a mammary gland, which I'm assume you have inside your body, and they have two of them."

"Two! Interesting. Are they bigger than a tinky?"

I laughed. "Very much so," I said, conjuring up an image in my mind of Olga sitting naked on my couch while we watched reruns of Star Trek.

"What do they look like?"

I was stumped. How do you describe a breast to someone who has never seen one? "Well, let me see.. Uh… do you know what a balloon is?"

"No, what is it?"

"Never mind. Uh… let's see. Well it's sort of like a round rock about six to twelve inches across, depending on the woman. But picture it flat about a third of the way around, with the flat part attached to the woman's chest about here," I said, pointing to my nipples.

She looked puzzled. "Do the women walk stooped over? Rocks are pretty heavy. Do they use them as weapons in fights? I can't imagine walking around with rocks on my chest. What happens if they bump into each other accidentally? That could hurt. And if they do fight with them, do they hit the other women on their rocks?"

"Wait," I said, holding up my hands. "I didn't mean to imply that they were as hard and heavy as rocks. Just the opposite. They're soft and light, as soft as my butt. Here, feel." I said, scooting around the table next to her and putting one of her hands on one of the cheeks of my butt. "Now squeeze a little," I continued. "That will give you the general idea. Except women's breasts are usually softer. Except for the nipples which often get hard during times of... of never mind."

"Umm," she said, "that feels good." And she began to caress it and move her hand around. I started to get aroused again.

"What's this?" she exclaimed. A breast has a crack in it? Is it in two halves? I thought you said that part of it was flat and attached to the body."

"No, no," I said firmly. "Stop." I took her hand and pushed it away. But I didn't lose my semi-erection. This was getting ridiculous, not to mention embarrassing, since a few nearby people in the restaurant were now looking at us... again, but obviously for a different reason.

"Let's go now," I said. "We'll go someplace where I can actually draw you a picture of a Homo sapien woman."

"I'd like that," she said.

I motioned to the waiter, who had been watching our little performance, to bring us the bill. As he started toward us with a smirk on his face, I came to the sudden realization that I didn't have any money, or even know what dolphin money looked like. In my haste to get away I had forgotten that Alia had said that the council was paying.

The waiter presented the check to me, and I looked it over as if I knew what I was doing. Alia watched me with a bemused expression on her face.

"Do you take credit cards?" I asked innocently. "Or American dollars? Or travelers checks?"

He looked at me quizzically; then at Alia. She finally came to my rescue. "The council is paying," she said. "I'm his official guide." She reached into her dakti and pulled out a handful of coin shaped objects, each of which appeared to be made of shells.

"That will be six oysters and a clam," he said. And that was how I found out what dolphinese money was. Relatively simple.

Alia put them on the table along with a few extra clams, or should I say clam coins. We got up and walked the length of the restaurant and out the door, numerous pairs of eyes following us. But I must admit that many of them were looking just at Alia, not us. I assumed they were males, and perhaps a few envious females.

"What would you like to do?" she asked after we got outside and started walking back down the hill.

"How about going back to the hotel so I can go to the bathroom and you can get us some paper and something to write with so I can draw you an Earth woman's body, breasts and all."

"Sounds good to me. I can hardly wait," she said, putting a hand on my butt and squeezing." "I think I like breasts."

I ignored the remark, intending to explain later. I also did not remove her hand. The sensation was too enjoyable.

"By the way," she said. "Why do you want to take a bath?"

"I guess I should have said toilet instead of bathroom," I said, and left it there, not wanting to get into a discussion of American bathrooms as opposed to the rest of the civilized world's toilets. Besides, I was enjoying the feeling of her hand rubbing and caressing my ass too much to distract her. And of course my erection grew as we approached the hotel.

Then all of a sudden she slipped her hand around to my front, reached under my dakti and grabbed my by now fully erect penis.

"Wow," she said. "Very interesting. Not as long as a dolphin's but much thicker. A very nice tinky. I like it."

I immediately stopped walking and pulled her hand away. "Stop," I said. "Please stop. This is not right."

"It is right," she said. "Is this considered wrong on Earth?"

"It depends on where you are," I said. "It's okay in private, but not in public."

She shook her head. "You Earthers really are strange. But I will respect your custom. Perhaps someday you will learn to respect ours," she said with a trace of irritation in her voice. We walked in silence the rest of the way to the hotel and went directly to my room. I opened the door and she left.

"I'm going to get a pencil and paper," she said. "The toilet is through that door to the right. By the way our custom is to flush it when we are finished. I hope you will observe that custom."

"Don't worry, it's our custom, too," I said. "We're not that different."

"Oh, yes you are." She turned and went down the hall toward the lobby.

I walked in and opened the door to the bathroom, not knowing what to expect. I hoped it wasn't going to be complicated because I knew from my readings and pictures I had seen on Earth that a dolphins anal and urinary openings were both in the front of its body.

I needn't have worried. There was an Earth-like toilet in the room, but it was in the middle of the floor rather than against a wall. And there were handlebars coming up from the floor around it, presumably so the dolphin could hold on while leaning over to do his or her duty. There was also a tank on the ceiling with a cord hanging down and a pipe running from it into the toilet. There was no seat. I did my duty, then pulled the rope. Sure enough the toilet flushed.

I went back into the bedroom. Alia hadn't returned yet so I decided to get a good look at what was to be my home for who knows how long.

The walls were made of brick-like blocks, pinkish in color, which I guessed were made of coral. The ceiling was made of the same material except that it was arched, whether for design purpose or to make sure it didn't fall down, or both. I didn't know.

The windows were clear and made of what looked like glass, and probably was since glass on Earth is made from silica, which is the principal component of sand, which I was sure Sea had plenty of.

The stand that held the washbasin, where I rinsed my hands after I got out of the bathroom, was made of what looked like bamboo. Even the top was made of bamboo strips touching one another to form its near flat surface. Even the door was made of the same wood.

I went back to the windows and looked out. The view, which I hadn't noticed in the action and emotion of my arrival was lovely and serene. There were dolphins swimming along in both directions of the canal. Some of them were pushing what looked like a cross between Earth sea kayaks, which are long and slim with a very shallow draft, so that they can be paddled easily and quickly, and Earth canoes, which have a lot space inside. Others were inside the boats, paddling.

Most seemed to be carrying cargo of one kind or another. I could make out what looked like the pinkish bricks, which were obviously used in construction. Others had boxes of various sizes in them, and still others carried bundles of bamboo. A few carried passengers.

I looked for sailboats but didn't see any. Probably because there was not much wind in the canal. But then I remembered that I hadn't seen any in the harbor either, or for that matter out in the sea. As an ardent sailor, that's something I always look for on water. I thought the lack of them was curious, since the dolphins were obviously advanced enough to figure out how to sail.

Then I checked out the bed. I sat down on it and bounced. It was soft and very comfortable. About the same as firm Earth beds. I lay down on it. Quite comfortable, except no pillow. I guessed that was because dolphins don't have much of a neck compared to humans.

Just then there was a knock on the door. "Come in," I called.

The door opened and it was Alia. She looked at me flat on my back and her face lit up with a broad smile.

"I see you changed your mind," she said, whipped off her dakti and dropped it to the floor. She stood in front of me sleek and stark naked, not that dolphins are ever very far from that.

"You like what you see?" She said, slowly undulating the lower part of her body, like a dancer in an Earth strip club.

I gulped. Yes, I liked it. But how could I? A dolphin. Not a woman.

After about 10 seconds of that she grinned salaciously, flopped down on the bed next to me, and reached over to pull off my dakti.

That was it! I pushed her hand away and leaped off the bed, disgusted with myself because I had another erection.

"I'm sorry," I said. "I'm just not ready for this."

"So it seems," she said, rising from the bed and standing in front of me.

I bent down, picked up her dakti and held it out to her.

"You'll need this," I said.

"What for?"

"To cover your… private body parts."

She shook her head and looked at me like the foreign object I was. "That's not why we wear them. We wear daktis to carry things like these." She shook it and some coins came out and fell to the floor. "We are not ashamed of our bodies as you Earthers seem to be. Perhaps some day you will tell me why you didn't want to make joy with me, since we are both obviously very attracted to each other.

"That's assuming we will see each other again," she said grabbing the dakti out of my hand. She tied it around her neck, turned around, stomped out the door that led to the outside and strode to the water's edge. Just before she got there she turned around and called to me.

"I feel sorry for Earthers if they're like you." And with that she turned back to the canal and dove into the water.

I quickly ran out to the canal, but she was out of sight. I thought I saw a grayish blur moving swiftly away from me just below the surface, but I may have been mistaken.

I went back into my room in a daze, confused, upset with myself and Alia, not knowing what to think; just feeling shitty. I lay back down on the bed and stared up at the ceiling.

CHAPTER 5

I closed my eyes and tried to escape by sleeping. I couldn't sleep.

I opened my eyes, got up and began pacing up and down the room. That didn't accomplish anything, so I went outside to the canal and inspected the clear blue water. Certainly not like a Venice canal. No pollution here.

I watched some crabs scurrying along the bottom, and a school of small fish darting one way and another in jerky motions as they often do on Earth.

I tried to picture in my mind's eye Earth dolphins swimming around, playfully chasing one another, jumping out of the water in acrobatic leaps, popping their heads up to look at me, and jabbering away like Flipper.

That didn't help, because pretty soon they seemed to grow arms and legs, and their squawks and shrieks and whistles turned into speech and they were calling out to me, "Earth asshole, Earth asshole!"

That was enough of that. I closed my mind's eye, looked up and down the canal for a few minutes and returned to my room. I plopped down on the bed again and tried to conjure up Alia standing before me undulating her body from top to bottom.

She is beautiful, I thought. I guess. But how the hell do I know? Is something wrong with me? Am I a bigot? Am I dolphinphobic? Or just scared?

While she does look like a dolphin, she also has arms, hands, legs and feet. That's human.

She can carry on an intelligent conversation like a human, well some humans, and she has a great sense of humor. Damn it! She's more human than most humans I know.

And yes, face it Danny, you find her sleek and sexy. But promiscuous, too. No I shouldn't use that word. That's an Earth word. Her actions are obviously not considered promiscuous here on Sea. And that's where I am, here on Sea.

I tried to recall what I had read about dolphins on Earth. Yes, they were indeed what we call promiscuous. They make "joy" very, very frequently. Obviously this is a trait inherent in the species. It's undoubtedly in their genes, both on Earth and here. And why the hell am I such a prude. That's not like me at all. I thought my rebellion against my parents was complete.

My conversation with myself continued…

But me. Why me? With all the male dolphins around why did Alia pick me? Is she looking for an adventure with a strange species? Is she bored with dolphin joy and looking for something new?

It can't be my looks, although I have been told that I'm reasonably good looking, sometimes even handsome, I must admit in all modesty. But by Homo sapien standards. I must be pretty funny looking to female dolphins, let alone one who is reputed to be one of the most beautiful on Sea.

Is it my intelligence, sense of humor and charming personality? Maybe it is. I would like to think I am all those things, and that they attracted her to me. Why? Why?

All I know is that I'm damned attracted to her. More than that; I'm infatuated, possibly more than that.

And it isn't just the idea of joy. Admit it, Danny boy, you've really fallen for her.

Not possible, Danny boy. You've known her for less than a day.

And she has a tail, and a blowhole, and no breasts. I fleetingly wondered if blowing into her blowhole would turn her on. Enough!

I opened my eyes and got off the bed. I decided to take a brisk walk along the canal and not think about Alia. I went out the door and started walking in the opposite direction from where I had come to the hotel.

It was quite pleasant, a mix of some very picturesque houses and shops and one story warehouse buildings. After about ten minutes I slowed down to look more closely into the shop windows. Suddenly my legs came to an abrupt halt. I turned to peer into the shop window that had stopped me. I took a deep breath. The aroma of chocolate.

Wow! I said to myself. Those do look like chocolates! I hadn't thought about chocolate since I left Earth. And I'm almost a chocoholic. I love chocolate; I wondered if Alia liked chocolate. I wondered where she was. I realized I didn't even know her last name, assuming she had one... or where she lived.

Enough of that. I went into the store. "Hello," said the clerk, trying not to stare at me. "I've heard about you. Welcome to Sea. Would you like a piece of chocolate?"

I was elated. It looked like chocolate, and they even called it chocolate. My elation became embarrassment when I realized I didn't have any money. I should have picked up the coins Alia dumped on the floor.

"Yes, I would. Most certainly. But I'm sorry. As you know, I just arrived here yesterday and I don't yet have any money."

"Oh that's all right," he/she said.

"I would like to make you a present of a piece. Consider it part of your welcoming. What would you like?"

"Why thank you. That's very nice of you." My eyes surveyed the glass display counters and came to rest on what looked like a chocolate truffle, my favorite. I pointed to it. "Could that be a truffle?" I said.

"It certainly is," was the reply.

"That particular one is double chocolate. We also have raspberry, blackberry, and —"

"Stop. I'll take the double chocolate. I love chocolate. And I'll come back and buy some when I get money. Thank you very, very much. By the way, where does the chocolate come from?"

"We make it ourselves from beans which grow in the hills on the other side of the island, the rainy side."

"I'll be damned. Just like on Earth. Thank you again."

I decided not to eat it in the shop in case I didn't like it, so I went outside and took a bite. Ah… it was delicious. Not quite like the truffles I used to buy at Chocolate Decadence, my favorite chocolate shop in San Francisco, but very close and very chocolatey.

I found myself wanting to share it with Alia. Cut out that shit, I said to myself. Just enjoy the damn chocolate. I did, but I still wondered — it's difficult to stop a chocolate-stimulated brain from working. So what if she doesn't like chocolate? What's the big deal? Lots of people don't particularly care for chocolate. If she doesn't, she doesn't.

I finished my truffle and continued along the walkway, determined more than ever to dismiss Alia from my mind. I had almost but not quite succeeded when a dolphin leaped out of the water and landed on its feet in front of me.

"So there you are," it said exuberantly. "I've been looking for you. I'm Ami, your new guide. I'm really happy to be your guide. It's going to be fun."

"New guide? What do you mean? Why? What happened to Al– my former guide?"

"She asked to be relieved. Said she didn't really think she was qualified. Frankly, I think she was angry. What did you do to make her mad?"

"Nothing," I answered. "Nothing at all." I took a deep breath.

"Well, Ami," I said. "I'm in your hands, figuratively speaking of course. By the way, are you male or female?"

"He looked insulted. "Male, of course. Can't you tell?"

"No, I'm sorry. Actually I can't. Can you tell me how to tell the difference?"

He looked thoughtful. "Do you mean by just looking at a person?"

"Yes, when I meet someone, how should I know? Because I'm a newcomer, everyone looks pretty much the same to me, and most of you wear aprons. Do the females wear more colorful ones, or do the number of pockets differ?"

"Please don't call them aprons. Aprons are what cooks and shop workers wear. We call an apron not used for work a dakti."

"Yes, I know. Do females wear different ones?"

"Some do, some don't. That's not really a way to tell us apart. Some women if they are good looking with a sleek shape, nice legs and tails, like Alia, might wear real colorful and short ones."

The image of Alia whipping off her red short dakti flashed into my mind. I eventually succeeded in blotting it out.

"What else?" I said.

"Well, some males, particularly those who do a lot of physical work, are broader and more muscular. Most are a little taller than women, too. But not always. And men's tails tend to be a little wider, too. But not always."

"Go on."

"Most women have a higher and more melodic voice than males, like Alia."

"Proceed, please," I said, starting to become exasperated. Alia, Alia.

"Surely," I said, "there are other women on Sea besides Alia."

"Of course," Ami said. "I was just using her as an example because you know her. If I upset you, I'm sorry."

"No, I'm not upset. Please go on."

"I guess you guys didn't hit it off too well. She seemed upset, too. I really am sorry."

"Please don't apologize. I apologize to you for seeming to be upset… and, it appears, for upsetting Alia."

"Think nothing of it. We dolphins are pretty emotional people, especially women. Sometimes we just don't get along with one another."

"I think I understand. But please continue."

"I'll try. You know I've never really thought of the differences. We just seem to be able to recognize them. I think it's a matter of vibrations. Kind of like an aura of femininess. Yes, that's it. It's a feeling you get when you are close to one. You feel it even more in the water, when you are swimming with them.

"And, of course, you also hear their clicks. Alia has her own particularly distinctive sound picture of clicks. Very alluring."

"Oh."

"Yes, I'm sorry I mentioned her name again. Naturally other females also have alluring clicks, delightful sound patterns, and they radiate what feel like warm, embracing vibrations. Alia's are particularly attractive."

"Uh… I take it then that you have been swimming with Alia."

"Yes, of course. We were in the same class at school. Sometimes we take trips together up and down the coast or out to the islands north of Sea. In groups naturally, and with guards to protect us from sharks. But we stick together. We know each other quite well, and we're very good friends.

"I see. That's nice. What kind of friends?"

"What do you mean?"

"Have you…uh…ever… made joy with her?"

He peered at me strangely. Then he laughed. "I do believe you are taken with her, aren't you? No, we're not that kind of friends. We have never made joy and undoubtedly never will. I'm not her type, and neither is she mine."

"Okay, okay. I understand, I think. Sorry I asked. It's really none of my business."

He smiled. "You Earthers are a curious lot. Are all Earthers like you when it comes to women?"

"I suppose they are. But me not as much. I'm a little different. I feel that everybody has a right to do what they want as long as it doesn't harm someone else. I apologize for asking."

"Please don't apologize for asking. I can see that you have a real concern. But you needn't worry. I'm a winky tinky."

"A what?"

"A winky tinky. It means I like tinkys."

"You mean you're a homosexual?"

"I'm not familiar with that word. Is it a variation of Homo sapien?"

"Sort of," I replied.

"But if it means that I only like joy with males, you are correct. I am, indeed, a homosexual. But our term winky tinky sounds like more fun."

"I'll be damned," I said. I had often heard and read that homosexuality was not unique to humankind and that it occurred in many animal species. But in dolphins, and on another planet? I suppose I shouldn't have been surprised.

"You act surprised, Danny. Don't they have winky tinkys on

Earth?"

"Yes, of course we do. But could you please explain the meaning of the word 'winky'."

He laughed. "Very simple, my friend. A male has a tinky, and a female has a winky. Most male dolphins like to put their tinky into a female's winky. But we winky tinkys are different —."

"I understand," I said. "Are there many of you on Sea?"

"Enough to keep life interesting and joyful."

"That's nice," I said., delighted that this relationship with Alia was winky tinky.

"So," I said. Changing the subject, what's next for me?"

"Nothing special for today. But tomorrow will be different. You have a morning appointment with the Administrator. He will talk to you about your stay here, and discuss with you what kind of work you would like to do, and he will give you some money to buy things until you start earning on your own. Although I do think he already has a job in mind for you."

"What kind of job?"

"I don't know. We'll find out tomorrow. In the meanwhile, how are you feeling? You must be tired. It's been a long day for you and it is getting dark. What do you say we go back to the hotel, maybe have a little something to eat, and then you can get a good night's sleep."

"That's an excellent idea," I said, realizing that it had been a long and eventful day, and that I really was tired.

"I think I'll skip the eating and go straight to my room. I'm not really hungry. If that's all right."

"Of course. You can do whatever you want."

We walked back to the hotel and parted outside my door, a little to my relief, I must admit.

"I'll leave a wake-up call at the desk for you. Would you like something to read before you go to sleep?"

"Oh, sure," I lied. What do you suggest?"

He reached into one of his dakti pockets, pulled out what certainly looked like a book, and handed it to me. It was dry, which surprised me since, he had been swimming just a short time before.

"How did you keep the book dry?" I asked.

"Simple," he answered. Most pockets in a dakti have an inner pocket with a flap that folds over and closes, making it waterproof. I'm sure yours has one, too."

I reached into mine and sure enough he was right. "Very clever," I said.

"Not clever, just practical. As you will realize when you read the book, dolphins are very resourceful. It's a basic history of Sea, and will tell you much about us. See you in the morning. Good night, Danny."

"Thanks, and good night to you, Ami."

Then he was gone, leaving me standing in the doorway with a book I couldn't read and fervently wished I could.

I went into the room and closed the door behind me. A candle was burning on the nightstand, and the bed was turned down. The cover was a light blanket that seemed to be made of soft skin that in the dim light was whitish in color. Fish skin? That reminded me that my body could use a washing. I still felt a little sticky from the salt water of my morning swim to the hotel.

I went over to the wash basin and just as I was ready to begin I saw a door next to the table I hadn't noticed earlier in the day. I opened it and looked inside. There was what looked like a shower-head with a bamboo tube running down to it from a tank hung under the ceiling. There was a cord hanging down from it just like in the bathroom, or rather toilet. There was also a hole in the slanting floor, which had to be a drain. This had to be a shower.

I gave the cord a short jerk and water came out of the head. It was a shower. Yes!

I looked to see if there was a source for hot water, but that turned out to be too much to ask. So What? Sea was a tropical island, and the water couldn't be too cold.

So I slipped out of my dakti, hopped into the room under the showerhead and pulled the chain.

Sea may be a tropical island, but the water was damn cold. I quickly stepped aside to see if there was any such thing as soap. Sure enough there was, on a little shelf coming off the wall. I wondered what it was made of.

I soaped myself and got back under the shower, just long enough to wash the soap off. There was no towel so I just stood there till I dripped and dried off partially.

While I was waiting I wondered why there was no towel. Then it came to me. A dolphin's skin probably shed water like a duck's back. They were probably dry within seconds.

I waited until I was nearly dry. I was too impatient to wait until I was completely dry. Then I went back into the bedroom, hopped into bed, and pulled the cover over me.

I lay there reflecting on what my life had been the last two days. I was always the adventurous sort, but this was a bit much — but not too much. I smiled and wondered about my new life. By now I was at least reasonably sure that I was not dreaming or hallucinating. The cold shower had helped to reassure me.

So, what remained? Was I in heaven? I doubted that. Whoever heard of cold showers in heaven? Besides, I didn't even know if heaven existed.

Hell? If I had gone that way, the shower would have been scalding hot.

Purgatory? Same argument.

Nope. Chances were pretty strong I was really on the planet Sea. And I liked it so far. Olga had done me a big favor by entering me in the Intergalactic Starmapping Society. My place in this universe was pretty damn good. I was fortunate that my sun, Star DiVinci, as the Society now called it, had a planet so pleasant and so much like Earth. As for the people, I really liked them so far. And it had chocolate! And it had Alia!

Oh no, I said to myself. No more. I will not think about her. I will think only about what tomorrow may bring, what I will see, what I will learn. My infatuation with Alia was simply a passing moment resulting from the stress of being in a new and strange environment. She was nice to me and I to her. Merely ships that pass in the night.

My eyelids began to feel heavy and I realized how truly tired I was. I leaned over, blew out the candle on the nightstand, lay back down, closed my eyes and fell asleep almost instantly.

To sleep, perchance to dream.

Boy, did I ever dream!

Dream Number One:

Alia was standing at the end of the bed facing me with a big smile on her face. She seemed to have real breasts. She made a half turn so I could see her from the side. She certainly did have real breasts, perfect ones projecting out at just the right angle. She also had a perfectly proportioned real butt, which she wiggled for me.

What she didn't have was a tail. It was gone. And her neck was more pronounced and human. Another thing she didn't have was a human woman's face.

I was taken aback at first, seeing that beautiful human female body with a dolphins head on its neck. But then I realized that it wouldn't be Alia if she didn't have her own head and face. And that it didn't matter.

I loved that face, its bright intelligent usually laughing eyes, and its smile. Loved? No way! Who said that? Impossible! How could I love someone I had known for less than a day? Love at first sight? Theoretically possible. Infatuation much more likely. Had I succumbed to the enchanting vibrations Ami said emanated from her?

Alia turned, faced me again, put her hands under her breasts, raised them and said, "Are these what you mean by breasts, Danny?"

I nodded my head. "Yes," I said softly.

She shook her head. "Not interested," she said. "A hindrance to freedom of movement, a burden to carry around, and undoubtedly as big — no bigger attraction to sharks as your Tinky. Goodbye, breasts."

And they slowly faded away.

"And as for these," she said putting her hands on her buttocks. "They serve their purpose for you. These bulging globs of fat take away from the sleek lines of every dolphin's body, especially mine. Why they're not much different from those ridiculous oversized external mammary glands breasts — just bigger and closer together. Yuk!"

And they, too, faded away.

"See what I mean," she said. "Don't I look nicer now?"

Then her tail reappeared, and she stood there in her own sleek, streamlined body. I thought she was beautiful. Then she smiled again, and faded away completely, her vision lingering in my mind for a few moments.

I awakened and lay there, staring at the foot of the bed where she had been, wondering if it were possible for a male Homo sapien on Sea to be brainwashed by a dream. Had she been sending out unseen vibrations to me?

Eventually I drifted off back to sleep, in time for…

Dream Number Two:

I was in the water, underwater as a matter of fact. There were dolphins swimming all around, like the underwater ballet you see in Earth films or on television or in an IMAX theater.

Then all of a sudden there was Alia. She had broken away from the group and was coming toward me. I swam to meet her, and just before I reached her she turned her body into me. I did the same, and our bodies touched and stayed touched as we swam around slowly together, both of us with ear to ear smiles on our faces. It put me into an exotically sensual mood.

Alia blew some bubbles out of her blowhole; I blew some out of my nose. Around and around we went, up and down, always touching, never going to the surface for air.

Alia flapped her tail and I flapped my legs together in unison. We swam over to the other dolphins and joined in, all of us together performing the underwater ballet. I had never in my entire life felt so graceful and in sync with my physical environment.

After a while we broke away from the group, still touching, and sat down on the sand at the bottom, observing the other dolphins. Ami spotted us, swam over, winked at me, smiled broadly, wiggled his tail, and went back to join the group.

Alia and I turned our heads to one another… and kissed. I closed my eyes to savor the moment. All of a sudden I heard a voice from my childhood shouting behind me.

"Danny's kissing a dolphin! Danny's kissing a dolphin!"

It sounded like my bratty kid sister. I pulled away from Alia and turned around. It was my sister.

"Shut up," I said. "It's none of your business."

"Mommy," she continued, "come see. Danny's kissing Flipper! Danny's kissing Flipper! Danny's kissing a dolphin."

"Look brat," I said, "if you don't shut up I'm going to throw you into your room and tie the door knob shut so you can't get out. When you get older you may understand this. In the meanwhile, buzz off."

I turned back to Alia, who seemed to have not heard anything, motioned to her, and we swam back to the group, touching and holding hands.

But just before we got there, the dolphins disappeared. I turned to Alia, but she, too, was gone, and my hand was empty. I turned around. My sister was also gone. The water was gone, too. Everything was dark, and I realized I had awakened.

I was sweating profusely. I laughed to myself sarcastically. Maybe I was actually dripping water from my swim with Alia. Fat chance.

I had no idea what time it was, but I resolved not to fall asleep again. My resolve didn't help. I was rehashing in my mind some of my comedy routines that had failed to elicit many laughs from my audiences, when I must have fallen asleep again. I guess I was so bad that I put myself to sleep. But this time no dreams, or at least none that I could remember.

The next thing I knew there was a knock on my door, and a male dolphin voice (I think it was a male — I thought I could now tell the difference, maybe) called out. Mr. Danny DiVinci, its time to get up."

"Thank you," I replied, loud enough so he would know I was awake. I got up and performed my morning ablutions. The toothbrush Alia had brought me did the job nicely, although I didn't particularly care for the taste of the soap, there being no toothpaste. I also didn't particularly care for the toilet paper in the bathrooms. It was more than a little rough and I made a mental note to research the subject, and try to improve it.

When I was finished I slipped into my dakti and while waiting for Ami leafed through the book Ami had given me that I couldn't read.

After a while he still had not arrived and I was getting bored. I got up and went to the window. It was a beautiful sunshiny day, so I went out the door and headed for the canal. Just before I got there Ami leaped out of the water in front of me, just as he had the day before.

"Good morning, Danny," he said cheerfully. "Sorry I'm late."

"Good morning Ami," I said, equally as cheerful, "Is it always your custom to leap out of the water in front of people when you come to meet them?"

"Only Earthers," he grinned. "Let's go."

I turned around and started back to my room.

"Wait," he said. "We have to swim over. It's too far to walk to make it in time for the meeting."

"If you say so," I said, still trying to sound cheerful, but not relishing the idea of a rehash of yesterday's adventure. I explained to him the swimming method I had worked out with Aba and Daba.

"No problem," he said. "Are you ready?"

"Totally," I lied, and dove in trying to execute as perfect a swan dive as I had ever done diving off the swimming rock in the Neversink River where I had spent my childhood summers.

I must have succeeded because when I returned to the surface he said, "nicely done. Very graceful. I'll have to tell my friends. We dive with our arms against our bodies the entire time. I like yours better. I think maybe we can learn a few things from you Earthers. Would you teach me how to do it?"

"I would be honored." I beamed, "Shall we go?"

"Let's do it," he said, hooking his arm around mine. And off we went, successfully using what I named the AbaDaba method of swimming.

When we arrived about ten minutes later I did my Earther swimming pool vault out of the water and landed hard on my butt. Ami did his gymnastic leap out of the water landing gracefully on his feet. He bent over, grabbed my hands and helped me to my feet.

We then went up the steps into the building I remembered from my interrogation the day before. It made me think of my FROS detention-mate, and I wondered what had happened to him, and what kind of punishment he received. I resolved to find out.

We walked past the large hall, which was now empty, and through a doorway just past it into a waiting room with a receptionist at a desk and chairs against the wall. Ami motioned me to sit down and went up to the receptionist. There was a door right behind her/him with some writing on it, which looked like two words, which probably said Administrator's Office, or more seriously The Administrator.

He spoke with the receptionist, came back and sat down next to me. "It will be a few minutes," he said. "In the meanwhile, let me tell you what to expect."

"Please do."

"The Administrator is the chief official of Sea. He or she, he in this case, manages the day to day affairs of Sea, and is an appointed rotating officer."

"Appointed by whom and rotating with whom and where?"

"Appointed by the Council of Administrators, but only by those council members who have not yet served as Administrator themselves. He can serve for a period of only three years. The he goes back to the Council, and another member is appointed. They rotate into the Administrator position. No member can serve consecutive terms or repeat as Administrator unless he has been out of office at least ten years. Council members themselves may not serve for more than 20 years.

"Who appoints the council members?"

"They are elected by the population when there is a vacancy as a result of serious sickness or death and, of course, should there be a corruption or abuse of power scandal, which is very, very rare.

"Can anybody run for Council?"

"Oh, no. First they have to go through extensive training in Administrator School, and then they have to spend five years on special council assignments, and another five as an assistant to a council member. Only then can they stand for election. By that time they are thoroughly trained, qualified and experienced in government, assuming, of course, that they pass their examinations all along the way."

"Naturally," I said, implying that our form of government was comparable, and that our elected officials were trained, examined and competent. We should live so long. "It sounds like an excellent system."

"It's not perfect, but it works. We rarely get a bad Administrator."

"And this one?"

"Excellent, I think. You have already met him. He's the one who was questioning you yesterday."

"Yes, I know." I thought back to that very serious personage. Tough, but fair. "Any suggestions, Ami?"

"Just be yourself, Danny. While he will still by trying to get the measure of you, he will also be trying to help you. Realize he's a good man trying to do his job, and that this is a situation neither he nor his predecessors have ever encountered before. Further more, he certainly has not been trained to know what to do. By the way, his name is Malti, but you have to call him Mr. Administrator."

Just then the door opened, and there stood the Administrator, resplendent in a brown purplish robe about the color of octopus skin, which it may well have been.

"Come in Danny DiVinci, and you, too, Ami," he said with a welcoming smile on his face. He certainly didn't seem the same dolphin as yesterday. It was a genuine smile, and then we shook hands.

He led us into a large room lined with bookcases. His desk was on the far end with three chairs in a semicircle in front of and facing it. There was another dolphin sitting in an end chair with its back to us. He escorted us to the area in front of the chairs and motioned us to sit down.

I didn't sit immediately. I just stood there staring at the other dolphin. It was Alia, and she was staring back at me very seriously. No dolphin smile on her face. Not even a hint of one. My heart skipped a few beats as I sat down in the middle chair next to her.

"Hello, Alia," I said.

"Good morning, Danny. I hope you had a restful sleep."

"What reason could I possibly have for not? And you?"

"What reason could I possibly have for not?" she echoed, still staring at me.

The Administrator looked at us from one to the other and back again. "You two seem to know each other well," he said.

"We've met," we said in unison.

"Alia was my guide yesterday," I said, "at least until Ami cam along late in the day."

"I know. I assigned her. Why did she want to change guides?"

Silence. I wasn't the one about to answer. Neither was Alia.

Ami came to our rescue. "Alia wasn't feeling well," he said, "so she asked me to take over for her."

"Just for the rest of the day," Alia blurted out. "I feel fine now," she added. "And well rested too."

My heart sang, and I felt that funny butterfly feeling in my chest and stomach. All was well; better than well... yes!

"I'm well rested, too." I added quickly and looked at Alia. She was smiling. I smiled back, and we both looked at the Administrator. He was smiling, too.

"Good," he said, "because we have a job for all three of you. The Council met last night and we decided that you, Alia and Ami, as our two leading councilors in training should accompany Danny here in an attempt to make verbal contact with the killer whales, or orcas, as you call them, Danny DiVinci."

"Call me Danny, please."

"All right, Danny. Is that something you think you would like to do?"

"Like to do? I would love to do that!"

One of the highlights of my life was the sea kayak trip I took to Robsons' Bight, an area in the Johnstone Straight between Vancouver Island and the mainland in Canada. It was a place where orcas congregated, especially during the summer when the salmon, their chief source of food, were beginning their runs up the rivers.

I loved those whales, whose common name, "Killer Whales", was a gross misnomer, since they have never been known to attack a human — in or out of the water. I still remember the picture in my grade school geography book showing a fiercely toothed orca with mouth wide open about to snatch an Eskimo off an iceberg.

Bullshit. Entirely false. But I wondered about the orcas on Sea. Maybe they really were killers.

"The orcas," the Administrator continued, "are large toothed predatory whales that inhabit, indeed rule, the waters of Sea. They have no natural enemies. All creatures of the sea if they have any sense, fear them, even the sharks.

They feed on large fish as well as seals and other sea mammals. They have never been known in modern times to attack a dolphin, although they did in the past.

"What do you mean by 'modern times?" I asked.

"Alia, would you like to explain that please."

She nodded her head, turned to me, gave me a prim school-marmish look along with a wink and spoke:

"About two hundred years ago, in 5485 to be exact, the Council had an idea. That idea was to make the killer whales — excuse me I mean orcas — feel they had more to gain by not look-ing at us as a food source, but rather a food supplier."

"And how did you do that?"

"Before answering that question specifically, let me tell you about a special place here on Sea. We call it Killer Whale Cove. I think we should rename it Orca Cove. What do you think Mr. Administrator?"

"I agree, my dear. I'll bring it up to the council. orca is a much nicer name for those very, very intelligent animals. I think the council will agree; we've all been uncomfortable with the killer name. Continue, Alia."

"Orca Cove, as I hope it will soon be called, is about eight miles down the coast. It has a beach of small stones, rather than sand, that gradually slopes into the water for about 200 yards, the approximate length of the cove. We think the orcas congregate there because they like to rub their bodies against the stones. We've seen them do it many times.

"Whether they do it for pleasure or to clean their skins we don't know."

"Very interesting," I said, trying to keep the delight out of my voice. "We have a place similar to that on Earth."

"That's extraordinary," said the Administrator. "And do you talk to them?"

"Uh… no. I wish we could."

"You mean you can talk to sharks and not orcas? Orcas are far more intelligent than sharks. We think they may be as intelligent as us. How unfortunate. That was going to be your mission.

"To talk with them and translate for us. To be our envoy. I am really disappointed. This could have been one of the turning points in our history."

"Wait," I said. "I think your disappointment is premature," Alia and I exchanged knowing glances. "It may still happen. On Earth I can't talk to sharks either, or for that matter, our dolphins. It's only here on Sea that I can talk to sharks.

"And if I can talk to sharks, which as you say are far less intelligent than orcas, I should be able to talk with orcas. Alia, please go on."

"All right. In 5805 the Council members had the notion that if we could feed them at Orca Cove over a period of time they would get the idea that we would provide a constant reliable food source, and that we were their friends."

"And it worked?"

"It took a few months, but yes it worked. At first we lost a few volunteer dolphins, but every time they ate one of us we withheld their food for several days. By the end of the third month they were convinced and stopped eating dolphins. And by then we felt we could trust them.

They actually became friendly, and have remained so ever since."

I was skeptical. "Why would what in essence was merely a

token feeding be so important to them that they changed their hunting and eating habits?"

"That's what we, or should I say our ancestors, wondered at first. There is certainly enough food in the sea for them, and they are such efficient hunters. We've watched them. They hunt in organized preplanned group attacks. Why should they give dolphins up just for the relatively little food they got from us? Fish that they could get for themselves anyway?

"The answer may have to do with the special nature of the cove. I explained what they do there, the rubbing on the rocks and in general lounging around."

"Yes, I remember."

"Well, the conclusion our ancestors came to, and we agree, is that Orca Cove is a recreational area for them, sort of a vacation retreat. And they simply do not want to be bothered to hunt. In effect, we helped them to recreate. Does that make sense?"

"Some," I said. "Maybe they just want to be friends with other intelligent beings."

I turned to the Administrator. "But what do you need me for if you already have the problem solved, and they have been friendly for 200 years?"

"True enough," he said hesitantly. "I know you are not familiar with our ways, but once you are you will find that we are a very non-violent people.

"While it is true that we do kill fish, it is because we have to eat them to maintain our health, although I must admit there is a tiny fraction of our population that thinks we can exist on plants alone. That may be theoretically possible, but it is against our core nature, and we think not healthy. Besides, they don't taste very good."

"I'll vouch for that," I chimed in.

"At one time in our history," he continued, "we ate other animals, not just fish. I am referring to air breathing mammals such as seals. We have come to believe that other air breathing creatures are our biological cousins. They can think, feel, play, take care of their young, and other dolphin-like things. We think killing them is very wrong."

"And that is where you come in, Danny, assuming that you can, indeed, talk with them."

"I'm listening," I said, beginning to get the drift of where he was heading.

"You probably don't know this," he continued, "because you are new here, but orcas do the very thing I was just talking about. In addition to feeding on fish, they also kill and eat seals, sea lions, and even other whales. They also kill and eat the children of these animals, especially other whales.

"We think this is terribly wrong, and we would like to start a dialog with them to convince them not to do this. There are plenty of fish in the sea. They don't have to.

"The only way it is possible to do this is to talk with them, appeal to their intelligence and morality, if they have any. We know they have the intelligence, but we don't think they understand that what they are doing is wrong."

"I understand," I said. "The orcas on Earth behave the same way." I had a vivid picture in my mind of a television program that showed orcas riding an incoming wave and chasing seals right onto the beach, chomping down on them, holding them in their mouths and waiting for the next incoming wave to take them back into the water. It made for good film footage, but left viewers like me with a feeling of repulsion.

"Then you can appreciate our view. We would like you, Danny, if you are willing to undertake this mission, to approach

the orcas in Orca Cove and convince them to meet with at a conference in the future. You will be the translator."

"I'd like to give it a try," I said. "And I do agree with what you
are trying to do. What's the plan and when do we leave?"

"Alia and Ami will take you there, of course with a unit of
guards to protect you from the sharks. But first they have to
arrange for transportation and supplies, and for volunteers for the
guards. So it will be an hour or so."

He looked from Alia to Ami and said, "You can go now, but
Danny, would you please stay."

Ami and Alia stood up, said their good-byes and left. Alia gave
me an engaging smile as she left, and I think I felt vibrations coming from her. At least I wanted to think I did.

"Certainly. What would you like to talk about?"

He sat back in his chair and peered at me for a few moments
before he began.

"I hope you won't be angry with Alia when I tell you this."

Oh. Oh. I thought. Did she actually tell him about our quar-
rel in the hotel room?

"I don't think I could ever be angry with Alia. She's an exceptionally nice person. I get good vibrations from her."

"Good," he continued. "You didn't ask her to keep what you
told her confidential, so in the interest of mutual understanding
she related to me what you told her about how you came to be on
Sea. It is an extraordinary story, to say the least, but it is an explanation, a little far-fetched, but possible. At least as possible as the
story you told at the hearing yesterday morning."

"It's true," I said. "And I'm not angry. I also apologize for what
I said at the hearing. I didn't think what actually happened would
sound plausible."

"A plausible explanation. So let us assume that is actually what happened. It seems to me that you are here for good, and that you have no way to leave."

"I agree."

"Good. Therefore, we have to work out several things. First, you need money so you can purchase things. Second, you need a means of earning money because we are not going to give it to you without your working for it."

"I agree, and am perfectly willing to work."

"Excellent. Now we have to agree on a way for you to earn money. In essence, a job."

"I understand."

"I have an idea, at least a temporary solution. How would you like to teach about your planet and what you know about the universe? You could have several classes of all ages from children to adults."

"I think that's a wonderful idea. I'd like to do it. Can I tell jokes in class?"

"Everybody on Sea tells jokes, well almost everyone. So you may, of course, too. Your salary will be the same as our regular beginning teachers. And it's a fairly good one, since we consider education to be very important. You can start a few days after you return from your assignment with Ami and Alia.

"That will give you time to look for a place to live and to plan your curriculum. Agreed?"

"Agreed."

"Good. And we will consider this assignment to be a preliminary job as compensation for the money we will advance you. Is that fair?"

"Very," I answered.

"Good. From here my secretary will take you to the financial office for your money to buy whatever you need."

"Thank you, Mr. Administrator."

"And Danny, please accept my most sincere good wishes for your success in this project. If successful, you will have made a truly significant contribution to civilization on Sea. So go, and may fortune be with you."

"Thank you, sir." For a brief fleeting moment I thought he was going to say, "may the force be with you." Wouldn't that have been something?

He escorted me to the door and spoke briefly with his secretary/receptionist. She, I think she was a she, took me to another office where I got my money, slipped it into a dakiti pocket, and headed outside, ready for another step in my new life.

Since my kayak trip among the orcas in Canada, I had really been intrigued by them. If these were the same or similar, the idea of actually talking with them was quite exciting. More than that, it was exhilarating.

I hurried down the steps to the water and was happy to see that Alia and Ami were already there waiting for me on the quay. They had some bound up parcels with them in addition to a large tightly woven basket with a handle about two feet across that looked more like a bucket.

"What's that?" I said pointing to it.

"That's for carrying live fish," said Ami. "We'll load you up when you wade out from the beach to talk with the killer — I mean orcas."

"You mean I can't talk with them from the boat?" I said, remembering their immense mouths full of sharp teeth.

"We think the boat would create an artificial barrier," said Alia, "but that you being in the water with them would put you in their element, and improve the chances of good communication."

"Suppose they think I'm something to eat?" I said, remembering the film of the orcas chasing seals up the beach.

"Orcas haven't attacked dolphins for over two hundred years," Alia said.

"But I'm not a dolphin. They've never seen a Homo sapien before."

"But you will be with a dolphin. Me," said Alia. "I'll wade out with you so they will see that we're together. You'll hold out a fish as soon as the first one comes near us so he will see that you mean well. The chances of him attacking you are slim. Especially if you greet him in a language he can understand."

"Let's hope you're right," I said. "I wouldn't want to give an orca indigestion. I'm ready. Let's see this boat we're going in."

We picked up the packages and bucket, and walked about 50 yards along the quay. "There it is," said Alia pointing toward the water. "It's one that Ami and I have used several times in exploring the coastline."

I examined it and was pleased. It was the same kind I had seen in my walk along the quay the day before, looking like a cross between a canoe and sea kayak. Long and narrow with a shallow draft, and open on the inside running the length of the boat for carrying cargo and passengers.

It was about 20 feet long and seemed to be made of some sort of skin wrapped tightly around a framework of bamboo strips touching each other. I was reminded that so far the only wood I had seen on Sea was bamboo and palm tress and bushes. No real tress, other than the palms.

"What do you call this kind of boat?" I asked.

"It's a baku, very comfortable and easy to paddle. A little tippy at first, but once you get used to it, very steady."

Ami got down into the baku and Alia and I handed him the packages, three doubled ended kayak type paddles that were on the quay next to it, and three long poles with their ends wrapped. Then he got out of the boat and climbed back on to the quay.

"I would say we're ready to go," said Alia. "I'll get aboard and help you in."

"Excuse me," I said. Shouldn't we have a little meeting first, so I know what the plan is?"

"We're sorry," said Ami. "We thought the Administrator had filled you in on all the details. Of course you should know."

Alia continued. "It's now about 10:00 A.M. and the distance is approximately eight miles. It's about a two to three hour paddle from here to when we actually reach the cove. We'll follow the coastline south. Just before we get to the cove we'll fill your basket with live fish, and water, or course, at the Denmar Fish Farm, and then proceed to our rendezvous with the orcas."

"What's the Denmar Fish Farm?"

"Denmar is the name of the fish we raise to feed the orcas," Alia explained. "Each one weighs about seven to eight pounds, and is about 20 inches long. Not a lot for orcas to eat, but large enough to keep them interested. Your basket will hold three or four.

"After picking up the fish we'll paddle into the cove and to the beach. There we will get out of the baku, you will take the fish basket, and together we will wade out. All clear?"

"I suppose."

"One more thing."

"There's more?"

"A lot more to come," she said, reaching out to take my hands in hers, and gazing into my eyes. "I just want you to know that I am no longer angry, that I understand why you acted that way, and… and I care for you very much." She leaned over, quickly kissed me on the lips and stepped back, still holding my hands.

"Alia," I said. "I just want you to know that I understand why you acted that way, and… and I care for you very, very, very much. And if you don't let go of my hands instantly and stop looking at me like that I'm going to pull your dakti off and make joy with you right on this damn quay in front of everybody."

"That would be unseemly," she smiled, pulled her hands away and blew me a kiss. "Let's go," she said, stepping carefully down into the baku and extending a hand to help me in.

"No thanks, I'm an old kayaker," I said, stepping down into the boat. I was so emotional from the last few minutes that I forgot the cardinal rule of getting into a boat like this: plant your foot on the midline. Instead, I thoughtlessly stepped on the side sending the baku into a precarious rocking motion that almost turned us over, and would have had I not realized what a dumb thing I had done and immediately plopped my butt down on the midline, and grabbed the rails to steady myself and the boat. I was really embarrassed but, Ami came to my rescue.

"I'm sorry," he said. "We forgot to tell you the proper way to get into a baku. You have to step onto the midline of the boat."

"Thank you," I said, realizing I blew it, and right in front of Alia. "These are different from the boats I'm used to," I lied. Sea Kayaks are just as tippy and I'm an experienced sea kayaker. "Earth boats don't rock so easily. I'll do better next time."

"I'm sure you will," said Alia. Something like that happens to almost everybody their first time. You'll get used to it."

Ami stood up, slipped out of his dakti and sandals, put them down and said, "I'll swim with the patrol. The baku will be easier to paddle with just two people, and I'll enjoy the swim with the patrol." Just then a dozen dolphins swam up to us and waved. They all carried the same kind of spears as my rescuers had that first day. Alia waved back to them. Then Ami did a terrible imitation of a swan dive into the water, landing on his belly, and splashing water into the baku.

When he came back up to the surface he looked at me and smiled. "Not very good, was it?" he said.

"No, not very good. But you'll learn. It happens to almost everybody their first time. You'll get used to it. Do we really need the patrol?"

"A necessity," said Alia. "We never go out past the harbor entrance without protection to ward off the sharks. The sharks are extremely ferocious and aggressive, and without the patrol they would try to turn over or bite through the baku to get to us. Sharks are afraid of dolphins, but only when we are in groups carrying poison tipped spears."

"I see," I said nervously. "You know I was rescued by a patrol like this."

"Yes," she said. "The patrol members are especially selected for their courage and speed in swimming. The harbor tower guards detected you splashing in the water and immediately alerted the patrol on duty. They raced out to investigate."

"I sure am glad they're fast swimmers," I said, remembering that frightening experience. "It's also a good thing the sharks took so long discussing which one would get to eat what part of me. The patrol got there just in time."

"You were very fortunate. Otherwise I would have never have met you."

"Nor I you."

"And I would have had to paddle this damn baku all by myself," she said. "So let's get going."

"Yes, captain," I replied. "Your wish is my command."

"At all times?"

"Not a chance." I grabbed a paddle and we pushed off, Alia in the stern, our cargo in the middle, and me in the front. I was elated for two reasons now. Alia was back and the orcas were ahead. It was going to be a great day.

The baku paddled very easily, almost a easy as a sea kayak. Before we left the harbor we practiced some turns and rocking the boat from side to side to get me acclimated and balanced. Then we pushed past the open gates at the harbor entrance, waved at the tower guards and headed south toward Orca Cove.

As we exited the harbor the patrol formed a circle around us. Then after we completed our turn and started hugging the shoreline, they kept about 20 feet seaward of us in a line from a few feet forward of the bow to a few feet in back of the stern.

I turned around to address Alia. "Do you always travel on the sea like this?"

"Always," she answered. "It's the only safe way to go by boat. The sharks are terrible and numerous. So please face forward again and dig into the paddling. I'm very nervous out here. The sooner we get inside the first reef the better I'll feel."

"Aye, my captain," I smiled, turned my head to face forward again and began paddling as fast as I could without appearing to be anxious, which I certainly was. I had always been afraid of sharks on Earth, which is why I never took up scuba diving. I always felt safe on a sailboat or kayak, but I never wanted to get in the water with them.

Now it appeared that on Sea we weren't even safe in a boat. We actually needed an armed guard. Interesting place, this Sea.

The shoreline was fairly straight once we rounded the point outside the harbor so we made good time paddling only about 10 feet off shore. There was virtually no surf because we were on the leeward side of the island.

We were about an hour out and approaching the first protective reef when all of a sudden I heard a shout. "Sharks!"

Then another. "Coming in from the northwest." The patrol immediately got a little closer to us and formed a phalanx in front of us, on the left side, and behind. We were close enough to the shoreline that there was no way the sharks could get to us from the right. Every spear was pointed out, and the patrol members alternated their positions, one on top, the next one underwater, to prevent the sharks from coming under us, the next on top, and so on.

"Stop paddling, Danny," said Alia, "until the guards chase them away, assuming they will be able to do that. Once in a great while they are able to break through to get at the baku."

At first I didn't see anything. Obviously the dolphins were able to detect them approaching because of their ability to hear and virtually see things by echolocation. Those sound waves they emitted through the water were obviously bouncing back in the shape of sharks.

After about two or three minutes I saw the first fin cutting through the water. Then another, and another, and three more. I was getting concerned, but not as concerned as I was about a minute later when a huge head with its mouth open displaying row after row of teeth that looked like long knives came out of the water and stared at us with its malicious beady eyes. It looked like the shark I called Big Teeth.

It was followed by five more, all with their heads out of the water, all with their teeth studded open mouths, and all of them pointing at us with eyes fixed and malevolent.

I had to control my bladder as I stared back at them, horrified. These were different from the sharks on Earth because they also had expressive faces, and those faces looked mean, malicious and merciless. No wonder I could hear their conversation. They were developed enough to have a language, and be physically able to speak.

Suddenly I heard a voice coming from the sharks. "There it is," the voice said, "the piece of meat in the front end of the boat. The one we almost had before the dolphins came." It was Big Teeth.

Alia looked as frightened as I felt. "What are those noises they are making?" she asked. "You spoke with them once before. Please try it again."

I visualized myself on stage with hecklers in the audience throwing verbal darts at me. I gathered my wits about me.

"Piece of cake," I said to her, with a bravado macho grin.

"Hey assholes!" I shouted to the sharks' heads. "Fuck off before I sick the guards on you, or turn this boat around and ram those wimpy teeth of yours down your pisshole throats!"

They turned and looked at one another, puzzlement on their expressive faces.

"What did you say to them, Danny," Alia said.

"I said if they had any sense they would return to their homes peacefully."

"Judging by their reaction they understand you, and seem surprised you could speak their language."

The sharks resumed staring at me. Then they worked their jaws up and down, chomping their teeth with loud clanking noises. Our dolphin patrol guards jabbed their poison tipped spears back and forth toward the sharks. The sharks made a feint at them, then backed off.

"So, chicken shits!" I shouted at them. Afraid of our little poison tipped spears, are you? Come any closer and you'll be crab food. But first you'll die in excruciating pain."

"Oh yeah?" said the biggest head with the biggest teeth, the one I called Big Teeth.

"Yeah," I answered. "You gutless shithead candy ass butt head."

"Oh yeah?" it said.

"You're repeating yourself. Are you so scared that your guts and brains have turned to shit?"

Big Teeth chomped his fearsome teeth again. "Listen to me, wiseass," he said. "We're gonna go now, but you ain't seen the last of me. Whenever youse is in or on the wata ya betta be lookin' ova youse shoulda fa me — cuz I'm gonna get ya."

And with that he ducked his head back in the water; all of them turned and began swimming away in the direction they came from. It was nice seeing fins cutting through the water going away.

"You and what army!" I shouted after them. "So long suckers." I really didn't think they could hear me and really didn't care. I turned to Alia triumphantly.

She was gazing at me with a look of astonishment that turned to admiration and then to pride. The dolphins in the water all turned around toward me and raised their spears in salute. I felt as pleased with myself as I did when I drew my first laugh on stage as a professional stand-up comedian, except this time I did my shtick sitting down.

I rose up in my seat and bowed, nearly turning the boat over because of the sudden change in balance. I quickly sat down again, faced forward and began to paddle.

"Come on, Alia, let's get with it," I called over my shoulder. "The orcas await us."

"Danny," she said. That was amazing. You were wonderful. I don't know what you said to them, but I'm so proud of you."

"Piece of cake," I called back over my shoulder. "Nothing to it."

As we paddled I could barely contain first my pride, then my anticipation. I was now completely confident I would be able to talk with the orcas. Certainly they were more developed than those narrow minded one-dimensional sharks.

We paddled for about another two hours, stopping every now and then for a brief rest and a swig of water from a canteen that Alia had brought.

It wasn't really a canteen, but served the purpose. It looked more like a segment of large intestine sealed at one end and with an opening and cap at the other. I resisted thinking too much about what animal, or more likely, fish, it came from and preferred thinking of it as a canteen. Especially when I put my lips to the hole, raised it in the air and took a swallow. It tasted a little fishy, but I chalked that up to my creative imagination.

We finally pulled up to a beach in ankle deep water, stepped out and dragged our baku up on the sand so it wouldn't drift away. Ami came up on to the beach with us while the guards stayed in the water. We were on the near side of a sharply pointed peninsula, and downhill from a gradual slope of sand.

"The farm is just about 50 yards on the other side of the hill." She reached down into the baku and pulled out the basket bucket and pole that had been inside. Ami grabbed the pole.

"The pole," Ami said, "is to hang the bucket on when we come back. It will be a little heavy with the water and fish in it, and we can each take an end.

I reached out and took the bucket from her. "Here, let me take that," I said in my most gentlemanly pretension.

"Is it an Earth custom for males to carry fish buckets?" Alia asked.

"Only when they are empty. Females carry them when they are full," I said.

"Sounds like a fish story to me," she said.

"Smells more like it to me," I said, sticking my nose into it. "Rotten fish."

"There's something fishy in Denmar," she said.

"What?" I exclaimed.

"Denmar. That's the name of the fish farm."

"Oh, yes of course," I said, still a bit taken back. I pointed my arm up the hill. "Lead on, McDuff," I said.

"Who's McDuff?"

"That's my newly coined affectionate name for you, my dear."

She started up the sand hill that separated us from Demar and Ami and I followed. It was just a short slight rise and within a few minutes we were on top overlooking an almost circular cove about 100 yards across, separated into segments by floating pieces of cork with the tops of nets hanging from them leading down into the water. They divided the cove into near rectangular segments.

"Very interesting," I said. "Can one of you explain how it works; and why is it so far from the city?"

"Certainly," said Ami. "To answer your second question first, the reason it's so far from the city is that Denmar farm is here only to feed the orcas. We do have similar fish farms close to the city. Orcas are very big and they eat an awful lot of food… every day.

"On Earth, too," I said.

"The cork floats mark off pens," he continued. "Each pen contains different size fish. Starting closest to us are the smallest. On the far end over by that dock," he said pointing, "are the largest. We get the fish two ways: by breeding them and by herding them."

"Herding?"

"Yes. When the stock starts to get depleted, we keep lookouts to spot large schools of fish. When one is located we send out a flotilla of dolphins, with shark guards of course. They spread out and in the manner of our ancestors gradually close in on the group on all sides and drive the fish into the designated pen area in the cove."

"Sounds like cowboys rounding up cattle on Earth," I

remarked.

"What's cattle? he asked, "and cowboys?"

"I'll tell you later. Please continue. How do you designate which pen they go into?"

"By size," he answered. "Most schools of fish are all about the same size. We can't have bigger fish eating the smaller ones, other than at feeding time, of course. So we try to keep them separated.

"Very interesting." I said. But with all these fish in such a relatively small area doesn't their waste foul and pollute the water?"

"Not at all. We also gather and breed bottom dwelling fish, crabs and other crustaceans that eat waste matter and put them into the pens. They also reproduce among themselves, so the water and the bottom stays clean."

"How do you catch the fish in such large areas?"

"Easy. The pens have moveable sides that can close in. It only takes three dolphins to do the job. Two to draw in the sides to pack them close together, and a third to open the gate into the next enclosure. In the case of the largest which we feed to the orcas, there is a dolphin on the platform you can see on the other side, who simply dips a big hand held net in the water and scoops them out to put into a receptacle, in our case the bucket you are carrying.

"Usually, when they are going to feed the orcas, they empty their nets into a water filled tank in a large baku we use for that purpose." He pointed to the dock again, where there were three oversized bakus tied up.

"The fish keepers then paddle around the corner and scoop out the fish with their hands and dump them into the water, or sometimes directly into the open mouths of waiting orcas. I've accompanied them several times. It's quite an experience."

"I'll bet," I said, trying to imagine a huge orca head a foot away from me with its mouth wide open. I'd seen it done in marineland type parks and on television, but those were tame trained orcas.

The ones I would be feeding in a very short time were wild ones. Wild ones who had never before in their whole lives seen a human, I mean Homo sapien.

I guess I looked a little apprehensive because Alia took my hand and squeezed. She must have read my thoughts because she said, "I'll be right there with you, Danny."

"I know," I replied. "But you're a dolphin and I'm a Homo sapien."

"But didn't you say that Earth Homo sapiens taste bad?"

"Yes, but in order for something to taste bad you have to try it first. Maybe I can explain it to them ahead of time."

"Good idea," she said and gave me another squeeze. "Let's not even think about it. Let's just go down, get our fish, and head around the point to Orca Cove."

And that's what we did. Three fish keepers, as Alia explained they were called, were staring at me as we approached. But they were very polite. One of them took the bucket from me, set it down on the dock, tied a line to it, threw it into the water and dragged it back on its side so that it half filled with water.

He pulled it out of the water and set it on the dock. Then he picked up a long handled net, dipped it into the water that was swarming with fish about two feet long, scooped one out, dropped it in the bucket and repeated the process four more times.

I tried lifting the bucket and it was really heavy.

"Not to worry," said Ami as he slipped the pole through the handle. You take one end and I'll take the other."

"Okay," I said, first turning to thank the fish keeper. "Good luck," said the one who had done the netting as he pushed his arm straight out and up with the palm of his open hand facing me.

"Put your palm against his," said Alia. "It's our gesture of wishing someone good luck and good wishes." Not very different from an Earth high five, I thought as we touched palms. I repeated the process with the other two fish keepers and they also wished me luck. They all seemed so serious.

"Well," I said cheerfully and with a smile. "Let's be off!" Ami and I each took an end of the pole handle and lifted the bucket. Alia helped us in turn to raise it to our shoulders, and we started walking around the cove and back to the hill. It was a little heavy, but not too bad. This old fashioned, indeed primitive, method of carrying heavy objects definitely worked.

When we were almost to the top to the sand dune, Alia tapped me on the shoulder and said, "I'll take it for a while."

"Thanks, but no thanks. I'm not even tired yet," I lied, hiding my struggling pace, determined not to show it while Ami was looking so strong on the other end in front of me.

And so we kept going. When we reached the top Ami yelled, "rest time," and we stopped and placed our burden on the sand. I didn't know whether he realized my fatigue and was trying to help me, or was a little tired himself.

I sat down and in an effort to prolong the rest period asked, "So what's the detailed plan? How do we proceed once we get the bucket in the baku?"

"First, of course, we have to paddle around the point, then around the next point into Orca Cove. Once they spot us they will undoubtedly swim right up to the baku. Just before they get close to us you should reach down, grab a fish and hold it out to them. That way they will see that you mean to be friendly. You will be in the middle with the bucket, Ami will be in the front and I'll be in the stern. Between the two of us and the fish they should not be upset at seeing the new species with us."

"Is that how you think of me, a new species?"

"Don't be silly. You're merely a new species to them."

"Merely?"

"You know I didn't mean it like that," she said. "To me you're … precious, my precious dear Danny, a little different, perhaps, but nevertheless very dear and very precious."

"I'll accept that," I said. "You're a little different, too, and very dear and very precious."

"Will you guys cut that out," said Ami. "It's obvious how you feel about each other, so let's concentrate on the task before us, okay?"

"Okay," I said. "But I would like to suggest one slight change in your plan."

"And what might that be, precious?" said Ami.

"Cut that out," I said. I thought we were going to be serious. I would like to give them at least one fish from the boat, and if there are no problems then paddle straight through them to the beach. Then we get out of the baku and you and I, Alia, take the bucket out of the boat and wade into the water together."

"Can I hold your hand?" Alia said.

"You can hold anything you want," I answered. "No, I take that back. Just my hand…for now."

"Yes, my hero."

"Don't be smart. This is serious business, and it could be dangerous, at least for me."

"Don't be silly. You're safe; all three of us are safe. Once you start sweet talking them as you did with the sharks, you'll end up being the best of friends. Right, Ami."

"Right," he answered. "We'll see what happens, but I'm not the slightest bit concerned. Anyone who can sweet talk sharks can surely do it with whales."

"It wasn't exactly sweet talk," I said. "It was more like street talk."

"Sweet talk, street talk, who cares? Just talk. I'll stay on the beach as an eyewitness to history being made."

"Or eaten," I said with a smile that was meant to be a joke but wasn't. " "Oh well," I said, "you only get to live once. Or in my case, it appears to be twice."

They both smiled. Then Ami looked at me seriously, put a hand on my shoulder, looked into my eyes, and said, "One thing you must remember, Danny. And this is extremely important… please promise me…."

"Yes."

"Do you promise?"

"Yes, I said I do. I don't know what you're talking about, but I promise anyway."

"I believe you," he said. "I want you to promise that if they get belligerent and rough with you, that… well… that you won't hurt them!"

"My eyes widened and Ami grinned. "Gotcha," he said with a laugh. After a momentary pause, Alia and I both also laughed.

"I'll try not to," I said, "But sometimes I just don't know my own strength. Let's get going and make history, guys."

CHAPTER 6

The lighthearted banter elevated our spirits. We picked up the bucket again, half walked, half slid down the dune to the baku, got in and started paddling. When we reached the mouth of Orca Cove the guard patrol stopped swimming with us. Alia informed me they would not come into the cove with us. Armed dolphins would risk breaking the peace treaty.

As we headed in we could see the orcas frolicking close to the rocky beach. I began to have a few doubts.

"You know," I said to my companions, "we've been assuming that I will be able to talk with the orcas. Suppose I can't?"

"Then we'll just have to feed you to the sharks on the way back," said Alia. "That one with the especially big teeth seemed particularly interested in you. And you him, incidentally."

"Thanks a lot" I said. "If I go, you go with me. Remember, I'm your hero."

"And my lover; well almost," she replied.

Just then the orcas noticed our presence and started swimming toward us as we were paddling toward them. There seemed to be about ten or eleven of them.

"Hey guys," I whispered quickly, "we forgot to discuss this, but should I start talking to them when they come up to the baku?"

Ami and Alia looked at one another. Both shook their heads. "We don't think so, Danny," said Ami. Let's wait until you wade out from the beach. We don't want to upset them until you're in the water in their element."

"I think you're right," I said, peering over the rail as inconspicuously as I could.

The largest orca came directly up to us. We were almost nose to nose, so Alia and Ami stopped paddling. Then the orca turned and came over to the side and looked us over from bow to stern. He was about two feet from us. Both his black and white head and dorsal fin towered above us. He was easily thirty to thirty-five feet long.

My emotions were a combination of awe, fear and joy. The orca's eyes fastened first on Alia, then on Ami, then on me sitting next to the bucket of fish. I was glad to see that he seemed to be curious rather than belligerent.

He kept staring at me. I stared back, transfixed. Then he opened his huge mouth. My joy vanished; the fear and awe remained. He closed his mouth. I was relieved but the joy did not return.

He opened it again. I held my breath.

Then a sound came out of it, and a deep menacing voice said, "Well, well, what have we here? A meal or a toy?"

I understood him completely and the joy returned. I reached down into the bucket, grabbed a wiggling fish and held it out to him.

"Eat first," I said, "and we'll talk later."

I didn't think orcas' faces could register surprise. Maybe not on Earth, but they sure as hell could here on Sea. His eyes bugged out, his bottom jaw dropped even lower and stayed there a few moments before his whole mouth closed. He stared at me for what seemed like a full minute, then quickly turned his massive body, and dove straight down under the water. He was back up less than 10 seconds later, and by up I do mean up. He leaped up in the air, his entire body clearing the surface by at least 10 feet, and came crashing down into the water sending a cascade into the baku, drenching us completely and rocking the boat from side to side. Then he casually swam back to the other orcas, leaving me soaking wet and holding a live fish in my lap, because I dropped it there when I grabbed the rails to help steady the rocking boat.

"Well," said Alia. "What was that all about?"

"Wow," said Ami. "He made a noise then you made a noise. Does that mean you were talking with him?"

"Not much of a conversation, but yes, he spoke and I spoke back. We understood each other. I picked up the fish and threw it into the water as far as I could.

"Yes!" I exclaimed loudly, "I can talk with orcas!"

"It appears that way," said Alia, but what did you say to him that caused him to respond the way he did? I've never seen an orca act that way."

"It wasn't what I said, but was the fact that I sort of answered his question and we understood one another. That's why he registered such surprise."

We watched as he went close to one orca after another in the cove.

As soon as he left the first, it raised its body about three quarters of the way out of the water as if standing on its tail and peered intently at us. On Earth that action of orcas is called "spyhopping". And one by one as he visited them they spyhopped. Soon all eight orcas were in the spyhop position staring at us. Actually, I guess me. It was a sight to behold.

"Hey guys," I said to Alia and Ami. "What do you say we head for the beach now that we have their attention. And, uh, don't hit any orcas on the way in."

"Good idea," said Ami. "Just ask the ones between us and the beach to get out of the way, and don't forget to say 'please'."

I didn't have to say a word because as we approached them,

they each came down out of the spyhopping position to lay horizontally on the surface and backed up to let us pass, never taking their eyes off us, particularly me. I felt like Moses at the parting of the Red Sea. I said a "thank you" to each one as we went by.

We got to the beach, stepped out gingerly because of the stones, and pulled the baku up out of the water carefully to avoid damaging its bottom on the rocks.

We looked out into the water and all the orcas were arranged in a line facing us about thirty feet out, all looking intently at us, their tall dorsal fins projecting straight up into the air. It was an extraordinary experience.

"Do you think they're friendly?" I said, "or is that a battle formation?"

"I think they're either friendly or just curious," said Alia. They don't look belligerent to me. Shall we test the water, so to speak?"

"Yes, I'm ready."

"Good luck, guys," said Ami raising his hand, palm out. We palmed him back, lifted the fish heavy bucket together, and struggled with it until we got into deep enough water where it floated. Alia reached into the bucket grabbed a fish, which by now was half dead from lack of oxygen and handed it to me.

"I suggest you hold it out in front of you to show your good intentions again," she said.

"Good idea," I agreed, taking it from her in my right hand. I took her hand in my left while she held on to the bucket handle with her free hand and we slowly waded out to the waiting orcas.

I could tell she was frightened by the tight way she clasped my hand.

"It's showtime," I said cheerfully.

"What does that mean?" she asked nervously.

"It means that this is the beginning. Let the adventure begin."

I knew I should have been at least a little frightened, too, but by then I had lost all my fear. I was elated. We waded out further until we were almost chest deep. The orcas moved close. Then suddenly the big male with his towering fin came right up to us, stopping about a foot from the extended fish, his mouth open.

I looked him straight in his eyes, or rather from one eye to another, since he was too close for me to see them both at the same time. I extended the fish further out to him. He ignored it.

"It's an old family tradition," I said. "First we eat; then we talk."

He opened his massive mouth, delicately took fish away from me and tossed it away.

"I say we talk now," he said.

"Is that a request or a command?" I said. "I hope it's a request because I don't take too well to commands." He was my audience and I had confidence my performance would win him over.

He looked at me quizzically. Another expression Sea orcas have that Earth orcas lack.

"Don't you realize," he said, "that you are not one of those animals," he motioned to Alis, "we have an agreement with? I am not obligated not to eat you. I could take you in one gulp like a seal."

"Have you ever met a talking seal?" I asked.

"No, of course not. Seals don't talk."

"If you took me in one gulp, I'd be talking all the way down into your stomach and I know some nasty words, too. Besides, where I come from nobody ever eats us because we taste bad. We also cause terrible stomach cramps. Do you have a good supply of antacid medicines? We also cause flatulence. Do you like to fart?"

He looked at me intently and shook his head side to side. "You are a very interesting creature," he said. "I've never seen anything like you around here. Where are you from? And by the way, we orcas take great pleasure in farts. We're quite good — the loudest in the sea." He looked at Alia. "And in the air, too."

"Well," I said, "the farts we cause are of the low frequency level, barely audible past three feet. We would probably destroy your reputation.

"And to answer your question, I am a Homo sapien, my name is Danny, and I am from a distant world called Earth."

"Do you have orcas there?"

"As a matter of fact we do. But they're different."

"How so?"

"Well... for one thing they can't talk. Or at least we Homo sapiens can't talk with them, although we wish we could."

"You obviously can here. We've never been able to talk with other beings here; so let's communicate... at least before we eat you."

"You mean you're still thinking of eating me?" My confidence was starting to wane.

"Not right now. We'll talk first and I'll eat later.

"Oh." Now I was starting to get a little frightened. He stared at me with cold hard eyes.

Then I saw another Sea orca expression. The cold hard eyes lit up with delight and a grin spread across his huge face that was wider than the widest dolphin smile I had ever seen.

"Old orca family tradition," he said. "Just kidding."

Relief swept through me. "You son-of-a-bitch," I said.

"What's a bitch?"

"Just an Earth expression of my appreciation of your sense of humor. You really had me going there."

"Going?" I don't understand your use of the word in that context."

I suddenly felt a jab in my ribs. It was my own hand along with

Alia's which I had been holding all this time. I had been so engrossed with the orca that I had almost forgotten she was there. She had pushed our clasped hands sharply into my ribs to get my attention. I turned to her with a big smile.

"We've been conversing," I said.

"So I gather. By the expression on his face I can tell you two have been getting along well. I didn't know that orcas could smile. Did you tell him a joke?"

"No. He told me one, sort of."

"How about introducing us?"

"Of course. Alia, this …" I turned back to the orca and paused, since he didn't tell me his name. "This is the leader of the orcas."

"The hell he is," came the higher pitched voice of a smaller orca with a much shorter dorsal fin gliding up next to him. "I'm the leader."

"Only when it comes to raising the children." said the first.

"No way," said the second. "We are a matriarchal society and I am the matriarch."

"You may be the matriarch, but if so I'm the patriarch. You seem to forget that we are no longer a matriarchal society. Those were the old days when males were subservient just because females gave birth and suckled us.

"Not anymore. Not since the time we found out how you females got pregnant. All along we thought it was just fun and games, rolls in the waves. No more… well it still is fun, but we're your equals now, so don't mess with my head. You can take your matriarchal attitude of superiority and shove it where the water don't reach. Right, Danny?"

"Uh."

"Well?" said the big male patriarch.

"Well?" said the smaller female matriarch.

"No speaka da inglis," I said. No way I was going to get involved in this family squabble with those two huge mouths within an arms length.

"What did you say?" asked the female.

"I said I didn't understand you. My knowledge of your language is limited at best. I don't have the slightest idea what you're talking about," I lied, remembering that on Earth the orcas were indeed a matriarchal society.

"May I present Alia." I withdrew my hand and held hers out to them. It was shaking more than a little.

"What's going on, Danny? They look mad. And all that noise. Are we safe?" she asked.

"Of course, I 'm right here with you. We stand-up comedians think very quickly on our feet, or as the case may be, in the water.

"What are you two talking about?" said the big male orca.

"We're talking about how glad we are to meet you both, and about how pleasant it is to be talking with you. We spoke about how we would like to meet the rest of your friends, or family, if that is what they are."

"Family," said the female. "We're all part of the same family."

Pod, I said to myself, remembering Earth orca society. Of course they are all part of the same pod, and all members of a pod are related.

"Sorry," I said. "I didn't realize." I addressed the big male. "I never did catch your name," I said.

"Never did throw it," he said with a laugh. This orca had a sense of humor, sort of.

"Are all orcas as funny as you?" I asked.

"Of course not. Most of us are killing machines. We're really killer whales."

"Oh stop with that, Bogi," said the female. "You know that's not true. We just kill to eat, as I'm sure you do. We're very good at it, but we don't kill any more than is necessary, and never just for fun. We're like your friend's species."

"They're dolphins."

"Like the dolphins. By the way my name is Oola. We see them kill fish. They even raise them in pens just to be killed and eaten. How about you Homo-what do you call yourselves, homosaps?"

"Homo sapiens."

"Yes, Homo sapiens. You do kill to eat, don't you?"

"Yes and no. Very few of us do the killing ourselves. We pay other Homo sapiens to do it for us."

"Pay? What's that?"

"It's like a reward. So they can pay still other Homo sapiens to kill most of the food they eat.

"We also have other Homo sapiens who are what we all vege-tarians. They don't eat meat or fish. They just eat plants for their food. And they pay other Homo sapiens to kill the plants for them. It's a healthy way to live."

"Hmm," said Bogi, "you certainly are a peculiar species."

"Danny," said Alia. "Would you please tell me what's going on?"

"It's a little difficult to explain. But we're leading up to the introductions. This is Bogi," I said, holding her hand out toward him while I translated.

"Delighted," he said.

I pointed her hand toward the female. "And this is Oola."

"Hello," Alia said, nodding her head.

"And this is the rest of our family, said Oola, calling to the other nearby orcas, who moved up to join the side by side by side in front of us. It was an awe-inspiring scene. There were five full-grown orcas and four juveniles. I could tell that one of the full-grown was a male by his tall dorsal fin.

Bogi explained to the other orcas, "Alia is, as you can see, one of the species we have the agreement with. They call themselves dolphins. Danny here is from another place far away where they eat other people's kills. Strange but true."

He introduced his family one by one, and when he was finished addressed me. "First let me state that we are delighted to meet you. It's an extraordinary experience to be able to talk with another species, as strange as you are. I hope we will have many conversations in the future. But now I have to ask why you are here. Why are you here?"

"It's your turn," I said to Alia. He asked why we are here."

"Good," she answered. "Tell him we are here as representatives of all the dolphins, and that our leaders would like to arrange a meeting with the leaders of the orcas. Tell him we consider it very important to have this meeting."

I translated and Bogi said, "Important, is it?"

"Yes," I said. "And because I speak both your languages I will translate what everyone says. So for the first time in history there will be true close communication between orcas and dolphins. I think it is not only important, but also very exciting. Don't you agree?"

"Definitely," he said. "Truly extraordinary. But it will take us sometime to gather other orcas. We are quite spread out all over the sea. There are only three other families around here that we share this cove with. There are hundreds elsewhere.

"Contacting them won't be too difficult since we can communicate underwater very long distances. Getting here will take most of the time. And don't forget they have to take time to hunt and eat along the way.

"We don't have a central form of leadership. Each family is

independent and has its own two leaders — the matriarch and the patriarch. Right, Oola?"

She gave him a resigned look. "Yes, Bogi."

Bogi continued. "I'll put the word out, and when we are ready I'll contact you and we'll set the time and place."

I translated for Alia, and she smiled. "Tell him we are delighted he agrees and are looking forward to this historic occasion. But please ask him how he will contact us, or you to be more precise."

"Good question," I said.

"Bogi," I said, "we need a means for you to let us know when the orcas are ready, since I am the only one you can talk to. We have to think of a way for you to let me know. Any ideas?"

He thought for a moment. "Hmm. How about this? We all gather just outside the entrance to the dolphins' cove where the gate and towers are. You can tell the dolphins in the towers to tell you when they see a few hundred orcas together there."

"Great idea," I said. "And we can have the meeting inside the cove — the dolphins call it the harbor — so we won't have to worry about sharks."

"We never have to worry about sharks," he said. "They wouldn't dare attack us. But the harbor is a good idea for the protection of dolphins that stray from our vicinity, especially the young ones, and our own babies, too, I have to admit."

I translated for Alia and she nodded in agreement to Bogi.

"Goodbye," I said with a wave. We're going to leave now. We really enjoyed meeting you, and we're looking forward to what looks like is going to be a truly momentous gathering."

Bogi and Oola nodded their heads up and down and wiggled the dorsal fins from side to side.

Alia waved and we started to turn toward the beach.

"Wait," I said. "We still have the fish." I reached across her into the bucket floating nearby, withdrew the remaining fish one at a time and tossed them toward the orcas.

"Children," said Oola. And the young ones dashed out and scarfed them up. Alia and I turned around and started to wade back to the beach.

"Wait!" shouted Bogi.

I stopped and turned around.

"I have a question for you; Danny," he said, looking very serious.

"I'll do my best to answer it."

"Good. Danny, can you tell me the reason the squid crossed the entrance to our cove?"

I gave him a puzzled look and said questioningly, "To get to the other side?"

He looked disappointed.

"Gotcha," I said with a laugh. Do you know that the dolphins also have that joke, and so do Homo sapiens on Earth? That may well be the oldest joke in the universe. See ya."

I turned around, took Alia's hand and headed back to the beach again. We could hear behind us a deep orca sound, which I took for a laugh. I waved and turned my head back around to the orcas just in time to observe Bogi soar out of the water into the air, do an acrobatic back flip and land back in the water with a loud splash that sent a large wave up our backs, over our heads and up on to the beach.

Then the rest of the orcas repeated the leaps and were gone, disappearing under the water. We watched a few minutes and saw nothing. They were gone from the cove.

We finished our wet walk to the beach and Ami pumped our hands in congratulations. After I finished explaining everything to both him and Alia I felt a need to be alone and excused myself.

I walked about fifty yards down the beach, found a sandy spot among the stones and sat down. I just wanted to be alone to contemplate and absorb the enormity of what had just transpired.

A first, not only in the history of Sea, but also in the history of Earth in a way, and quite likely in the history of the cosmos. And I, Danny DiVinci, washed up Earth comedian am responsible for it. I was incredibly elated and just sat there for a few minutes enjoying the feeling, and for the first time in a long time, myself.

But then a dark idea hit me. The very same idea that had come to me so many times the last few days, and which each time I had tried to dismiss. This is real. I am really here. But this whole thing sounds impossible. I always considered myself a realist, and this was unreal. Being on another planet, talking with dolphins and orcas, and even sharks. And how did I do it? With something called the Universal Translator which lets me converse with other species on another planet in near perfect English, just as on Star Trek. It's not possible. You're dreaming, Danny. But it all seems so real.

I dropped my head down toward my lap and closed my eyes in dejection. I stayed in that position for several minutes, not wanting to open them.

The next thing I knew my chin was being raised by a hand. I opened my eyes. It was Alia; she was looking at me with tenderness and what I could only interpret as adoration. She bent over and kissed me on the lips.

"I know what you're thinking, Danny," she said. "And it is not true. You are not dreaming; you are not imagining. Everything is real. Ami is real, Bogi, and Oola and all the rest of their family are real. And I am real… and I think… I think I am in love with you."

I gazed into her eyes. "And I think, no, I know, I am in love with you."

"Am I real?"

"Yes."

"Are you here on this beach on Sea with me?"

"Yes."

"And are we both in love?"

"Yes."

"With each other?"

"Yes."

"Then stop moping and come with me. We have a surprise for you."

She reached for my hand, helped me get to my feet, and we went back to where Ami was starting to push the baku into the water.

"So what's the surprise?" I said.

"Since it's already late in the afternoon," Alia said, and it would be dark before we got back to Sea, how would you like to spend the night in Cali, the town I come from? We can stay at my parents' house. I'm sure they would like to meet you. It's only a few miles from here."

"Sure," I replied. "Sounds like a great idea. Let's go."

Alia and I took our respective position in the baku and Ami pushed us out into the water before swimming out to rejoin the dolphin patrol waiting outside Orca Cove.

We paddled for about an hour and a half following the coast-line south along what seemed like an endless stretch of sand beach once we were out of the cove. The fact that there were no sharks around allowed me to do a lot of thinking along the way. And it was all about Alia and me.

All right, Danny, I said to myself, lets be objective about this whole thing, as difficult as that may be.

Point one. She obviously has strong feelings for me.

Point two. I obviously have strong feelings for her.

Point three. Could she really be in love with me? Do dolphins actually experience love? And if they do, could she be in love with a strange creature from outer space that looked like me?

Point four. Were my strong feelings for her actually love? Could I be in love with a not so strange creature in outer space? I know I have been over this before, but this is complete objectivity time. She is a dolphin, sort of; and I am a human, not sort of.

Point five. Why are we going to meet her parents? She hadn't mentioned it before. Is it simple a convenience so we don't have to go back to Sea in the dark? Or does she want them to meet me as a prospective mate? Do they even have such things as mates on Sea? Are her parents going to look upon me as a strange creature from outer space, or are they going to see me as I really am, a man or rather male in love, maybe, with their daughter?

Questions, questions, questions. Objective questions. But no answers, not even nonobjective ones. So what did I learn? That trying to be objective about feelings for a woman was fruitless... and dumb. Not to mention impossible.

CHAPTER 7

The long sand beach ended just as the light began to fade and we came to a large rock jutting out into the water. We rounded it and found ourselves paddling into a narrow opening in a reef and into a small harbor, not much more than a cove with a picturesque village nestled in the flat area at the base of green hills. It was Cali, Alia's hometown. The next stage of my life on Sea was ready to begin.

We pulled up to the quay and Ami leaped out of the water to hold and tie up the boat while Alia and I got out. That dolphin certainly likes leaping.

Our guard patrol climbed up onto the quay instead of leaping and dispersed to look for quarters for the night. They first deposited their spears in the baku.

"This way," said Alia taking my hand. Let's go into that shop a little way down."

"What are we buying?" I asked.

"Nothing in particular. I just want to say hello to the proprietors."

"I hope they don't think I'm a freak," I said.

"Don't be silly. They already know about you. There was a story and a picture of you in today's paper. A very good likeness, I might add, from head to toe. The paper has an excellent artist."

"I hope he showed me with my dakti on."

"Of course, silly. We know now how modest you Earthers are. But the article did explain about your body parts."

"Great. Now everybody will be mentally undressing me." I laughed inwardly, remembering how Earth men would often mentally undress a good looking woman they encountered. I guess the inward laugh wasn't so inward.

"What's so funny?" Alia asked as we arrived at the shop and she opened the door. My favorite aroma in the whole world, or should I say cosmos, greeted me: chocolate! Yes, it was unmistakably chocolate. I'd know it anywhere, anytime, anyplace.

"I'll explain later," I said breathing in through my nose deeply. "Ah… chocolate."

"Do you like chocolate?"

"Does a bear shit in the woods? Does a whale shit in the sea?"

"What does that mean?"

"It means that I absolutely love chocolate."

"You do?" she said, as the proprietor came walking out of the back room.

"Me, too! I adore chocolate!"

That did it! Every lingering doubt I had in my mind about loving Alia vanished immediately. I knew I was truly and objectively in love with her. Looks and species could never separate us. This was it. Love. True love. Alia and chocolate. I felt love, as I had never believed possible before.

As I was savoring these thoughts and feelings, the proprietor, an older female (I could now tell the difference) called out, "Alia! My darling! I didn't know you were coming." She came out from behind the counter and hugged and kissed Alia, who returned the affection in kind.

"Mama," Alia said. "It's so good to see you again."

"Mama?" I said.

"Yes, I wanted to surprise you. I come from a long line of chocolate makers. I was practically raised in this shop. You have no idea what it means to me that you love chocolate."

"Oh my God," I said.

"Alia," Mama said. "Please introduce me to your... uh... friend. I've heard and read much about him. After the story in this morning's paper, it's been the topic of conversation all over town. I don't know how many people have come in to talk about it and congratulate me for the Administrator picking you to be his guide."

Alia took my hand. "Mama," she said, "this is Danny. Danny, I'd like you to meet Mama."

"Hello Danny, or should I be calling you Danny DiVinci?"

"Danny is fine, Mama," said Alia, squeezing my hand. I could tell she was a little nervous.

"Hello. Mama. I'm very happy to meet you," I lied. Now I was nervous, and squeezed Alia's hand tighter.

"So Danny," Mama said, staring intently at our clasped hands. What do you do in that Earth place?"

"I... uh... tell jokes for a living."

"That's a living?" She didn't look very impressed.

"Mama," Alia said. "You can ask questions later. Let's go see Daddy. Is he in the back?"

"Of course, that's what he does." She said, eyeing me suspiciously. She led us behind the counter into the back room. Alia still held my hand as we walked past displays of all kinds of ravishing looking chocolates neatly laid out in rows according to variety.

"Shoko," Mama called as we went through the door. "Alia's here. She's brought a friend."

Shoko had his back to us sitting on a stool inspecting a piece of chocolate he held in his hand.

"A very special friend," said Alia.

"A very, very special friend from the looks of it." said Mama.

"Excuse me while I finish this beautiful piece of chocolate," he said, dropping his hand and dipping it into a revolving bowl of melted chocolate that he kept turning with a foot pedal similar to one on an old Earth sewing machine. He still had his back to us.

"He's not only special, but also a little different," Mama said. "Very different."

"So what's new? Alia has always been a little different herself."

"Thanks Daddy. I hope that's a compliment."

"You know I love you, honey. Anything you do is fine with me."

"Shoko," Mama said. "His name is Danny."

"That's an unusual name. Different."

"Exceptionally different, dear. Do you remember what was in the paper this morning? His name is Danny DiVinci."

"The alien! Shouted Shoko, spinning around on his stool and springing to his feet to face me. He dropped the piece of chocolate on the floor. It was a truffle. He looked me up and down from head to toe, then up and down again.

"Hi," I said. I felt as if I were in high school again meeting my prom date's parents for the first time.

"That piece of chocolate you dropped looks like a truffle, and too good to waste."

I bent over, carefully picked it up and placed it on a nearby table. The outer layer of chocolate was still partially melted and soft, so it stuck to my fingers. I put my fingers to my nose. "Smells good," I said.

Then I put my fingers into my mouth and licked the chocolate off. "Exceptionally delicious." I said. And it was. "Better than the chocolate I had in Sea last night."

He stared at me blankly and then at my other hand which was still in Alia's. "Oh, my God!" he exclaimed.

"That's what he said, too," Mama admonished. "You both should know better than to take the Lord's name in vain."

"Sorry," I said, "it was just an Earth expression of surprise."

"Sorry shmorry," Shoko said. "I was surprised, too. And I'll take his name in vain any damned time I want to.

"You have much to thank the Lord for," said Mama.

"Thank you, Lord," said Shoko, "for teaching me how to make chocolate… at the bottom of the sea."

"Shoko!" exclaimed Mama crossly.

Alia was visibly distressed. "Mama, Daddy," she said, "please not now. I haven't seen you for months. Can't you discuss it another time? Besides, Danny is here."

"You're right, honey," said Shoko. "I'm sorry."

"Me, too," said Mama. "So, Danny, what brings you to Sea?"

Alia answered for me. "That's a long story, Mama. A better question is what brings us to Cali."

"All right, what brings you to Cali?"

Alia answered again. "We were in Orca Cove, and I thought since we were so close, I could introduce you to Danny and we could spend the night."

"Orca Cove," said Shoko. "Isn't that a little dangerous? What were you doing there?"

Alia smiled, gave me a proud look and turned back to her parents.

"Danny was talking with the orcas."

"Or course, what else would he be doing there. Did they tell you any good jokes? Did they give you a new recipe for chocolate truffles?" Shoko said sarcastically.

"Well, as a matter of fact," I started to say, before Alia cut me off.

"Daddy," she said, "I'm serious. What the article in the paper didn't say is that Danny has the ability to actually talk with some of the more advanced animals on Sea."

Shoko's mouth dropped open. Mama stared at me wide eyed.

"I'll be damned!" Shoko said.

"My lord!" Mama said. "Sorry, I didn't mean it that way."

"Yes," said Alia, "he actually did have a conversation with the orcas. I was there and saw and heard it. Not exactly hear, because I didn't understand what they were saying, but it was obvious they were talking. Danny even introduced me to them. They communicated very, very well."

"Remarkable," said Mama. "And he seems to be communicating very, very well with you, too," she said, staring down at our clasped hands again.

"And vice versa," said Shoko following Mama's eyes. "Did you ask the orcas if they had any new recipes for chocolate?"

"Daddy," said Alia. "This is serious. Danny arranged a big meeting between the orca leaders from all over Sea in the harbor at Sea. Danny will translate for both groups, so we will actually be able to communicate with them also instead of just giving them fish to eat to keep them from eating us. We will be working together. And all because of Danny." She gave my hand an extra hard squeeze. "I'm so proud of him."

I could feel myself blushing.

"Look, Mama," said Shoko. "He's changing color. That's a nice shade of red. You don't by any chance have octopus blood in you, do you?"

"Daddy!" said Alia.

"Sorry. So what else is new?"

"Not much Daddy, except for Danny, of course."

"Of course," he answered, turning to face me. "So what's new on Earth, Danny? And if you say Alia, I'm leaving."

I smiled and decided a change in subject might be in order. "I know Alia hasn't had a chance to tell you," I said; "as a matter of fact I haven't even told her yet, but I think you will find this interesting. All through college I worked for a company making chocolates."

Everybody looked at me in surprise.

"That's where I developed my great love for chocolate; and one of the things that pleased me the most about Sea — except for Alia, of course — is the fact that you have chocolate here, even truffles, my very favorite. I can't tell you how delighted I am."

"That's wonderful," said Mama.

"Amazing. You and I are going to have to spend some time together," said Shoko, putting an arm around me. "I think I might get to like this alien. Maybe he's not so alien after all."

The ice was broken; everybody was smiling.

Mama glanced up at the clock on the wall. "It's time to close the shop. Since we weren't expecting company and don't have dinner prepared, how about us all going to a restaurant?"

"Sounds good to me," said Alia.

"Me, too," I said, hoping that Alia would remember that I wouldn't be able to read the menu.

"Let's do it," said Shoko. Just give me a few minutes to close down the chocolate tempering bowl and set up the melter for tomorrow morning."

He turned back to his table and equipment while Mama led Alia and me back into the store, where she spent the next few minutes describing and pointing out the varieties of chocolates they sold. They were remarkably similar to Earth's except for some different kinds of nuts and fruits that grew uniquely on Sea.

When Shoko was ready, Mama locked up the shop and the four of us walked down the quay to the restaurant in pairs, Alia and I walking behind, quietly hand in hand, Mama and Shoko not hand in hand, engaged in animated conversation.

Once I thought I heard the word "alien", another time "choco-late," and several times "crazy daughter." It was obvious they were discussing Alia and me.

I saw their heads shaking and nodding at various times, and I'd swear the flukes of their tails wagging up and down as if they were swimming, but not so low that they touched the ground. I didn't know dolphins did that when they were emotional.

Finally we arrived at the restaurant and were ushered to a table, stares following us all the way.

"Ignore them," said Shoko. "You would think they had never seen an alien before."

I held out a chair for Mama in a gentlemanly fashion, then for Alia, and sat down myself, facing Shoko. He looked at me and nod-ded.

"So, Danny, tell me what kind of chocolates you used to make. The two of us were discussing chocolate covered nuts when the waiter arrived with the menus, handing one to each of us I pre-tended to read mine.

When the waiter turned to me to find out what I wanted, Alia said, "Danny, I know you are not familiar with our food. May I make a recommendation?"

"Please do."

"How would you like braised crabs' legs in garlic sauce? That's one of my favorites."

"Sounds good to me," and I nodded to the waiter. After every-one had ordered, Shoko and I compared chocolate making meth-ods while Alia and Mama, I assumed, discussed mother and daugh-ter things, probably involving me.

During dinner, which was excellent, I described my life in show business, leaving out the bombs at the end, and told them how I happened to pick Sea as the planet I wanted to come to, leaving out Olga and Whiplash, embellishing on the kindness and power of the gatekeepers, not mentioning the golden arches at all, or much of anything else.

After we finished our main course the waiter brought dessert, Shoko had ordered, which was a delicious chocolate cake, along with cups of a steaming liquid. I put my cup under my nose and breathed in. It smelled like coffee. I blew on it and took a sip. It tasted like really good coffee.

"Excellent" I said.

"Do you have such a thing on Earth?" asked Mama.

"Do we ever," I replied. "Shoko, I have an idea for you for a new kind of chocolate. From what we discussed, I don't think you make it. How about combining ground coffee with melted choco-late? That's a delicious combination."

More than delicious, I remembered. More like habit forming, I thought, remembering how I used to eat some every morning for both the taste and the energy it gave me. I also ate some before going on stage in the evening.

Shoko looked at me and nodded his head up and down. He turned to Alia and then Mama and said: "You know I think I am really going to like this alien."

"Earther," Mama said.

"Man," Alia said, "possibly mate," she added slowly.

"Mate," I said looking into Alia's eyes. I turned to her parents sitting across the table and said to them, "Mate, yes. I do believe I am in love with your daughter."

"Love, shmove," said Shoko. You've only known each other since yesterday."

"I know," I said. "I don't understand it either. I only know what I feel."

Alia looked at me and then at her parents. "I don't understand it either. I just feel it, too."

Shoko shrugged his barely perceptible shoulders. "Well," he said, " I guess that's the way the chocolate melts."

Mama didn't shrug. She merely looked sad as she said to Alia, "I hope you know what you're doing."

"I do know what I'm doing, Mama. We are just going to be mates, not lifemates."

That's interesting, I thought. I guess mate means something like a trial marriage, or live-in relationship. Lifemate was the real thing... for life. I liked the terminology. Mates for life.

"And you," Mama said to me, "Do you really know what you are doing?"

"Not really," I said. "I just know how I feel about Alia, and after all, we're just going to be mates, not lifemates. At least not yet. There is a difference."

Alia looked at both of them intently. "Mama, Daddy, do we have your blessings?"

Shoko said, "Does it make any difference?"

Before Alia could answer, Mama gave me a hard look and said, "Do you believe in God?"

"Mama!" Alia exclaimed. "Please! Danny, you don't have to answer that."

"That's all right," I replied. I don't mind. Mama, on Earth we have a different God than you do here. Your God lives at the bottom of the sea, our God lives in heaven, in the sky. So to be perfectly honest with you," I said, diplomatically, not being perfectly honest, "I would have to say that I don't believe in your Sea God. I don't know enough about him — or her or it — and don't know how the two are connected."

"Does that satisfy you, Mama?" Alia said.

"For now," answered Mama. "We'll discuss it another time."

"Perhaps yes, perhaps no.," said Shoko.

"Is it all right if we stay at the house tonight?" asked Alia.

Both parents nodded their heads. "When we get home I'll get your room ready, darling," Mama said.

"I guess that means we have your blessings," said Alia.

Both of them nodded their heads in agreement, Shoko somewhat enthusiastically, Mama with resignation.

Shoko motioned to the waiter for the check, paid the bill, and we got up to leave.

"Would you like to take a walk along the quay?" Alia asked me.

"Sure, that sounds like a good idea," I answered. When we got outside we thanked Shoko and Mama for dinner and Alia said to them, "Do you mind if Danny and I take a walk? We'll see you back at the house."

"Not at all," said Mama. "We'll see you later."

"Do we have a choice?" asked Shoko.

"Of course not," smiled Alia. She took my hand and after a wave we started walking in silence in the opposite direction from the chocolate shop.

It was quite picturesque. Little shops on the shore side of the quay, most of them closed but with lights in the upstairs windows, which I assumed were living quarters.

On the water side, bakus were tied up along the quay, a few larger than others with low cabin type arrangements from which light came, indicating dolphins below. There were lantern posts about every 50 yards with flickering lights inside. I wished I had seen the old lamplighter lighting them, assuming he was old.

A few pedestrians strolled in each direction, some with children in tow, some obviously young lovers like ourselves, not that I was so young.

There were also still a few dolphins out in the water swimming and playing, even thought it was dark out. I remembered the sort of mysterious enjoyment of night swimming in my teens and twenties. And I thought I would like to do it again, with Alia. The water was certainly warm enough around here. I was musing on what it might be like when I heard, "Hello, Danny. Hello."

It was Alia bring me out of my thoughts and into my real world.

"A limpet for your thoughts," she said.

"You weren't thinking about my parents, were you?"

"No, I was just enjoying the walk and the sights. I like your little town."

"Me, too. But it's very quiet, too quiet for me. So… are you going to say anything about my parents?"

"It's been an interesting experience."

"And…."

"They're very nice, and they obviously love you very much."

"I love them, too. But at times they can be very trying, especially Mama."

"They only want the best for you, to make sure you know what you're doing. Do you know what you're doing?"

"No, I only know that I've never felt this way before." Her answer produced that feeling of butterflies in my stomach. "And you?" She continued.

"No."

"Not even for a Homo sapien female?"

I thought immediately about Olga, and a few before her. I smiled inwardly. "Not even close. And you? Certainly being so beautiful you must have attracted many males." Hmm, I said to myself. When we first met I didn't understand why dolphins thought her beautiful. Now I did.

"None like you," she said. "You make minnows dart around in my stomach."

"It's for damn sure you've never met anyone like me," I laughed, "with my permanently external tinky."

"Never," she echoed my laugh. "I certainly hope you know how to use it."

"We'll find out tonight won't we?"

"I can hardly wait," she said looking down at my groin.

I was beginning to get an erection. More than beginning; it was almost complete, when after glancing around to see if anyone was looking, she reached under my dakti and took hold of it. "My, my," she said. "It's like a sea cucumber, and still growing."

"Thanks a lot for the comparison."

"I meant it in a positive way."

"I know." I looked around to doubly make sure no one was watching us. No one was. I tried to think of somewhere to touch her. Since dolphins have only internal mammary glands, breasts were out.

Then I had a very disturbing thought. We were going to make love later, and I didn't even know where her vagina was. Was it between her legs like in Homo sapien women, or further up her abdomen, and if so, exactly where? And what about her tail?

I also wondered if touching the area of her mammary glands would stimulate her. And then I realized I didn't know where the opening to her mammary glands was, or if there were two… or even more.

"Hey, what's happening, Danny," Alia said. "It's getting smaller."

I realized that all those thoughts were causing me to lose my erection. "Maybe it didn't like being called a sea cucumber," I said.

"Danny, you know that can't be true. What's the matter?

"It's nothing."

"It must be something."

"I'd rather not discuss it."

"Dearest Danny, if we're going to be mates we have to be honest with one another. So please tell me."

She took her hand away from my tinky. What a silly name for such an important part of a man's anatomy. But I'm sure the dolphins don't think of it as being silly. "Can we just keep on walking?" I said.

She stopped walking and said, "I'm not moving from this spot until you tell me."

I took her head in my hands and kissed her gently on the lips. "All right, I'll tell you. But please don't take it the wrong way. I love you with all my heart and this has nothing to do with my feelings for you. Promise me."

"I promise."

"Well, it's a technical problem."

"What do you mean?"

I overcame my embarrassment and told her. She listened quietly and then was silent for a long moment. Then she took my hands in hers. Let's go to my room," she said. "And bring your sea cucumber with you."

I thought fast. "Are there sea anemones in the waters of Sea?"

"Yes."

"Then if you'll bring your anemone I'll bring my cucumber. Agreed?"

"Agreed."

CHAPTER 8

Alia's parents' house was in the direction of the shop, a few minutes beyond and slightly up the hill from the quay. The front door was unlocked and Alia opened it. It was dark inside.

"Mama and Daddy must have gone to their room. I know the way even in the dark. Here, take my hand." When we arrived at her room she opened the door and closed it behind us.

"Wait here," she said.

I heard her opening what sounded like a drawer. Then she struck a match and lit a candle that was sitting in a shell. I was glad to see that they had such things as matches on Sea and resolved to find out how they made them. I don't know why I would think of such a thing at a time like this, but I guess I was subconsciously nervous and was trying to take my mind off any problems that might be coming up.

That was really stupid. Come on, Danny, I said to myself. Better to think of a sea cucumber and a sea anemone. No, not that either. Better to think of Alia.

And I did as she came to me and pressed her body against mine. She took my head in her hands and kissed me slowly on my lips. Then she put her tongue in my mouth and worked it around passionately. My tinky responded as if it were a spring let loose.

"Umm," she said after withdrawing her tongue from my mouth. "I feel something down there."

She reached around behind me, untied my dakti and stepped back as it fell to the floor.

"Well, I see I don't have to worry anymore," she said slipping out of her dakti and stepping forward to press our bodies together again.

She kissed me again on the lips. Our mouths opened and I thrust my tongue into hers and worked it around and then we touched tips. Within seconds my whole body began to tingle.

She pulled away and began licking. First my face, then my neck, then my nipples, then my navel, then downward to my tinky for a few moments. By now I was quivering.

She stood up. "My turn," she said.

"My pleasure, but I may need a little guidance."

"I'll be here."

"I know," I said as I began to stroke her face with my tongue, and started working my way down her body. I got to where I thought her mammary glands should be on an Earth woman. She was obviously enjoying it, but there was no added effect.

So I kept going down, and down, and down toward her pelvic region. Then she took hold of my head and pushed it to the right. There was a slit. I stuck my tongue inside. There was a nipple and I licked it. She quivered.

Then she moved my head to the left. Another slit and another nipple. I worked my tongue around it. She quivered again. I assumed these were her mammary glands, unless she had two vaginas with nipples in them.

Then she took hold of my head again and moved it back to the center-line of her body, and pulled it downward a few inches. And there it was. I thrust my tongue inside and elicited a sensual moan to go along with her quivers

Then she pulled my head away, raised it and we kissed again and tongued our mouths. Then she withdrew, took my hand and led me to the bed.

"Now it's our turn," she said as she lay down on her back.

"Come to me, my love," she said.

I lay down on top of her and we kissed passionately as my tinky searched for her winky and my toes wiggled on her tail, which was also flat on the bed under her legs.

It seemed to take forever to find her winky. Was it up? Was it down? It couldn't be sideways because that was where her mammary glands were. I was getting desperate, but then she took hold of my tinky and guided it in to the right place.

It was a perfect fit. We made joy passionately for all of about 20 seconds before we both came.

"Oh, no," I said as it began to happen.

"Oh, yes," she moaned. "Oh, yes, yes, yes!"

After our spasms subsided I just lay there in ecstatic exhaustion.

"Don't move," Alia said.

"Not a chance." And we lay together quietly for several minutes.

Then I raised my head and looked into her eyes. "Alia, darling, I love you more than you can possibly know."

She smiled. "And I love you more than that."

"Not possible."

"Oh yes it is."

"Oh yeah?"

"Yeah."

We both began to laugh as I rolled off her. We lay there side-by-side, face-to-face.

"Well," I said. "I guess we are now officially mates."

"Hello, mate."

"Hello, yourself, matie."

"How was I?" she asked.

"Incredible," I answered. "I know I came way too quickly, but how was I, anyway?"

"Wonderful," she answered. "That was too quickly? Why all dolphins come quickly."

"Then baby, you ain't seen nothing yet. Wait till next time."

"I'll be ready when you are."

And I was about an hour and a half later, and then again about dawn. Not bad for a 39 year old washed up stand-up comedian

Between times Alia slept soundly. But even though it had been an eventful day, to say the least, I still had trouble sleeping.

At one point I lay on my back staring up at the ceiling, thinking about the Gatekeepers. By now I no longer had any doubts about whether or not my life here was real. I knew it was.

As a comedian, washed up or not, I am a pretty creative person, but not that creative. It would have been impossible to imagine all that had happened, let alone dream it. And as for hallucinations, I knew from my reading that hallucinations seem real, but not this real and for this long. Impossible.

And what about the love I felt for Alia? Besides, who the hell could hallucinate a tinky and a winky? Child words used for things children know nothing about. Well not many, anyway.

And heaven? Do angels fuck? Maybe in the extremist Muslims' heaven, but not in any others I ever heard of.

No, it was all real, and the Gatekeepkers? Who were they? What were they? Agents of God? Did God tell Olga to buy me a starname in the Intergalactic Starmapping Society? Did he know that that star has a planet with an atmosphere like Earth's? Did he send the sharks to eat me and the dolphins to rescue me? Or did he send a message to the Dolphin God at the bottom of the sea on Sea?

And hell? If this is hell, Satan surely screwed up.

Lots of questions. No answers. And I knew there never would

be. Besides, who cares? I loved my brief life on Sea so far... and Alia... I couldn't love anyone more.

Eventually, I slept.

We were awakened by a knock on the door. It was Mama.

"Time to get up, sleepy heads. Breakfast is ready," she said cheerfully.

"Sounds like she's in a good mood," I said.

"I hope she stays that way."

"She will now that I'm here," I said with a chuckle.

"Don't bet on it."

We washed our hands and faces and other parts in the basin on a stand in the corner, put on our daktis and went out of the room.

I was glad to see that Ami was joining us. "Hi, guys," he said. "I hope you had a good night." I detected a slight smirk on his face. Mama must have, too, because she frowned at him then turned a happy face to us.

"Come into the kitchen, darlings," she said. I caught the plural and was pleased. "Alia, I have made your favorite breakfast."

Alia grinned. "It must be broiled sea urchins with sliced baked sea cucumber. Oh thank you, Mama."

I gulped. Sea urchins, sea cucumber. At least it wasn't sea slug stew. Actually the breakfast turned out to be delicious. Now Alia and I had another thing in common.

We made idle chatter about the weather, what was new in Sea and Cali, and about this year's cocoa crop. Then Shoko brought the subject around to Earth. "So, Danny," he said. "You told us that Sea is very similar to Earth, except for the amount of water here, but are there dolphins on Earth?"

It was a question I half expected but wasn't looking forward to. "Yes," I said hesitantly, "but they're different."

"How so?"

"Well, for one thing Homo sapiens and dolphins can't talk with one another."

"Go on."

"And on Earth the dolphins don't have arms… or legs."

"Those can't be dolphins," said Mama indignantly.

"They are what we call dolphins. There are many varieties, but they all look similar to you folks, except for the arms and legs, of course."

"What do they have instead?" asked Shoko.

"Instead of arms they have what we call flippers. And they don't have anything at all where your legs are. Their bodies go straight back from their flippers to their flukes, which you call tails.

"How primitive," said Shoko.

"But they are very intelligent," I stammered. "Some people, I mean Homo sapiens, think as intelligent as humans — I mean Homo sapiens."

"How do you know that?" asked Ami. "Can they read or write?"

"No."

"Well they can't be very intelligent then," said Mama.

"Perhaps they don't have any need to read and write, like our orcas," interjected Alia. "If they have no arms or hands they wouldn't be able to write. And if they can't write, what is there to read?"

"Aside from which," I chimed in, "Homo sapiens didn't know how to read or write until comparatively recent times. That doesn't mean they weren't intelligent before."

"Sounds logical," said Shoko. "But how do you know they are intelligent?"

"Uh… we observe them in the water."

"We observe fish in the water," said Mama. "But that doesn't make them intelligent. So how can you tell?"

"Uh... we interact with them."

"That's good," said Shoko. "How do you interact with them?"

"Well, they are very friendly toward Homo sapiens, some of them."

"So seals are friendly, too, and we train them to do tricks for us," said Shoko, peering at me questionably.

"I looked back at him and nodded my head. "Yes... we train them, very easily, I might add."

"To do tricks?" asked Mama.

"Sometimes."

There was shocked silence around the table.

Ami broke the ice. "I can do tricks," he said pushing his chair back and swiftly moving to an empty spot on the floor. Then he proceeded to do a few back flips and a handstand before he scurried back into his chair.

"Not funny," said Alia. Mama and Shoko merely shook their heads.

"Sorry," said Ami. "Just trying to lighten things up a little. I guess it wasn't funny. Was it, Danny?"

"No."

Shoko gave me a hard look. "And I suppose," he said, "you Homo sapiens therefore think you are superior to dolphins."

"On Earth, yes. Most Earthers do, but not me. Certainly not here. The dolphins on Sea are the same as Homo sapiens on Earth. Through evolution we have both evolved into what we are today, the dominant species on our respective planets."

"What's evolution?" asked Shoko, "and what does evolved mean? I don't know these words. Does anyone else here know them?" There was a shaking of heads.

I was surprised, although I shouldn't have been. On Earth we didn't know about evolution until about 150 years ago, and even now huge numbers of our population either don't know about it, or if they do, don't believe in it.

"I'll do my best to explain. What I'm going to tell you applies to Earth, and since our worlds are so similar, probably to Sea as well. I know it's going to be a little hard to believe at first, but please bear with me and think about it before jumping to any quick reactions. Agreed?"

There was a nodding of heads as all eyes were fixed on me.

"Well, to begin with," I said, "the word evolution means... a sort of gradual, very gradual, process of development and change of all the living species. They change from primitive forms of life to more complex and advanced ones by successfully adapting to their environment. Those that don't adapt eventually die off while those that do reproduce, passing the things that permitted them to adapt to future generations, and so on. Gradually, the species itself changes because of the new adaptations.

"When I used the words gradual and gradually I mean sometimes millions or even billions of years. Is everyone with me so far?"

Heads nodded again and I continued.

"Now comes the hard part. In the beginning, Earth was completely covered with water, which was probably also true of Sea, and the only living things were so small you couldn't see them. Then they got larger and more complicated as the more successful ones adapted to the environment of the planet, which was also changing."

"Do you mean that early on there were no fish or dolphins?" asked Mama.

"Correct. Fishes and dolphins evolved from these tiny almost invisible living things over billions of years.

"On Earth we know that even the ancient ancestors of modern Homo sapiens lived in the sea. Over time they evolved into wormlike animals, fish, and then what we call amphibians, which had legs and were able to come out of the water on to land. Then after billions more years Homo sapiens evolved from them and more advanced animals that lived entirely on land. Does that make sense?"

"Possibly," said Shoko.

"Maybe," said Ami.

"I'll have to think about it," said Alia.

"Impossible," said Mama. "What about here on Sea?"

"Probably very similar, except that because Sea itself is almost all water, dolphins are the end result of evolution, the most evolved and advanced of all life forms. Whereas on Earth, where there is so much land, Homo sapiens are the end result of evolution, at least so far."

There was silence as I looked around the table. I addressed each person in turn.

"Shoko?"

"Very interesting. I'll think about it while I'm waiting for the chocolate to melt."

"Ami?"

"I suppose it's possible. But so what?"

"Alia?"

"Sounds plausible, we briefly talked about this before, but you will have to go into a lot more detail before I accept it."

"I will. I promise. Mama?"

"Eel poop," she said with the emphasis on the word poop. "Impossible. God created dolphins in his own image. So how could we, as you say, have evolved from worms!"?

"Not necessarily so," said Shoko. "We should think — "

Alia interrupted him. "Daddy, before you and Mama get into an argument Danny and Ami and I have to go. We have a long trip back to Sea and a lot to do."

She got up from the table; Ami and I did the same immediately. Shoko and Mama took a little longer. I could see that Shoko wanted to pursue the subject, but Alia took him by the arm and we all walked to the door, where we said our goodbyes.

I thanked them for their hospitality. Mama nodded her head, but Shoko took me by both hands and pumped them. "You're alright, Danny," he said.

"I hope everything works out between you and Alia. And I do believe Homo sapiens are the highest form of life on Earth. After all, they have chocolate."

"The only species on Earth that does," I laughed warmly. I liked him.

"And Mama," I said. "There are a lot of Earthers who believe as you do, that we were created in the image of God."

"Then how come you don't look like a dolphin?" she asked.

"Mama," said Alia. "Goodbye." They kissed and hugged. I saw Mama whisper something in her ear and Alia whisper back. Alia hugged and kissed her father, Ami and I shook both their hands, and with hand and arm waves we headed down to the quay to our waiting baku and dolphin escort.

On the way down I asked Alia what Mama had whispered to her, and what she had whispered back. She smiled sheepishly. "None of your business. Strictly women's talk."

"You mean there are already secrets between us? We just became mates. I'm shocked and profoundly disappointed. This may be grounds for de-mating."

"De-mate all you want. I'm not going to tell you."

"All right. In that case I won't tell you my secret."

"What secret."

"The secret I haven't told you. If I told you, it wouldn't be a secret."

"Are you playing a game with me, Danny?"

"Yes, It's called 'lets make a deal'. You tell me yours and I'll tell you mine."

"Is that a popular game on Earth?"

"Very. Would you like to play?"

"All right. You first."

"Okay. My secret is that all that shouting back and forth with the sharks was strictly bravado. I was scared shitless, if you will pardon the expression… and I still am when I think about it."

"We don't have that expression here, but it's a good one. Very apt. But that's hardly a secret. I knew it was an act all the time."

"Alia, are you trying to wiggle out of telling me yours?"

"We don't have that expression here, but it's appropriate, too. Especially considering my secret."

"Which is?"

"Since your secret wasn't really a secret to me, I'm only going to tell you half of mine. You'll have to guess the rest."

"Do I have a choice?"

"No."

"Okay, let's hear it."

"My reply to Mama's two part whispered question consisted of these eight words: wonderful, shorter but thicker, better and longer lasting. And that's all I'm going to say." She smiled lasciviously. I smiled back lecherously. "Well, we'll just have to keep that between us."

CHAPTER 9

The trip back to Sea was uneventful, a welcome change. The orcas were gone from their cove and we saw nary a sign of a shark. We stopped for lunch on a beach near where we gathered oysters and clams and barbequed them in a pit we dug. They were excellent, every bit as good as Earth clams and oysters.

We arrived back in Sea late afternoon and headed for the Administrator's office. He wasn't in, but we left word that our mission was successful and that we would report to him in the morning.

"Your place or mine?" I said as we were leaving.

"Mine is much cozier than that hotel room." Alias said. "Besides, I'd like to show you where I live."

"It's another deal."

After stopping at a little shop to pick up food for dinner and breakfast the next morning, we walked to Alia's tiny house. It was two blocks up the hill behind the quay and about a block from the Administrator's office.

The house was indeed cozy with a small living room lined with books on one wall and a deck with a lovely view of the harbor over the roofs of the houses below. There were two comfortable looking chairs on the deck, so I sat down in one of them. After she put the groceries away, Alia came out and sat down in the other.

"I think you will like the bedroom, too. The bed is very comfortable."

"I know I will."

"Would you like a drink?"

"Sounds good to me."

She got up, was gone for a few minutes and returned with what appeared to be two spiraled conch shells with a little shell base attached to the bottom. She handed one to me. I raised it to her.

"Raise yours, too," I said. It's an old Earth custom."

She did and I clinked mine again hers. "Here's to us," I said. "Long may we be mates."

"Yes," she answered. "To us, and perhaps someday... life-mates."

"I'll drink to that, my love." I raised the shell to my lips and took a small sip, relishing the tender moment.

"Ugh," I sputtered and shuddered. "That's... different."

"I guess you don't like it."

"I wouldn't say that exactly. It's just not like anything I have ever drunk before. I would imagine it's an acquired taste, like scotch."

"What's scotch?"

"It's an Earth drink that everybody hates the first time they try it. Then some people get used to it and really like it. Others continue their distaste for it. Do you like this stuff?"

"Not really. I just thought you might. It's the Administrator's favorite drink. He might offer it to you sometime and I didn't want you to be surprised."

"Am I allowed to refuse?"

"Of course... if you don't mind hurting his feelings, which, of course, may be to your disadvantage."

"Thanks a lot. What do you call this wonderful drink?"

"Squid Squirt."

"Squid Squirt!"

"Yes, it's made from the distilled juice of a squid's tentacles when they're squeezed, and aged in flasks made from palm wood.

It's an additional use we have for the squid we raise for food. It's very potent, so don't drink it too fast."

"I don't think you have to worry about that." I put the shell to my lips and took another sip. It was awful again. I felt like vomiting, but didn't think that would be very romantic. "Would you be offended if I didn't finish it," I said.

"Do I look like the Administrator to you?" she said swiveling her hips seductively.

"I'll take that as an invitation."

"You don't have to be invited."

"Then let's christen your bed."

"I don't know what christen means, but I think I get the idea."

"It comes from a religious experience. In ordinary everyday use it means the first time."

"I think this experience will be more religious than ordinary," she said as she got up, took my hand and led me to the bedroom.

The experience may not have been religious, but it certainly was spiritual, I thought as I lay on my back in a state of blissful exhaustion after we made joy. And I felt sorry for every priest I had known since my childhood Sundays in church. Well, maybe not quite every one.

My Saturday rabbis in the temple of my youth were another thing. They at least could get a double dose of spirituality, and feel that they were fulfilling their duty to God at the same time.

Being raised with a Catholic father and a Jewish mother had its advantages. I could reject the formality of two religions instead of one. Or was that really an advantage?

Oh well, what difference did it make? Here I was a stranger in a strange land, where I didn't feel like a stranger anymore. I really liked it here... and Alia... she was making my new life complete and fulfilled.

I looked over at her. She was fast asleep and didn't look like any woman I had ever known or seen or heard of or imagined. But she was a woman, all woman. A woman in mind, a woman in soul, the woman I had bonded with, the woman I was in love with.

She must have sensed me looking at her because she opened her eyes and smiled. "I feel that way about you, too," she said softly.

"Oh yeah"

"You must have been dreaming."

"Perhaps, but I do know what you were thinking."

"All right, what was I thinking?"

"And feeling, too. That's the most important part." She then proceeded to tell me exactly what I had been thinking and feeling.

I sat straight up and turned so I was facing her head on. I stared unbelievingly into her eyes. "You're psychic," I said.

"I don't know the word, but it's obvious what you mean. Yes, I am, and so are all the other dolphins on Sea. That's how I knew your secret about the sharks."

"You mean you can all read minds?"

"No, not exactly. Only if there are strong feelings between the people involved with the thoughts. And actually, if we try hard enough we can project thoughts even over distances."

"Extraordinary. Will you teach me how to do it?"

"Yes, of course. At least I'll try, though it's not something that can easily be taught. The person has to have the capacity within him or herself. But I know I can teach you how to read and write dolphinese. That's different."

"I hope so. It's very embarrassing not to be able to do that. The Gatekeepers really screwed up there."

"But look at everything else they gave you. If it hadn't been for them you wouldn't be here now. They gave me you, and that's the greatest gift."

"Oh, Alia," I said. I could actually feel her love emanating from her body. I concentrated on projecting mine back.

"I feel it, Danny. I can feel it. You did it."

She sat up and we collapsed into each other's arms; and then we made complete and overwhelming love like never before.

And then we slept, a blissful sleep through dinnertime, through the night and part of the morning.

Chapter 10

We were awakened by a knock on the door. Alia got up to answer it and returned a few minutes later.

"It was a messenger from the Administrator. He would like to see us right away, or as he put it, at our earliest convenience. He wants to see me first alone and then both of us together. We must have slept late because Ami has already reported in. We should probably both go together so that you will be there when he wants to see you."

"Let's do it."

I got up out of bed and we each washed, showered and did our other ablutions, gobbled down a quick breakfast of what looked like an Earth breakfast burrito, but was actually, as I later found out, a tasty fish sausage wrapped in an edible leaf from the rainy side of the island.

When we arrived at the Administrator's office, Alia was ushered right in, and I was told it would be about an hour before he would be ready for me, and that if I wanted to I could go outside and walk around. They would send someone to find me as long as I didn't go too far.

I like that idea, since I hadn't seen much of the land part of Sea except for our walk to the restaurant on my first day and Alia's house yesterday.

The city, which on Earth would actually be called a town, was quite attractive. It was laced with canals like Venice, before it rose into the hills. There were narrow trailways on each side of the canals wide enough for two or three people walking side by side, or someone pushing a wheelbarrow type cart, which I saw a few times. The pathways appeared to be covered with ground up shells. There were bakus in the water, mostly carrying cargo.

Wherever I went I was, or course, stared at. I expected that but knew that in time they would get used to me. The stares were brief and everyone was polite. There were many hellos, waves, friendly nodded greetings, and lots of smiles.

The house and buildings were colorful and seemed to be constructed of various shades of coral or rock. None were of wood. There were shops of various kinds selling foods and general merchandise. I discovered to my delight one that sold chocolates.

I went into it, bought a chocolate truffle and nibbled on it as I strolled through the streets. The only disconcerting part of my walk was when I passed a stand that had two different kinds of newspapers with my picture on their front pages. I wished I could read then, especially the smaller one, which looked like a supermarket tabloid. I was sure it contained a story about my external tinky.

I had just about finished the truffle when a dolphin caught up to me and said that the Administrator was ready to see me. I thanked him and headed back to the Administration building. He dove into the water in the adjacent canal and headed in the same direction.

The receptionist greeted me cheerfully and ushered me to the door to the Administrator's office. She knocked and he came to the door himself.

"Come in, Danny," he said warmly. Sit down. Would you like a drink? I have some of the best Squid Squirt from the finest distillery on Sea."

This was the moment of truth. I glanced at Alia, who was sitting there with a huge dolphin grin on her face. It was so huge that it was almost a caricature. To drink or not to drink? That was the question. Was I going to be noble, or true to myself? Neither. I was going to bullshit him.

"Thank you, sir," I said, but on Earth it is against the rules to drink before lunch. In fact, in some circles it is considered sacreligious, at least in my family. So in respect for my parents, I'll have to refuse for now. But after lunch," by which time I hoped I would be in a different place, "I would be delighted... and honored."

He looked me straight in the eyes and smiled, "You don't like Squid Squirt, do you? You're not a very good liar, you know."

"Uh... you're very perceptive."

"I know. It's part of our training to be Administrators. Sometimes, it hurts to be able to understand so much. I do love Sea Squirt though. It's a weakness of mine. But... as disappointed as I am, I'll excuse you because you are an Earther." He turned to Alia, who still had that shit-eating grin on her face.

"And as for you, young lady, you could have told me he doesn't like it."

She didn't look like she was being admonished by the highest-ranking person in Sea. She was still grinning.

"I just wanted to see what would happen, Uncle Malti."

"Uncle!" I exclaimed. "Uncle Malti?"

"Yes."

The Administrator laughed. "Yes, Alia is my naughty niece. Shoko is my brother."

"I'll be damned."

"If that means surprised, you obviously are," he said "Alia has told me all about you. Welcome to the family, Danny." He put out his hand, took mine, and shook it. "And you are still not a very convincing liar."

"On Earth it wouldn't be considered a real lie, but rather what we call a white lie. It's an untruthful statement made to avoid hurting someone's feelings or avert an uncomfortable situation."

"I understand. And now niece and mate of my niece, let's get down to serious business. First, Danny, do you have any idea how long it will be before the orcas are able to meet with us?"

"No, they didn't say. But judging by Earth standards, which I know may not be accurate here, and by what Bogi told me, I would say that by the time the ones from far away get here, it will be at least one or two months, possibly longer. But I'll try to stay in contact with Bogi's family and report back to you."

"That would be helpful. What do you think our chances are of convincing them of our point of view?"

"I don't know, but I wouldn't count on it. Frankly, I think the true value of this meeting will really be in the communication between you two species. I think the orcas who live in an area where there area a lot of fish, as here around Sea, will go along with you. But in more remote parts of Sea, they will have to hunt for food, and that food will probably include mammals."

"Hmm, you may be right, but we'll certainly give it a try. Whatever the outcome, it will be a truly exciting event. I'm sure we will also learn much about the more remote areas of our world. We don't know much, hardly anything, about what's out there. We've never been very far from our group of islands, and have just assumed that the reset of the planet is water."

"Why is that?"

"We have never been visited by any other dolphins, or any other intelligent species for that matter. You are the first non-dolphin we have ever encountered."

"I understand that, but what I don't understand is why you haven't explored the rest of your world. Certainly, you must be curious. Intelligence breeds curiosity."

"Yes, of course we would like to know what's out there. But there is one overwhelming reason we have never been able to venture far from our island. I believe you are well acquainted with that reason."

"I am?"

"Alia, dear, would you please refresh his memory."

"Danny," she said, "I'm sure you remember the sharks."

"How could I forget?"

"Well, the sea is teaming with them, and they are all as ferocious and blood thirsty as you saw. We can only send patrols out so far before they tire and can no longer protect adequately. Then they become victims themselves. And because of their size and strength, the sharks can easily overturn or wreck even our largest bakus."

But can't you build bigger and stronger boats that they can't turn over or wreck. There is wood on the island. Surely at least on the rainy side there are trees large enough to make sea going boats out of."

"I'm afraid not, Danny," said the Administrator. "You haven't seen our whole island yet, but when you do I'm sure you will not find a tree or shrub more than two inches thick. They grow profusely on the rainy side, but thinly. And palm trees are too heavy.

"Believe me, we have tried. But the sharks have always been able to bite or butt them, even if we put the wood in layers, in which case they are smashed or at least leak enough to make the boat sit low in the water for the sharks to just push their heads over the sides to get at the occupants. And our poisoned spears aren't enough to stop large numbers of them. We have lost many good dolphins in our efforts. The sharks are just too big and too vicious. Nothing can stop them except orcas. The sharks are afraid of them."

"I understand. Well it certainly will be a momentous event when the orcas get here."

"And we have you to thank for it, Danny," said the Administrator.

"Please don't thank me. I've enjoyed every minute of it."

"Even the scary ones?" Alia chimed in.

"Well, maybe not quite every minute. But sir, I would like to thank you."

"For what? It was your accomplishment."

"For two things. For having the trust in me to try to do the job, and... for allowing Alia to be my guide." She looked at me, and I looked into her eyes. We held our gazes so long it made "Uncle Malti" a little uncomfortable.

"All right now," he said, let's talk about other things."

"I'm ready."

"Excellent. Alia and I have already come up with a plan, and we would like to see if it is agreeable with you. Alia, by the way, is one of my aids for special projects. Everybody knows it's what we call nepotism, but they also know that she is exceptionally capable."

"I agree. Incidentally, we have that word, too."

"Before her appointment to my administration she had been a teacher in our college, specializing in the history and culture of our people. Since her appointment she has continued in that field, but more from the research aspect.

"Her job is to increase and improve our knowledge of people and the world around us so we can better educate our young people, and adults, too, of course. And, I might add, she has been doing an excellent job."

"You flatter me, uncle."

"Perhaps. But you deserve it. And Danny, here's where you come in. Before you left for your meeting with the orcas, I said we would have to find a way for you to earn money to support yourself. Here's how you can do it. Alia, would you please explain to him."

"Of course, Uncle." She turned back to me. "Danny, I told Uncle Malti about your theory of evolution — "

"Wait, " I interrupted. "I'd like to claim credit, but it's the theory of one of the great men in our history, Charles Darwin. In fact, the theory is often called Darwinism. And I might add it has been substantiated by tens of thousands of scientists since his time."

"Be that as it may," she continued. The Administrator, although he's far from convinced, thinks there might be something to it, and he would like you to work with me to study it in relationship to our dolphin history, and that of other life forms on Sea.

"At the same time I could teach you about Sea and our way of life and history, and you can do the same about Earth. What do you think?"

"I can't think of anything I would rather do. I'm far from a trained researcher, but I think I can contribute. When do we start?"

The Administrator looked at me with satisfaction. "As soon as you leave this office," he said. "And by the way, Ami is also one of my aids, so you can call on his services at any time, if he is available."

"Good," I said. "I like him."

"And, oh yes, Danny. One more job for you. I would like you to teach a class, actually two classes a week about Earth, its history, people, customs, position in the universe, etc. Whatever you think is important to explain your world. I'm sure our people will be fascinated, as will I. One class would be for adults, the other for children. I will attend myself. And, of course, you will be paid for them as well as for the research with Alia. Agreed?"

"Absolutely," I answered. "Absolutely delighted." As a matter of fact I was more than delighted; I was almost ecstatic. To be with Alia so much, and to get paid for it! Maybe I was actually in heaven. Nah.

CHAPTER 11

And that was the beginning of the happiest months in my life. By day Alia and I explored the hills and valleys and shorelines of Sea; by night we explored each other.

Early in our explorations we found fossils and remains of sea animals such as clams and mussels and conch shells, usually in caves and outcroppings on the tops of hills in the center of the island, indicating that it was once completely or almost completely covered by water and that the dolphins must have been completely aquatic animals at one time.

But did they have arms and legs before they went back to the sea, or did they develop them after the water receded and they came to the land? We had no way of telling. Eventually we gave up that line of pursuit, and decided to search for other advanced life forms on Sea.

We found nothing in and around the lower elevations of the island, so decided to search the very highest regions. Alia gave me a brief description of the high country. More sparse vegetation with dozens of caves, some of them going deep into the hills. She thought that might be our best bet.

She also recalled that Abu Abu, whom she hadn't seen since she was a child, lived there. He had left his teaching past at the college and moved back to the part of the island of his childhood to follow in his father's footsteps as a sort of shaman medicine man.

"Perhaps if we can find him he may be able to help us. We can ask some of the local people up there where he lives."

I was a little uneasy about the local people because of our previous visits to the hill people. They tended to be out of communication with Sea and at the time of our visits didn't know of my existence. They hadn't seen the newspapers and there didn't seem to be much word of mouth up there.

Some of them had been frightened of me, thinking me a monster or fiend. If I had been alone without Alia to explain who I was, I might have been attacked and killed. But after she explained and I spoke with them, they actually became quite friendly.

But now we were going into still higher country. I hoped they had heard of me by now.

Alia explained what they were like and why we might learn something.

"By comparison with the people along the coast," she said, "these dolphins can be considered primitive. Most of them rarely come into Sea, and some still practice the old forms of religion. They may have some ancient legends which, incidentally, have never been written down. Even if we don't learn anything to help in our search we can write down their legends and take them to the college library.

"I think that's a great idea." I was particularly pleased because by now Alia's every-day-without-fail lessons in teaching me to read and write dolphinese could finally be put to use. "Let's do it."

Finding shaman medicine men did not prove difficult. It seemed that every tiny village had one. They either lived in huts like their fellow villagers or once in a while in caves on the highest hill in the area. These were the ones we decided to focus on, while at the same time trying to locate Abu Abu. I remember several of them very well, but Abu Abu's especially vividly, both because of what we saw in his cave and because of the medicine man himself.

On the fifth day of our search we finally found Abu Abu. The local villagers gave us explicit directions to him and informed us that he lived in seclusion in a cave directly behind and connected to another cave.

We entered the front cave and had to crawl on our hands and knees to get into the second one. It was dimly lit by candles and Abu Abu was sitting on the ground in sort of a lotus yoga position with his legs crossed over his tail sticking out in front of him. His eyes were closed and he was chanting softly as if in a trance or deep prayer.

We didn't want to disturb him, so we watched for a few minutes. He still didn't move so we decided to explore the cave, especially the walls. Our way was illuminated by our own candles, which we had lit before entering the outer cave.

The walls were both fascinating and unexpected. The first thing we noticed were books, several shelves of them. Also on the walls were what appeared to be cave drawings similar to what I had seen in pictures on Earth made by prehistoric cave dwellers, except these were of sea creatures — all kinds. The only thing they had in common were fins or tails or flippers in various combinations.

In one corner was an array of bones in stacks separated by what appeared to be parts of the bodies they presumably came from. There was also a pile of skulls off to the right. I held my candle up close to the skulls and almost dropped it when a deep unfriendly voice directly behind me said,

"Nosey, aren't we?"

Alia, who had been peering at the skulls standing along side me, did drop her candle.

We spun around to face the source of the voice and almost touched him.

He was huge and towered over us.

"Let me see your faces," he commanded. "The gods don't like supplicants sneaking in and nosing around without announcing themselves at the door. Raise your heads and let me see your faces."

Alia raised hers first. "Hi," she said weakly.

He looked her over from the top of her head to her feet and then behind her to the end of her tail. "What are you doing here?" he said.

"Just visiting. We're doing research for the Administrator, and looking for you," Alia replied.

"Uninvited. And what about you?" he said turning to me. "Raise your candle to your face."

I did as he asked and saw his eyes bug out in astonishment. He lowered his own candle slowly down along my body to see my legs and feet. He bent over closer and then around my body behind me.

"My God, no tail!" he exclaimed, his voice a few octaves higher than before.

He raised the candle back up to my face and examined it closely.

"External ears!"

"That's not all he has that's external, Alia chimed in."

"I'm sure he's not interested, Alia. I don't think he knows about me. Would you please tell him?"

"Everything? She grinned.

"Everything that's important to him," I said, emphasizing the word "him".

"Okay, but first let me introduce you two. You had me scared at first Abu, but not now. Danny, this is our old family friend Abu Abu. Abu Abu, this is my mate Danny."

"Old family friend?" said Abu Abu.

"Yes, Abu, I'm Alia. We haven't seen each other since I was a child, but I do remember you."

"Of course, of course. I'm sorry I didn't recognize you all grown up, and I'm sorry I frightened you. In my position people should be a little afraid of you."

Alia introduced us and explained who I was and where I came from. While she was speaking he never took his eyes off me, paying particular attention to my head.

When she was finished he motioned us to the center of the room. Then he went to a side we had not examined, opened a curtain and in four trips behind the curtain brought out three chairs and a table. "Please sit down," he said.

Then he went back a fifth time. When he returned a minute later he had changed from the Ghandi-like rag dakti he had been wearing into a multicolored robe similar to an Earth bathrobe. It was the first real robe I had seen on Sea. He noticed us staring at it.

"You like it?" he said. "In all modesty I must confess I made it myself, and painted it by hand."

"It's lovely," Alia said.

"Perfect for a holy medicine man shaman" I said sarcastically, sensing a Hollywood-like phoney.

He got up from the table again without saying a word, and disappeared behind the curtain. When he came back he was holding three glasses and two bottles, which he proceeded to set down on the table.

"It's refreshment time," he said cheerfully. "Sea Squirt or wine?"

Alia and I looked at each other in astonishment.

"Wine," I said.

"Me, too," Alia added.

"I'll have a Sea Squirt myself," Abu Abu said as he poured the drinks. When he was finished he raised his glass to the toasting position. We raised ours to meet his.

"Here's to shaman medicine men, scholarly researchers and not so strange beings from outer space," he said, clinking our glasses and swallowing his in one gulp. We sipped ours slowly while he sat back and observed us, especially me.

"So," he said. "What's new in Sea? Other than you, of course," he said glancing at me.

"Only you," I said with a smile. "We came here expecting a humble shaman medicine man and here we are being entertained by a bon vivant in a hand painted robe whom Alia had previously known as a professor."

"I don't know the expression 'bon vivant', but I get your meaning. You were obviously expecting someone different, a stereotype perhaps. Well I am not your typical shaman medicine man; nor are some of my fellow shamans around here. I never have been, never will be. I can be straight with you folks because you, Alia, are from Sea and we are old friends and because you, Danny, are from God knows where.

"I really am a medicine man shaman, a good one, too. And to the local folk I look and act like one. But I don't have to fake the look with you. So drink up and tell me what you are researching."

We told him what our assignment was, including Darwin's theory of evolution, and how it might apply to the dolphins of Sea. All the while we were talking he was nodding his head with what we took to be agreement with our ideas. He paid particular attention to the evolution theory parts.

When we were finished he was still nodding his head. "Yes," he muttered, "it makes sense, a lot of sense, and explains an idea I've been wondering about. There's something I'd like to show you, but first let me tell you about myself, and a few others like me."

"Yes, please do," I said, and Alia nodded her head in agreement. "Quite frankly we are amazed that you claim to be a holy shaman medicine man."

"We are," said Alia, " I thought people like you all lived simply. You seem to be doing just the opposite."

"Right and wrong," he said. "Right in that I don't live simply and that I am not holy. Wrong in that I truly am a medicine man shaman, and a damn good one.

"I was thoroughly trained by my father who was trained by his father, and so on, back for who knows how far. I know all the herbs, plants and natural medicines, where to find them, how to prepare and administer them. I am an expert.

"And most of those for whom the medicine doesn't work I cure by the power of suggestion and my reputation."

"Dressed the way we first saw you, I assume," said Alia.

"Of course. And by the way, the scene you saw when you entered my inner chamber was an act. I didn't know who you were. I heard your voices when you first entered the outer cave, so I quickly changed into my holy man mode, which is how you found me."

"And the chanting and almost dream state you appeared to be in…." said Alia.

"Purely an act for your benefit. Alia, you may know that even though I am a thoroughly trained medicine man I also went to regular school and then onto the university, where I studied and taught literature."

"Literature?" I exclaimed. I had just learned something new. "Do you mean fiction? Novels?"

"Yes, that's what literature is. Don't you have it on Earth?"

"Yes, I just didn't know it existed on Sea." I turned to Alia.

"Sorry," she said. "I just never got around to telling you about it. It's not my field, but I do love to read."

"Ah well," said Abu Abu. "That's what we writers have to face… neglect and indifference from all but a very small segment of the population of Sea."

"You're a writer?" I said.

"A real writer? Said Alia.

"Of course," he said with a shrug of his shoulders. "Why do you think I work at this lousy boring job living in a cave miles from civilization? I'm writing the great dolphinian novel. And when it's published and I become famous, I'm out of here. High living and party time for me in Sea."

"I can see you're really dedicated to serious literature," I said sarcastically.

"Serious shmerious," he said. It depends on what the critics say. I just do my best, and whatever comes out comes out. Would you like to see where I work?"

"We'd love to," said Alia.

"Sure," I said.

He got up. "Follow me." He walked to the curtain and pulled it aside. He lit an oil lamp and we were once again surprised. There were bookshelves crammed with books, many more than we had seen before. There were also a comfortable looking chair, a writing table with an oil lamp on it and a chair next to it. The table was strewn with papers. There was also a low door in the back.

We both looked at him and shook our heads.

"I see you don't approve," he said.

"No, it's not that," I said. "We're just more than a little surprised. How did you manage to get all these books up here so high up in the hills?"

"Through that door," he said with a laugh pointing to it. "It's my escape hatch. It leads to still another cave with an exit outside on the other side of the hill. I use it when I want to go down into Sea, unseen, or to go partying."

"Partying?" said Alia. "Whom do you party with? Surely not

the villagers."

He gave her a stern look. "Of course not. Give me a little cred-it, please. I party with the other medicine men of my generation in the nearby villages. We all pretty much have the same approach. Several of us are writing because this kind of work allows us plen-ty of free time. And the pay we get for our medicines and treat-ments gives us sufficient income to live on and buy books and bev-erages on trips to Sea.

"But enough of this mundane conversation," he continued. "Follow me." He led us back through the curtain and over to the pile of bones we had seen before.

"As you know, or perhaps you don't know, one can write only a few hours a day. The creative juices can flow for just so long. And since we party only under cover of darkness at night, I have found something to keep my busy mind busy."

He pointed to the bones. "These," he said proudly.

"Oh, I said, "did you kill all those animals?"

He looked at me critically and said, "If you will stop being sar-castic, I will explain."

"Sorry," I said. I could see that he was very serious.

"I have been collecting and studying these bones," he said, looking at me sternly. "I study these bones to try to learn some-thing about the history of Sea and about its inhabitants."

"That's my field." Said Alia. "That's one of the reasons we are here."

"Yes, so you said. And that's why I would like to look through these bones with you."

"I would be delighted," said Alia.

"Me, too," I added.

"Good. You might find this particularly interesting." He picked up what looked like a leg bone from one pile, a femur if my memory serves me correctly.

"This is a leg bone from a dolphin," He reached into the pile and picked up another leg bone about the same size and held them together.

"Look at them closely," he said. "I don't believe the second one is from a dolphin."

We examined them and they were distinctly different.

"You may be right," said Alia, a puzzled expression on her face. I agreed.

Abu Abu continued. "But if it is from a different animal, what animal? We are the only animal we know of that has legs… and feet," he said reaching down and picking up more bones and laying them out on the ground. There were two sets, each in the form of a foot, but obviously different from one another.

Both he and Alia looked puzzled and thoughtful. My mind was starting to click.

"I don't suppose you know how old they are," I said.

"I have no way of knowing. I found them either in the deep recesses of caves or at the bottom of pits dug by villagers. They may have been there for hundreds or thousands of years.

"Or millions," I added. "I don't suppose you've heard of carbon dating."

"What's that?"

"It's a way we have on Earth of telling approximately how old bones like those may be."

"I wish we did," he said. "But don't you think it's beginning to look like there may be something to your theory of evolution, that we may have evolved from these other animals?"

"Not necessarily," I replied. "It's also possible that at one time the sea was lower and that the island of Sea was much bigger, and that those animals lived here. Then the sea rose again, and the animals retreated up into these hills to escape it, and ultimately drowned when the water covered the island."

"Sounds logical," he said. "Now let's look at some skulls." He reached down to the skull pile, picked through it and brought up two, one in each hand. He extended the first to Alia. "This is a dolphin head. Correct, Alia?"

"It looks like one to me."

"And this," he said extending the other.

"I think so."

"Agreed." He handed one to each of us, then bent down and pulled one out from the bottom of the pile. He raised it up and held it out to us triumphantly.

"My God!" I exclaimed. It looked like a human skull, or at least an ape close to us.

"It looks like a Homo sapien head," I said.

"Yes. At least it is what I assume one would look like with the flesh and eyes and ears and nose removed."

"Yes," I said. "You are probably right."

He smiled broadly. "Of course I have never seen a creature who could possibly have a skull shaped like this… that is until you came along."

He looked at my head as if he wanted to peel all my skin and eyes and ears and nose off. Alia looked dumfounded. I didn't know what to say as he kept staring at me.

"Well," I said casually. "It certainly looks like some kind of sapien head, but not necessarily Homo sapien. And I sure am glad dolphins are non-violent people."

"We weren't always non-violent," he said, his eye darting back and forth between the skull and my head. "As a matter of fact, some of our long past ancestors were what we call 'head hunters!' Right, Alia."

"That's true," she said, looking at Abu Abu. "I remember that from my studies at the university. And it wasn't very long ago either. Was it, Abu?"

"Like about a hundred years ago," he said.

"More like 50," she said.

I was starting to get a little uncomfortable and took a step backwards.

"Where are you going, Mr. Homo sapien?" said Abu Abu with menace in his voice, taking a step closer to me. "I just want to examine your head a little more thoroughly... while it is still attached to your body."

I took another sep back with clenched fist ready for action. But I was stopped by Alia's laughter and Abu Abu's guffaw.

"Danny," Alia said with a huge smile.

"We're just kidding," said Abu Abu. "You have to admit we had you going there for a minute."

"Going where?" I said innocently, unclenching my fists. "I know you were never head hunters. You probably just made up the word, although there is such a word on Earth, and even now there are still some Earthers who hunt heads."

"There are?" said Alia.

"Why do they hunt heads?" said Abu Abu.

"For the hunted head owner's brain. They sell the heads to other people, who in turn eat the brains, then discard the head itself. Unless, of course, they shrink it, in which case it becomes a collector's item. They're particularly fond of dolphins' heads."

"Danny!" said Alia. "You must be joking."

"As a matter of fact I am." I laughed. "Can we get back to these skulls? I don't know enough to differentiate between Homo sapiens and other closely related species on Earth."

"You mean there are other animals similar to you on Earth?"

asked Abu Abu.

"Not quite. There are other animals who look a lot like us and from whom we may have evolved, but probably we all evolved from some distant ancestor we had in common. But none of these other animals are as evolved as Homo sapiens.

"If they have a language it is not nearly as complex as ours, and although they are intelligent, they are not nearly as intelligent as us; nor do they read or write. Though they can feel and they certainly do think. They just haven't evolved to our advanced state."

"Then do you think this skull belongs to a creature as advanced as us?" said Alia.

"I doubt it," I answered. "Homo sapiens — at least on Earth — are a very resourceful species, and survivors, even under the harshest condition. I think that if they had been here they would have adapted and survived."

Abu Abu looked at me quizzically. "But they have no tails — at least these bones don't indicate them. So how could they survive in the sea?"

"Good point," I said, "They would need land."

Abu Abu and Alia looked at each other, and I'm sure the unspoken idea that passed between them was that although they knew of no other land on Sea, the dolphins had not explored the entire planet. I know that's what I thought briefly, but dismissed the idea, not because I thought it was impossible, but because I didn't want to think about anything that might mess up my slice of paradise on Sea.

"Undoubtedly," said Abu Abu. "Nevertheless, I will continue my studies. I'll let you know if I turn up anything else or have any new ideas."

"Please do," said Alia.

"Yes," I agreed. "You can let us know on one of your spiritual trips to Sea."

"You mean 'spirits trip', don't you?" The three of us laughed, and Abu Abu said, "Danny, Alia calls me Abu, and I wish you would, too."

"Delighted, Abu." It has been intriguing, fascinating, and an experience meeting you."

Thank you. I wish you the best in your life on Sea, and with Alia. And you, Alia, with Danny. See you in Sea. Would you like a drink before you leave?"

We politely declined, thanked him for his hospitality and took him up on his offer to lead us out through the rear exit and point us back to the village.

CHAPTER 12

On the way back down the hill we discussed what to do next. First we decided to contact Bogi and his family to see how he was making out in gathering the orcas together. We also wanted to spend some time with him and their family. Alia was intrigued with the idea of playing with their children, while I wanted to learn more about the orcas and really get to know one on a one to one basis.

The second thing we wanted to do was to explore the waters around the island in search of evidence of other species that might have once lived there.

But first we had to find Bogi and his family. When we got back to Sea we reported our findings to the Administrator. He questioned us closely about the skull and bones, but didn't pursue the subject beyond saying "Very interesting. Yes, very interesting."

We did not mention anything about Abu's living style. After all, he was an old family friend. He agreed to supply us with dolphin guard patrols on our trips as long as we agreed to stay close to shore.

Finding Bogi and his family was easy. They were again in Orca Cove. He reported contact with many orcas who agreed to the meeting. But it was still several months away.

So we pursued our explorations, but also spent several days socializing with the orcas. We always thoroughly enjoyed our time with them, not only because they were nice and fun to be with — Alia especially enjoyed playing with the children. Even though they were bigger and stronger than she was, they played many games of tag, which she usually won because she could swim and maneuver faster.

We learned much about their lives and habits and culture and extraordinary ways of communicating across long distances. Even though I spent much time translating many conversations, we realized how much we thought alike, and it didn't take long before we established a strong bond of friendship.

Bogi and I became especially close friends, not so much because of male bonding, but rather because of our conversations when we were alone, about the different physical worlds we lived in, and the similar ideas we had about our worlds and their inhabitants. He was particularly interested in the orcas on Earth and the variety of sapiens.

We also told many jokes to each other, changing the physical settings of course.

But there was one conversation which I found quite disturbing, and which still haunts me. It started out innocently enough with Bogi asking if I would like a ride on his back to a cove around the bend. I readily agreed because I got a real kick out of rides like that, despite lingering guilt feelings about orcas trained to do that in Earth aquariums and marine shows. I climbed on with a boost from Alia, and we took off.

Just around the corner of the bend we came to some large steep boulders falling off straight down into deep water. Bogi picked one at just the right height where I could slide off and onto its ledge. He asked me to hop off his back and take a seat on the rock so we could talk eye to eye, which I did.

"This sounds serious," I said.

"It is serious. Not an emergency, so don't worry."

"I'm glad of that. What are we going to talk about?"

"Me, or rather us. Not you and me but rather orcas in general and me in particular. Because we live so close to Sea, I guess it affects me, and Oola , too."

"This does sound serious."

"In its own way it is. It's something I have been thinking about for a long time, but which really came to a head since we have gotten to know Alia and you so well."

"Oh, I hope we haven't offended you in any way."

"No, definitely not. You haven't offended us at all. We really enjoy our time with you. It's just that... that... that we are envious of you."

"Envious? I don't understand. You are big, strong, powerful, humorous, warm, interesting, free and independent, and virtually lords of the sea. And highly intelligent, as intelligent as us, perhaps more so. What more could you want?"

Bogi looked me straight in the eyes, hesitate and said, "What you call arms and legs, and hands and feet. We are creatures of the water, trapped for all of our lives, never to venture on land."

"Holy Shit!" I exclaimed.

"There's nothing holy about it, and sometimes it is indeed shitty."

"Sorry," I said. An Earth expression. Please continue."

"Yes. You said we are highly intelligent. That's true, and I suppose that's the main reason for our problem. We are not able to utilize that intelligence the way dolphins can. We cannot build things. I have heard you and Alia referring to things called books that give you information and enjoyment, and stimulate your mind. We don't have those and never can. Nor can we talk with the dolphins to learn things they know. While we are indeed free, our lives are very limited by our environment, which we cannot change. In a sense we are trapped."

It didn't take long for what he was saying to sink in. Even on Earth I had watched dolphins and orcas in the wild, in captivity and on film, knowing how intelligent scientists considered them to be, and often wondered how they felt being confined to the water and not being able to live full lives like humans. I wondered if they had the capability of understanding their situation, and if they did, how they felt about it. Now I knew.

"Oh, Bogi," I said. "I understand. I really do." I reached out and embraced his huge face, as much as I could get my arms around it, and patted his forehead. "I wish there were something I could do about it. If I were God, I would."

He laughed, a deep uproarious and somewhat phoney one. "Impossible," he said, "we are made in God's image and you don't look like an orca. Let's not talk about our situation any more. I just wanted to get it off my chest because you are such a good friend. We have to enjoy what we have, so forget it and let's get back to the ladies and children."

He turned the side of his body to the boulder, I stepped out to his back, plopped down on my rear, grabbed hold of his dorsal fin, and we headed back around the corner and into the cove. I knew I could never forget that conversation and that I could never do anything about the arms and legs, but I could do something about the reading, I thought, on our way to join the others.

I would make it a point, now that I could read dolphinese, to make arrangements to read to the orcas. But I couldn't do it all the time and forever. No, we had to establish a means of communication between orcas and dolphins so other people could read to them, and eventually if someone could figure it out, for them to read books themselves. And who knows, perhaps to write them by dictation.

But first had to come a means of communication — a language of some sort that could be used by both orcas, and dolphins. It would have to be reasonably complex so that ideas could be exchanged and expressed. Yes, a language. It could use sounds, since both species could vocalize. It could also use movement of dorsal fins, heads and hands.

It would take a lot of work, but it could be done. I would be the intermediary, and coordinator, since I spoke both languages.

When we got back to Alia and Oola I proposed the idea. The reception was enthusiastic. Both Bogi and Oola came right up to me, pressed their faces against mine pulled their lips back and gave me what I can only consider to be Orca kisses. That had to be a first in the history of the Universe, and had the makings of a great tabloid story: "Orcas kiss man. Man lives to tell about it."

Alia must have considered them kisses, too, because she came up to me, playfully pushed on the Orcas' faces and planted a big one right on my lips. "I love you, Danny," she said.

"We love you, too," echoed Bogi and Oola.

"And I love you guys," I said.

Alia and I talked all the way back to sea about how we could accomplish this truly momentous task. It would be another, historical first, along with the upcoming meeting between the orcas and dolphins.

But we still had some underwater explanations to complete before the big meeting. After that we would jump into out project feet first.

As you can well imagine, when it came to exploring underwater, dolphins had several advantages over me. In addition to the fact that they were aquatic creatures for eons, they could see underwater far better than I, they could swim faster and go deeper, and they could stay under far, far longer. So there was no way I could keep up with Alia, but I could try.

So before we started on this assignment, I called upon my limited skin diving experience. Alia and I worked out a few aids, which she then had made for me.

First, there were fins the shape of dolphin flippers I could strap on to my feet. She had them made to measure from a thick, rubbery, flexible seaweed that I could slip into and fasten with a strap made from that same seaweed. They worked beautifully and increased my underwater swimming speed by many times.

Next came a snorkel. That was easily made from a hollowed out piece of bamboo with a seaweed mouthpiece.

A diving mask wasn't difficult either, since the dolphins had glass that they made from the silica in beach sand. They cut the glass large enough to cover my eyes and nose and mounted it in a flexible frame made from the same rubber-like seaweed used for the flippers. It had a strap similar to the flippers.

Unfortunately, an aqualung or other type of breathing apparatus was beyond our combined technical skills.

But what I had worked and I had a lot of fun with it. The only thing that bothered me was the shark protection spear we always had to carry in case the sharks got through the guard patrol that invariably accompanied us.

I still couldn't keep up with Alia, but it certainly made our exploring easier. Because the tropical waters of Sea were so clear we could see a long way down, well beyond the approximately 12 feet depth I could dive to. Alia, of course, went far, far deeper.

We were looking for bones of all types, things buried in the sand, anything that looked like it didn't belong there. We didn't accomplish much, but had a wonderful time doing it.

However, we did accomplish one totally unrelated thing. We worked hard at practicing the skill of thought transference between us. As I mentioned before, it came easily to Alia — dolphins used it often among themselves — but it was something I had to work very, very hard at.

It required a great deal of concentration on my part, an intent focusing of my thoughts going out and an equally intent focusing of my mind to absorb what was coming in. I got pretty good at it, but only with Alia. I never could get it to work with other dolphins.

Why? The only conclusion I came to was that it was really a form of energy that could be directed and received, and that I was on the same wavelength with Alia and no one else. Sort of like a short wave radio transmitter tuned into a certain frequency.

It was quite extraordinary for me to practice it. We would spot something on the bottom and Alia would dive toward it, while I hung just below the surface breathing through my snorkel. Since I had a much wider field of view from my position, if she had trouble finding the object once she was on the bottom, I would focus hard on such things as "a few feet to the left, it's off to your right, straight ahead", and so forth. It really worked.

And then she would send thoughts back from the bottom such as "it's just a fish head, it's only an odd shaped rock," and so forth.

We also tried it on land while I was taking a break between teaching my "Earth Classes", or while Alia was attending a boring faculty meeting, or from one room to another at home, which was actually her house. We even tried it in the midst of making love. Amazing!

I look back upon those months as being truly idyllic, by far the happiest, most glorious time of my life. Alia and I were so much in love, the bond between us so strong, that at times I was so happy I thought it would go on forever.

But idylls are like idols. Neither is forever; both can crack...and even break apart.

CHAPTER 13

My idyll began to crack one morning when Ami rushed into my classroom shouting. "They're here, Danny! The Orcas are here! They're at the harbor gates. One of them is making loud noises to the gate guards. He's probably asking for you. Please come immediately."

I quickly excused myself to the class, suggesting they go down to the quay to witness history in the making. Ami and I made a dash to a waiting baku at the quay, carefully hopped in and paddled to the harbor entrance.

We could see a group of Orcas on the surface just beyond the gate and behind them extending way out into the sea, hundreds more. The largest one at the gate was shouting at the guards, who, of course, couldn't understand a word he was saying. But I could.

It was Bogi, and he was yelling, "Do you think this puny gate can hold us? We can jump right over it."

Then he spotted me. "Hey, Danny," he called. "The chickens are about to cross the road."

Then he wiggled his skyscraper dorsal fin in greetings, and dropped down beneath the surface, followed immediately by a half dozen other big orcas. Within 10 seconds all of them shot out of the water full speed in unison, flew over the gates in formation and landed about 10 yards from our baku, almost overturning us with the wave they created and soaking me from head to toes with its water.

We were still rocking when the orcas came back up to the surface. When the rocking slowed down Bogi meandered over, wiggled his dorsal fin again and said, "the dorsal fin wiggle means hello

in the new language. Hello, Danny. Sorry for the big splash. I guess
we don't know our own strength."

"Oh yes you do," I replied, "You were just showing off."

"You're right. How are you? And Alia?"

"We're fine, thank you. And you and your family?"

"Just great. Are you all ready for the big conference?"

"We will be as soon as I can get the Administrator and the
council out. How many orcas are here?"

"About 300 here outside the gates and another two hundred
over at the cove waiting for word from me. How are we going to
handle this?"

"Here's what we have done so far. The council had a meeting
and decided that if there aren't more than about 500 of you we can
have the conference here in the harbor."

"Sounds good to me. If you will have someone open the gates
I'll send word back to the others."

"We do have one request, however," I said. "Please don't take
offense, though… because we don't know your habits. We would
appreciate it if there were no defecation in the harbor. Shit pollutes,
you know. The dolphins here spend a lot of time swimming in the
water, and I don't think they would enjoy bumping into mammoth
whale turds. Do you?"

Bogi thought for a moment and laughed. I see your point. It's
not something we worry about in the open sea, but the harbor is
different. He laughed, "I'll tell everybody if they have to go to just
raise a flipper out of the water and be excused to swim out the gate.
How about farting?"

"Bogi!"

"All right, I'll pass the word on. Seriously though, Danny, we
are all looking forward to this meeting, to an even better relationship with the dolphins. And they are really excited about your idea

for reading and language. I think this is going to be a beneficial meeting."

"I agree."

"It will also be a productive one if we can coordinate a mutual problem we both have."

"What do you mean?"

"The sharks."

"The sharks? I thought they were afraid of Orcas and never bothered you."

"They are afraid of us and never bother us, except, and this is a big exception, when one of our children decides to wander away from the immediate vicinity of its family, which, because they are so curious, they are very prone to do."

"If the sharks don't think a child is within our protective range, they will dart in, grab it, and immediately start tearing it apart and devouring the pieces. By the time we would realize what was happening they would be gone; and we're not fast enough to catch them."

" I never realized that, and I'm sure the dolphins didn't either. The sharks are afraid of them too, but only if they are in groups and armed with their poison tipped spears."

"Yes, we know. That's what gave us an idea."

"What is that?"

"We were thinking that perhaps we could lure the sharks into a trap they can't get out of. The dolphins could be lying in wait for them and then suddenly spring out and start piercing them with their poison spears. The struck sharks in their pain throes would attract other sharks and trigger a mass of feeding frenzy, attracting still more sharks, and so on. We would stand guard outside the trap to prevent sharks escaping, but at the same time let new ones in to join the frenzy."

"That sounds like a good idea," I said. "Perhaps we can at least reduce the numbers of these awful creatures around here so dolphins and orcas can use their natural habitat in safety. Let's discuss it with the council at the meeting. In the meanwhile, why don't you get your delegates while I alert ours and tell the gate guards to let you in, not that they could stop you? But please…keep an eye out so no sharks sneak in."

"Guaranteed. We'll see you later."

"And Bogi, please let the gate guards open the gate and you swim out gracefully. I don't think they were very happy with your performance."

"Happiness is our main goal in life." he said with a smile as he turned away. I motioned to the gate guards who opened the gates and immediately closed it behind the departing Orcas who swam majestically and serenely out.

Chapter 14

A few hours later the great moment arrived. Hundreds of Orcas were on the surface in the harbor, arranged in a huge semicircle, their fins sticking straight up in the air. Ten were separate in a straight line in front of them.

The dolphins were also in a semicircle, its edges almost touching the Orcas ends to form a while circle. The council members were also in a straight line directly in front of the ten orcas, with the Administrator in the middle and me in my baku by his side, ready to translate. The water was deeper than the bodies of both species so all were gently moving their tails in the equivalent of humans treading water to stay in one place. What a sight!

The Administrator raised an arm in the air, motioned for the guards to close the gate, waited for silence, and said, "Welcome orcas, to our home. We hope this is the beginning of a long and mutually beneficial relationship."

I translated, and the orcas wiggled their dorsal fins in assent. Bogi spoke on behalf of the Orcas. "We have long respected your accomplishments on this piece of land, which we now call Dolphinland but which Danny informed us you call Sea. We, too, hope this is the beginning of a new era in our lives. Dolphins, we salute you."

I quickly translated. Then as if they had rehearsed beforehand all the Orcas wiggled their dorsal fins in unison and each raised its right flipper out of the water and shook it back and forth. It was truly an inspiring scene, and I was more pleased and proud of myself than I had ever been, even after my best performances on stage. I only wished I had a camera or camcorder to record this momentous event.

I looked for Alia in the crowd of dolphins, but couldn't spot her. Then I heard and felt her thoughts. "I'm so proud of you," she said. I smiled and sent a thought message back. "I love you."

"Not as much as I love you," was the return.

"Oh yeah?"

"Yeah."

Before we could pursue the conversation the administrator began speaking and I translated.

"Danny has told us of your plan to eliminate, or at least sharply reduce, the shark problem around here, and we agree. And we also have a proposal to you. We —," He broke off abruptly. "What's going on out there?" he shouted to the gate guards who were agitatedly calling from the towers and waving their arms.

"It's the sharks," one of the guards yelled. "They're surrounding some more orcas who are trying to hold them off. One of the orcas looks wounded. His back and sides are bleeding and there are things sticking out."

"Open the gates!" the Administrator shouted. "Danny, translate for the Orcas."

As soon as I did the Orcas turned en masse and raced to the gate as it opened. I paddled my baku as fast as I could to try to stay close to them.

Most of the orcas didn't wait for the gates to open. They simply dove down, flew up into the air, and landed on the other side right in front of a circle of six approaching orcas, with a seventh one in the middle, all surrounded by a horde of circling shark fins knifing through the water, but not attacking. The orca in the middle was oozing blood. That's evidently what made the sharks so brazen as to come that close to the orcas.

As soon as the sharks saw the rest of the orcas they began to scatter. I gingerly paddled my baku into the group of orcas in front of me to reach the new arrivals and to find out if the wounded one needed medical attention. I didn't bump into anyone because they parted to let me through.

I arrived at the circle as one of them was excitedly telling the group what had happened. I was a little too far away to hear exactly what he was saying, but as I approached closer and he was able to see me he stopped talking and stared malevolently at me.

"You're one of them!" he screamed, "I'll kill you!" He opened his mouth wide and started charging toward me with hate in his eyes. I was terrified.

But just before he reached me Bogi darted out in front of him and blocked his way. "Stop!" he shouted. "He's our friend."

The orca stopped but continued to stare hatefully at me.

"Wait here," Bogi said to me.

I sat there waiting uneasily in my baku while Bogi swam into the protective group, spoke with them, and examined the wounded orca from all sides.

He came back to me. "Danny," he said, "Follow me. I want to show you something."

I did as he asked while Bogi cleared the path ahead of us talking quietly to the orcas in front of us. I couldn't hear what he was saying, but they didn't appear unfriendly as we passed. When we got to the wounded orca he spoke soothingly to him.

"Don't worry, you'll be fine. Your wounds are not deep. I want you to meet Danny, he's a good friend and wants to help us." I waved my hand in greeting. The orca didn't respond; he just stared at me.

"Take a look at his wounds, Danny," Bogi said. I examined them from the position where I was and inched closer. Blood was oozing slowly up from holes in his back and on the side facing me. The wounds appeared to be superficial, but his face did show pain. He looked to be frowning at me through his pain.

I stared uncomprehendingly at the holes. They were definitely real holes — not shark bites, which would have torn the flesh.

"Come around to the other side," said Bogi.

I paddled around the orca and when I got to the other side I stopped cold, astounded. Protruding from his side with their heads buried in his flesh were several arrows.

"No. No. No." I moaned. "It can't be."

I moved in closer to get a better look. The shafts were straight and appeared to be made of some sort of wood. There were feathers on their ends like Earth arrows, to help them fly straight through the air.

"So Danny," said Bogi. "It appears you are not the only Homo sapien on Sea. Our friends were attacked by animals who looked like you."

He motioned me around to the front of the orca where he could see me. "Fasi," he said, "Danny really is a friend. He is not one of those who attacked you. He does not know them. He didn't even know they existed."

"Hello, Fasi," I said. "I'm really sorry to see that you're hurt. We'll get somebody to take care of your wounds." I had barely gotten the words out of my mouth when a dolphin came swiftly swimming up to us. He was carrying a small bag, similar to an Earth medical bag. "I'm a medical dolphin," he said, placing the bag into my baku. "I'll take care of you." I translated.

The orca's back and sides were too far out of the water for the doctor to reach the wounds, so he jumped into my baku, almost overturning it while I did a balancing act.

He cleaned each of the holes, which I assumed were made by

spears, with a rag dipped into a jug of clear liquid he had in his bag, and then dabbed them with an ointment that stopped the bleeding.

"Now for the hand part," he said. "Paddle around to his other side, would you. We have to pull out those little spears. I hope they're not toxic."

"They're called arrows," I said, "and are not likely to be poisonous. And be gentle; the ends are buried in the orca and probably have things on their ends called heads to keep them in position. You'll probably tear flesh pulling them out."

"You seem to know something about these...arrows."

"A little," I answered. "Unfortunately." I addressed Bogi. "This would be better coming from you than me. Would you please tell Fasi that pulling the arrows out might be very painful."

He did as I asked.

"See if you can get him to lean over so we can get a good grip on the arrows to pull them out." I translated what the doctor said to Bogi, who passed it on to Fasi.

The orca leaned over toward us. The doctor and I grabbed an arrow and pulled. It did not come out easily, and when it did it carried a lot of flesh with it. The orca winced in pain as we did it. After it was out the doctor dressed the wound. We repeated the process with each of the other arrows.

"Done." said the doctor. "I think he'll be fine. Nothing penetrated deeper than flesh and fat. Ask him how he's feeling."

I decided to do the talking myself.

"How are you doing, Fasi?" I said.

"I feel better already."

I translated for the doctor. "I'm glad," he said, looking around to see if anyone else needed attention.

No one else did, so the doctor slipped out of my baku into the water and before he swam away told me to tell Fasi he would like to see him tomorrow to check the wounds.

I translated for him and turned to Bogi. "Do you mind if I ask Fasi and the others who were with him some questions?"

"Not at all. I've got some myself, but you first."

"Thank you. "Fasi, or anyone else, could you describe what happened, and then in detail what the attackers looked like."

"I'll tell you," said one of the orcas. I was closest when they were doing things to Fasi, and closest to the beach."

"What was happening on the beach?"

"It was horrible. They were killing dolphins by stabbing them with short things that were pointy on one end and wider than spears between the handles and points."

"I think you're describing something called knives. The dolphins have them also. Please continue."

"After they stabbed them they sliced open their stomachs, reached inside their bodies and pulled out pieces of odd shaped meat. They put them in their mouths, sometimes chewed them and sometimes seemed to swallow them whole. And all the while the ones who weren't doing those things were making loud noises and jumping up and down. There were also a few of them banging on something round, in a rhythm that seemed to get them excited. It was disgusting."

"Why did they attack you?"

They all looked a little embarrassed. Another one spoke. "We were so absorbed in watching what was happening on the beach that we didn't see a large baku that had snuck up behind us until it was too late. Fasi was the first one they came to, and the animals on it started jabbing him with their spears. A few of them pulled back on a half round thing that looked like a bent piece of bone, and sent those small spears that you pulled out of Fasi flying through the air and into him. They sent them at the rest of us but they missed.

"Then when they saw Fasi bleeding, the animals in the baku started shouting one single sound and repeating it over and over again. The rest of us surrounded Fasi, made threatening lunges at the baku and got him out of there as fast as we could. Then we headed here to complete our journey for the meeting."

"Exactly what did the attackers look like?" I asked.

"They looked like your except their skin was lighter, almost white like the white parts of our bodies; and their hair was the color of the sun."

I groaned at the familiar physical description of ancient Earth Vikings from the North.

"Where did this happen?" asked Bogi.

"On a small island three islands that way," he said turning his body to the north.

"Do you know how many bakus there were there?" I asked.

"We didn't count them," said one of the others. "But there were two different sizes; small ones pulled up on the beach and very large ones with things that looked like thick spears sticking up into the air."

I groaned again and looked at Bogi. He shook his head. "I don't know what to think," he said. "Nothing like this has ever happened before. No animals have ever attacked grown orcas before. Do you think they are really Homo sapiens? What do they want?"

"Bogi," I said with a heavy heart. "If they're not Homo sapiens, they are very close. I hate to say this but I think the subject matter of our gathering has changed. Will you come with me while I tell the Administrator and council what happened, and what I think."

"Of course, and I'd like to bring a few other orca leaders with me, if I may."

"Certainly," I said. He called out several names, one of which I noticed was Oola. The others cleared a path for us as we made our way back into the harbor where the dolphins were still congregated. On the way I sent a thought message to Alia asking her to be by my side. If I ever needed a soul mate it was now.

When we arrived the concerned Administrator asked, "What happened? Is the orca going to be all right?"

"He'll be fine," I said, "But we may not be."

"What do you mean?"

"Can we have a private meeting? Just you and the council and the orcas. I'd like Alia to be there, too, if that's all right."

"Of course," he said, and motioned to the council to gather around. Alia joined us. I motioned for her to get up with me on the baku, which she did.

"Mr. Administrator and council members," I said somberly, "I have something terrible to report."

I related the events as I understood them, all the while translating for the Orcas in their language. When I finished there were tears in the eyes of some of the dolphins, looks of fear and horror in others. Alia held my hand tightly. There were tears in her eyes, too. "Abu's bones," she said.

"It appears so," I answered.

"What are you two talking about?" asked the Administrator.

"I'll explain later," I said, turning to Bogi. "Is there anything you would like to add?"

"Yes," he said. "First I would like to state that although these savages appear to be Homo sapiens, we should in no way blame Danny. We don't believe he arrived on Sea with them or in any way even knew of their existence. Correct, Danny?"

"Yes."

"And second," Bogi continued, "and I think I speak for all the orcas, this assembly, although it hasn't gotten very far, is about friendship between dolphins and orcas, and I want you to know that whatever happens we are your friends and will help you in all ways possible." He turned to the orcas with him. They all agreed.

I translated for the dolphins, who were obviously pleased.

"Thank you," said the Administrator and the other members of the council, nodded their heads and smiled. "Does any one have any ideas as to what we should do next?"

"I do," I said. I then told them about the bones in Abu Abu's cave and that what happened today obviously means that those creatures did not die out. That they must have found a place on Sea where they could survive, and that place seemed to be the far north.

"Now I'd like to tell you a little history of Earth, because if these indeed are primitive Homo sapiens, as they appear to be, there is much to fear. For almost their entire history on Earth, Homo sapiens have been instinctive hunters and killers. Hunting for food or for power over other Homo sapiens and killing, usually without mercy or conscience, has been a way of life for thousands and thousands of years.

"There were exceptions, of course, throughout our history, but not many. That's the basic truth. Things are much better now, particularly in the last 100 years as Earthers have become more civilized, but it still goes on.

"I think that the first thing we should do is learn more, find out what kind of Homo sapiens they are. We already know they kill for food, and seem to enjoy it. Dolphins and orcas also kill for food, but not for pleasure.

"I think that since I look like them and can probably speak their language I should pay them a visit to try to reason with them, and if that's not possible, try to find out what their plans are so that we can come up with a plan to counter theirs. What do you all think?"

"I think it is very dangerous," said the Administrator.

"It is," said Bogi, "but I think you should do it. I'll help. All the orcas will help."

I turned to Alia. She shook her head no, then yes. "It's the only option we have," she said taking both my hands in hers and holding them tight.

"It is absolutely necessary," I said. "We must find out what we're up against."

"How do you propose to do this," said the Administrator, resignation in his voice.

I turned to Bogi. "Any suggestions?"

He thought a moment and said, "How about this. You go in a baku with a long rope. We'll throw it around my dorsal fin and I'll tow you as fast as will keep the baku stable. The sooner we get there the better. You will still need protection from the sharks, so we will travel with an escort of orcas."

I translated for the dolphins. All within hearing nodded in agreement.

"I have another idea," said Bogi. "We'll ask another group of orcas to go ahead of us and gather in front of the savages' bakus. They can start jumping out of the water and making noises to attract their attention. Then we'll sneak around behind them in the direction they're not looking and you can cast off the rope. I'll dive underwater and make sure the sharks won't get to you while you try to get aboard one of their bakus."

I translated for the dolphins.

"It should work," said the Administrator.

"It better work," said Alia. "But there may be a problem."

"What's that?" I said.

"Getting off their baku," she said. "Suppose they won't let you go?"

I translated for Bogi.

"Then," he said, we'll raise such a ruckus that they won't be paying any attention to you. You can jump overboard, climb on my back, and we'll get away as fast as we can."

I translated for the dolphins. All agreed.

"Good. While I am gone I strongly urge you to gather as many shark spears as you can with as many dolphins as you can to wield them. I think you should also make as many new ones as possible. We may have to fight the savages."

There were some murmurings of discontent.

"Look," I said, "I know you are a non-violent people, but there is nothing wrong with violence in self defense, and to defend the lives of your families."

Heads nodded in assent again. I continued, "I also think it would be a good idea to practice throwing the spears. We might not always be close enough to poke the savages. Also, everyone should carry a knife; we might all be fighting at close quarters, fighting for our lives."

Where was all this coming from, I thought? I was beginning to feel that I was in a John Wayne movie and that I was John Wayne.

No, I hated John Wayne movies, and John Wayne even more. The characters he played had absolutely no sense of humor, and he always wore elevator shoes with six-inch heels to look taller than everyone else around him.

My mind was racing. No, definitely not John Wayne. Then I remembered... George C. Scott in Patton. Yes, I would be Patton. Stand up comedians have to think fast, and I was thinking fast.

I turned to Alia. "Alia, darling, I think those look-alike Homo sapiens are probably very primitive and superstitious. I have an idea to play on this. What do you think of you going back to Abu Abu, telling him what has happened and asking him to bring down all the skulls he can, along with people with poles to hold them up in the air. His partying cohorts might enjoy it. If it is dark maybe we can put lighted candles in them, and scare the hell out of the savages."

"I like the idea," said Alia. "I'll go as soon as you leave. I'm sure Abu will be excited to do it. And you, my dear, please don't let your excitement lead you into taking unnecessary chances. Promise me you will be careful."

"I promise. I will be careful. Heroics are not my lifestyle. Maybe I can tell them some jokes."

"That might be dangerous, my darling. Please don't."

"All right. I'll be a straight man. I didn't travel all these miles in space to meet the love of my life just to be killed by some damn earth-like pseudo humans. I'll be more than just a straight man. I'll be a damn careful one."

By the time I had paddled to the mouth of the harbor, Bogi had his group of volunteers. There were about two dozen in all, with six hanging back to form a perimeter around Bogi and me to protect us against any possible sharks that might still be in the area.

I flipped the middle of my length of rope over Bogi's dorsal fin and held both ends in my hands like the reins of a horse, so I could release the tow when we got there and still retain the rope in my baku for the trip back. Off we went.

It took only a few minutes to adjust Bogi's speed to the stability of the baku. We traveled at a pretty fast clip because the long narrow shape of the baku made it stable when being pulled forward in a straight line.

We zipped along swiftly northward along the shoreline I hadn't seen before. It was more rocky than the South with fish farms and just an occasional cove with a beach. The first one was only about two miles north of Sea in a sheltered cove. I made a mental note of it as a possible landing site for the savages.

We soon reached the northern end of the island of Sea and kept going. A few miles out was the first small island, about two miles long. The next island was a little smaller, but there was still no sign of their boats. We headed for the third and last island, rounded its southern point, and saw them.

I spotted the savage's ships when we were still a good mile away from them. I call them "ships", rather than bakus, because that's what they were. Sailing ships. There were five of them and they all had masts sticking up into the air.

I tugged on the rope to get Bogi's attention and motioned him to come alongside so we could talk. I also waved my arms for our escorts to come close. When Bogi arrived I asked him to call the group that was going to detract the savages.

When everyone was gathered around I told them what I thought. "Those bakus out there," I said pointing at the ships, "are not bakus as we and the dolphins know them. They are what on Earth are called sailing ships. They are each capable of traveling long distances and carrying many savages, so we have to be extra careful. And remember Fasi. They can shoot arrows at you. I don't know how far they can shoot them, but please remember that and be careful.

"And Bogi, you can't get too close. Ships like that often have what are called lookouts on them. And even if the savages are distracted they may have someone watching all around, so you can't get too near. I'll have to paddle the last distances myself. I'll tug on the rope when I'm ready to let go. Is everyone ready?"

There was a chorus of assents and good lucks, and we were off again. As we got closer I realized the ships were all 75 to 100 feet long and had one stubby mast each. There were also slots in the sides of the hulls, probably for oars when there was no wind. Both their bows and sterns were pointed, and their masts were a little forward of their centers.

I also saw that there were still savages on the beach, but that most of them were on the ships. I asked Bogi to head for the largest one, because I assumed that was where their leader would be. At a signal from Bogi the "demonstration" orcas took off and within a few minutes went into their act. It immediately attracted the savages' attention, who seemed to be enjoying the show immensely.

I would have enjoyed it myself — it was like watching a giant marineland demonstration of killer whales — if I hadn't been so nervous and focused at what might happen when I got there. As we got closer to the largest ship I noticed there was a lookout at the top of its mast.

As soon as I saw him he must have seen me, because he began waving his hands wildly and calling out. Bogi and I were still more than a hundred yards away when I tugged on the rope and let one end go. I gathered it into my baku and paddled toward the ship. Bogi and our escorts immediately dove underwater.

As I got closer to the ship it was obvious that the whale show was no longer the focus of the crews' attention. I was.

I saw arrows being strung into their bows and aimed at me. Spears were raised and pointing toward me.

I raised both my arms in the air to show I wasn't armed. As I got next to the ship I waved to them frantically and smiled the widest and most cheerful stage grin I was capable of. No one smiled back.

"I come in peace," I yelled.

No one made a sound. They merely peered over the side at me,

and for the first time I got a look at their faces. They were the
whitest I had ever seen on a human other than in pictures of albinos. They also looked definitely human, Earth human. They had
long very blond hair and no beards that I could discern. They were
also bare-chested, and their skin had red splotches all over, which I
assumed was sunburn.

One of them, who unlike the others wore a white vest, which
looked like fur, leaned out toward me.

"What mean 'in peace'?" he said menacingly.

I was relieved that he understood my language and I his. At
least we would be able to communicate.

"It means I am a friend and wish to do you no harm," I called
back.

This produced laughter. Was this a good audience or not? The
speaker in the white vest, who I assumed was the captain or general or whatever, spoke when the laughter died down. He had a deep
throaty voice, like the giant in Jack and the Beanstalk.

"You no can harm us," he said. "We harm you. Who you are?
What you want? How you be friend if we no know you?"

"Let me come up on your ship and we can talk," I called.

He motioned to his crew and a rope ladder was tossed overboard near me. I paddled over to it, tied my rope around the bottom run and climbed up onto the ship. When I got to the deck
arrows and spears were still pointed at me. I guess they weren't a
good audience.

"You honor me," I said. "How can I possibly harm you?" I
raised my arms. "See, no weapons."

"Search him," the Captain commanded.

"Search me?" I started to say. "All I'm wearing is —" Before I
finished someone grabbed my dakti and ripped it off.

The sailors, who had by this time had all gathered around to watch, started laughing.

"Look," said one, "him have hair around his grundig. And it black like burned wood."

"Grundig, my shit hole," said another. "It about the size my nose."

This produced gales of laughter. I looked down and my penis was in its mini-size, obviously the result of my fear and nervousness and embarrassment. At least I could make them laugh after all.

I held back the impulse to cover it with my hands and instead decided to think of Alia in our most intimate moments. It worked…to a degree.

"Well, well, well what we have here? Said the captain. "It like blowing up piece of snow bird gut, littlest part."

More laughter than before. Obviously because it was the captain's joke. "Give back his rag," he said.

One of the sailors handed it to me and I put it on slowly. Slow enough to get a good look around. There were about 40-50 men and the first thing I noticed was that they were all big, very tall and very thin as if they hadn't been eating much. All except the captain, that is. I said before that his voice was like the giant in Jack and the Beanstalk. Well, so was his body. He was huge, at least 6'8" or 6'9", and looked like he weighed more than 300 pounds. I guessed he ate well.

After I finished tying my dakti on I looked directly at the captain.

"So," I said, "what's new in the snow country? How do you like this warm weather down here? Delightful, isn't it?"

The captain looked me up and down, from head to toe and back again. He turned to the man next to him. "Hmm," he said, "do you think he good enough to eat?"

I was horrified at the question. These were supposedly human beings, not sharks.

"No! No!" I answered. "Humans like me taste terrible. You can ask the sharks."

"What sharks know?" the captain said. "Them no talk. Just dumb fish."

"He maybe right," said the man next to him. "He have small grundig and black hair, like Glugalug clan. They no taste good."

"Glugalug clan?" I said.

"You quiet," said the Captain. Maybe just throw you to sharks. See if you lie."

"Yuh, Yuh, Yuh," said one of the sailors nearby. "Good fun to watch." There was a nodding of heads and a chorus of "yuhs" from the rest of the crew.

"Yuh, much fun to see," said the Captain. "But wait for sea. No sharks here in cove. Signal other boats and men on beach that we going south to next island and others if are any."

"Wait," I said, if you are going to feed me to the sharks can I first ask you a few questions?"

"Yuh, if promise no give answers to talking sharks. Huh! Huh! Huh!" he said laughing. The rest of the crew chimed in with their own huh huh huhs.

"I promise. My first question is who are you and where do you come from?"

"Me Klug, we from snowlands far north."

"How far?"

"Many round moons north. We go long time no meat. Only birds, fish. Dolphins on beach taste real good. Good reward us meat hungry men."

"Why did you come so far south?"

"We look new place to live. Most meat in Snowland hunted dead. Dolphins here taste real good. Think maybe more in south.

Good warm air. After eat more we go back. Tell people good eatings. They come back with us. No more questions. We go now."

He motioned to his men. "Tie him till we throw to sharks."

"Wait, Klug," I said, holding up a hand. "I have only one more question."

He motioned to his crew. "Wait," he said, "Sharkshit have last question."

"Thank you," I said. "I shall give the sharks your best regards. My question is… why don't you go fuck yourself?"

And with that I kicked the sailor closest to me in the balls, turned, made a mad dash to the rail, leaped over head first into the water, hoping that Bogi would be down there to rescue me.

While I was under the water I opened my eyes and there he was. He pulled up along side me and I grabbed his dorsal fin. Then we headed for the surface. As soon as we were in the air he said, "take a deep breath." I did and we dove quickly down again.

I hoped he remembered that I had to breathe every 30-45 seconds. He did, and we surfaced again about 50 yards from the ship, just in time to see a flurry of arrows headed our way.

"Down quickly," I yelled.

"Hang on," he said as we were going under just before the first arrows reached us.

The next time we surfaced we were a good hundred yards away, out of arrow range, I was glad to know. We stopped to see what was happening. The men that had been on the beach were hustling into the small landing boats they used to get there, and the sailors on the ships were getting the sails ready to raise, and pushing oars out their slots.

Bogi called the other orcas to us and we decided that on our way back to Sea we would stop wherever there were dolphins. I would tell them what happened and warn them to leave immediately for Sea where we would mass to defend ourselves. I explained to the orcas what the savages were planning.

There was very little wind, so the savages would have to depend primarily on rowing. We assumed they would stop at the next two islands to see if they could find more dolphins to eat, and then do the same along the coast all the way to Sea. This would give us at least a day or two to prepare for them, so we headed for the next island to borrow a baku for me, since I had left mine at the ship.

We warned the inhabitants, and they made hurried preparations to leave; they had heard nothing of the massacre to the north.

We did the same all the way down to Sea, where the gate guards let us in immediately. There were still some orcas there, including Oola. We headed for the quay, where I let go of my towrope.

"I'll tell the dolphins," I said. "While I'm doing that why don't you inform the orcas?"

Good idea," he said, and headed out to the middle of the harbor for his briefing to them.

By the time I reached the quay landing, several of the council members were already there, as was Alia. I got out of the baku and we embraced and kissed, and held hands until the Administrator arrived a few minutes later.

After he got there I related all the events that I had seen and heard, leaving out, of course, the part of my mini-tinky moments, and what I did to cure that temporary penis condition. There was a stunned silence when I finished.

I looked at Alia and sent a thought message to her. "I love you."

I didn't mention how my thinking of her may have saved my life by putting my captors in a temporary good mood, relatively speaking, of course.

I wondered if they were ever in a good mood other than the time they were gorging on animal flesh and innards, or contemplating the thought of it, and cannibalizing other savages like themselves. Were they really Homo sapiens?

I tried to dismiss those ugly thoughts from my mind by recalling the comparatively amusing aspects of my experience with them.

My thoughts were suddenly interrupted by a message from Alia. I'm glad I was of some use to you on your expedition," the thought said. "And by the way, can they really fuck themselves?"

"Very funny," I projected back. You were eavesdropping. And how can you think such thoughts at a time like this?"

"Guilt by association," came the answer.

"Danny, Danny! Are you all right?" It was the Administrator's voice. "You seemed to be drifting off."

"Oh, I'm fine. I was just thinking."

"Thinking of a way to stop the savages, I assume."

"Yes, of course," I lied, and realized that we had better get our heads together and figure out what to do. We had to come up with a plan before they got here. I also realized that because the savages were Homo sapiens in the dolphins' eyes, and I was Homo sapien, they were thinking that I was the most qualified to do that.

All right, Danny, I said to myself, it's time to be John Wayne again. No not Wayne, General Patton. No, not Patton either. He was always aggressively advancing. We were going to be defending. Besides, I didn't have two pearl handled pistols. I wished I had.

No, not Patton. Then it hit me, Sitting Bull. Yes, Sitting Bull. Defending against those beasts who want to kill us and steal our land. Well, maybe General Custer didn't want to eat the Indians, but he sure as hell wanted to kill them and take their land. We would make this the savages' last stand. The Little Big Horn would be ours.

"All right," I said. "Let's have a pow wow and review the facts that we know first."

"I don't know what a pow wow is" said the Administrator, "but if it's a meeting I think it's an excellent idea to review the facts."

"Agreed," I said. "One, we know that they are truly savages and that they enjoy killing. Two, they are heavily armed with spears and arrows, and probably swords.

"Three. They can kill us at a distance with their arrows, and at close range with their spears and knives, and swords if they have them, which they probably do.

"Four. We can do a good job of fending them off with our poison tipped spears, even though they are flimsier than their spears, because ours are longer than the ones I saw. Just one prick will incapacitate them with pain and agony.

"Five. This one is not positive, and we will have to overcome it. We are a non-violent people, and they are physically bigger and have an advantage because of their killer instinct.

"Six. This is one you are going to have to think seriously about. We must remember what their captain told me about them looking for a place to live. That means to me that they didn't know of our existence before. It also means that we can't let any of them escape to go back to tell others of their kind of our existence and of Sea."

There were shocked exchanges of looks among the dolphins.

"Are you implying, Danny," said the administrator, "that defending ourselves by repelling their attacks is not enough. That if we are successful in doing this that we must then kill the survivors."

"Yes, but only if they attack," I replied sheepishly, and a little guiltily. "Or at least incapacitate or imprison them so they can't get away. I know that is against your nature, but it must be done. If any of them escape to tell about us, there will surely be an invasion in the future, and probably by many more savages than those here now."

"We can't do that."

"You must. The survival of all the dolphins may be at stake. We don't know how many there are in the northern cold where they live. Believe me, I've been in places on Earth like where they live and it is a very difficult life. Especially if there isn't enough to eat. Sea would be extremely inviting to them."

"Excuse us, please, Danny." He turned away and had a brief discussion with the Council members. When they were finished, he turned back to me and spoke.

"We have decided that what you said can be discussed when the time comes, if it does. Our first and faraway most important task is to defend ourselves. Let us discuss this matter openly. Danny, we have already mobilized all of our spears, and we are busy having people make more and brewing the poison for them."

"Good," I said. "I don't think we are strong or experienced enough to invade and capture their ships. And even if we could, they have so many weapons that we would sacrifice many, many dolphin lives."

"Agreed," said the Administrator, "that means we have to make them come to us." There was a nodding of heads in agreement.

"Perhaps we can entice them into the harbor," said one of the Council members. "We can all be hiding on shore and when they land fall upon them with our spears."

"I like that," I said, and there was general agreement among the gathering. The Administrator said something to the Council members and then turned back to me. "Excuse us," he said, and motioned to the Council members to step back a few feet to have a meeting. It was a short one and a few minutes later they came back.

Then he spoke loud enough for everyone around to hear. "The Council has decided that since Danny is the most familiar with the savages and that they are also Homo sapiens and probably more understandable to him, and that there must be a leader of our defense efforts — we cannot have a council meeting every time something comes up — that we must appoint an overall leader to be in command, and that you, Danny, are obviously the most qualified. We would like you to be our leader of defense. Do you accept?"

"I do," I said modestly, and with satisfaction that the dolphins respected and trusted me enough when so much was at stake. Yes, I would be Sitting Bull, a Sitting Bull whose only warrior experience was on a stage trying to make people laugh and fending off hecklers. A big difference, but I would play the role to the best of my ability.

I stepped back, spread my legs, and folded my arms across my chest in the classic Indian Chief stance. I addressed the gathering while looking around for someone I knew. I spotted Ami, and called him over to me.

"Gentlemen, and ladies, I like the idea of trying to entice the savages into the harbor, but if they don't come in, I think we need a back-up plan. They may not venture in because they will see the gate and possibly worry about being trapped. The more I think of it, I don't think they will come in. They'll see all the houses and realize there are so many dolphins here that they will be outnumbered. If so, they will go somewhere close by. My guess is the cove just north of here.

"Therefore, let's station about 200 people on the shore there. Ami, will you please take charge of them. If the savages refuse to land here, we'll let you know by sending a runner. And would you please let us know if they stop there first."

"Will do, Danny. By the way it's called North Cove." He selected his troops; they each picked out a spear and knife the council had ordered assembled on the quay, dove into the water, assembled in formation to ward off sharks, and departed. They had decided to go by water because it was quicker.

Then I called for sets of volunteers to be lookouts at various points all the way up the shoreline to the northern end of the island of Sea. They were to swing back as fast as they could as soon as they spotted the ships. That way we would have a fairly good idea of the progress of the savages toward Sea. I asked Bogi if he could request an orca escort for them to protect them against shark attacks on their way back. Of course he agreed, and within an hour eight groups of lookouts took off.

By this time it was approaching dark and I was pretty sure the savages couldn't get here before the next day.

The Administrator ordered the harbor gates closed and the guards in each tower doubled. I then asked him for a rough count of how many armed dolphins we could count on, and he informed me that as of now we had about 700 and that the number would substantially increase as the newly poisoned spears were finished.

I thought that gave us a good chance against the savages. They had better arms and were undoubtedly seasoned fighters, but we had more troops and were defending our homes.

I smiled inwardly as I realized that I was using the pronouns "us" and "we". I really did now think of Sea as home, and although I obviously didn't look like a dolphin, I considered myself to be one — a dolphin citizen of Sea, of this dolphins' world.

"Yes, you are," said a voice within me. "And I'm so proud of you." It was Alia again, eavesdropping on my thoughts.

"Thanks," I thought. "But don't I have any privacy with you?"

"What? I can't understand you."

"Bullshit," I thought to her.

"What's bullshit?" said the return voice within me.

"Bull is an Earth animal. All right, eel shit."

"Don't be coarse."

"Alia, would you please come over to me so I can see you."

"I would be delighted," came the reply. I immediately felt a tapping on my shoulder. It was Alia; she had been standing right behind me. I spun around to face her.

"Hi," she said with a big smile on her beautiful face. "I've missed you."

"How can you miss me when you're inside my head? I thought I would have to concentrate real hard to project my thoughts. You've been picking them up as if I have a microphone inside my brain."

"I can only pick up non-projected thoughts if I am physically close to you, or from a greater distance if you are in a highly emotional state. I am much better at it than other people, and we are mates, which helps considerably."

"How far do you think we can project to and receive from each other?"

"I don't really know. At least across the island. It's a lot more powerful between bonded people, especially mates."

"And lifemates?"

"I don't know personally, never having had a lifemate; but I understand it is considerably more powerful between lifemates."

"Do you think we may be ever be lifemates?"

She gazed at me affectionately, leaned over and kissed me on the lips. "I think we're getting there," she said softly. "And you?"

"I don't know exactly what a lifemate really is, but if it's what I think and what I feel, I'm very close."

"Me, too," she whispered and kissed me on the lips again.

"Not in front of the troops," I said, returning her kiss emphatically amid catcalls and whistles from many of the dolphins and orcas within sight.

"Hey, Danny," called Bogi from out in the water, "do you think the savages waiting to kill you would approve of this frivolity?"

"It's not frivolous, but you're right. I'd better get back to work. Alia, I think I would like to get a look at North Cove, in case we end up confronting them there. Do you think you can guide me?"

"As well as I can guide you around my body," she answered with a sensual leer.

"Cut it out," I said. "This is not the time or place. Let's go... please."

"Yes, sir, Mr. Danny DiVinci," she replied. Let's go Sitting Bull."

"You don't even know who Sitting Bull is, or rather was."

"No, but you do, and therefore, so do I."

Not possible, I said to myself. Or is it?

Alia asked for two torches, and within minutes we each got one, lit them from others on the quay already burning, and were on our way.

The path to the cove was well used and between that and Alia's guiding we arrived in a little less than hour.

Between our torches and those of the dolphins already stationed there I was able to get a pretty good idea of what it was like. It was a small cove, less than a quarter mile across with bluffs on each side and a beach along the inner curve. The beach itself was about 100 yards wide, and directly behind it were thick bushes that ranged from about three to five feet in height.

By the time we finished inspecting and got back to Sea, it was quite late, probably past midnight. I thought I should spend the night on the quay so asked for some mats. Alia elected to stay with me. We were both very tired and collapsed on them immediately. I gave instructions to be called as soon as the first word about spotting the savages came in.

Someone was kind enough to rig a shelter over us. I didn't think I would be able to fall asleep, but much to my surprise, after about an hour of thinking, I did. We must have slept for five or six hours because the next thing I knew it was daylight and someone was shouting,

"They're here! They're here!"

CHAPTER 15

I tossed the shelter aside and leapt to my feet.

"Where?" I said loudly.

"At the north end of the island," I was informed. "And the wind is now blowing hard from the north, so they will be here soon."

About every 15 minutes a swimmer and his orca patrol came in through the quickly opened gates reporting that his watch had spotted the boats.

Finally another watcher came in, this time on foot. "They've come into North Cove, and stopped," he said. "They're searching the shoreline from their huge bakus, but have not come ashore."

I hoped they wouldn't, because although our men were hidden in the bushes behind the beach, there weren't enough of them to repel a full-scale attack.

Then another runner came in on foot and reported that they were leaving the cove and heading south… toward Sea.

It was time to put my plan into action, the one I had formulated before falling asleep.

I sent a half dozen bakus out to go back and forth in front of the harbor and to make sure the ships saw them. As soon as they were reasonably certain the savages spotted them they were to head back into the harbor. The gate guards were not to close the gates. If the ships followed the bakus into the harbor, then they would close the gates, thereby trapping the savages.

I also dispatched a dozen bakus to paddle back and forth inside the harbor as a further enticement.

Finally, the guards signaled that the ships were in sight, then ducked down behind the rail so they wouldn't be seen. The outside bakus came back into the harbor and joined the others paddling back and forth. All was going according to plan.

Then they were there. Five large double ended sailing ships poised outside the harbor. They had taken down their sails and the rowers were slowly moving their oars to maintain position.

I could see the savages up on the decks peering intently into the harbor at the dolphins paddling around in their bakus, and at the houses and buildings behind the quay.

The quay itself was empty. All of us were hiding behind the first row of houses, poisoned spears at the ready. I could feel the tension in the air.

We waited... and waited... and waited. Nothing happened. They obviously suspected a trap and weren't coming in. I had planned for this possibility.

They soon hoisted their sails and turned their ships back toward the north. Since it was already late afternoon, I assumed they were heading for the anchorage at North Cove.

And, calling upon my sailing experience, I knew that even though it was only two and a half miles away, the wind was still blowing hard enough that they would have to tack back and forth many times before they would be able to get there, assuming that's where they were going. We therefore had at least three hours to prepare.

As soon as they were out of close sight, I gave the signal to come out of our hiding places. I dispatched several dolphins with shark guards to swim along the shoreline and to inform us if the ships had changed direction.

Then I conferred briefly with the Administrator and council

telling them what I wanted to do, and dispatched all but a hundred of our troops, who would stand guard in case the ships returned, to North Cove. They were to take sleeping pads, food and blankets because I didn't expect the savages to attack at night. I didn't think the battle would take place till morning.

I turned to Alia. "Has Abu Abu arrived yet?"

"He and his friends are waiting in the Administration Building."

I asked a messenger to request that they join us on the quay.

A few minutes later Abu Abu arrived with his entourage, each of whom held a stick with a skull on the end, as I had requested. He held the one with the Homo sapien head.

All of them were dressed in colorful robes similar to the one Abu Abu had worn last time we saw him. They didn't look like villagers.

"Hello, Abu Abu," I said, raising my hand to touch palms.

"Hello, Danny," he said, not raising his. "I won't palm with you unless you call me plain Abu."

"Okay, Abu," I said, and we palmed. "It looks like your suspicions were correct. There were Homo sapiens on Sea and still are, unfortunately."

"So I heard. I would rather have been wrong." He turned to his group. "These are my fellow medicine men shamans from the nearby hills around my humble abode. All are excellent and knowledgeable medicine men, fair minded judges, and well acquainted with their respective village spiritual beliefs, and, I might add, excellent party hosts."

He introduced them one by one, and we all touched palms.

"What's the plan, Dan?" He asked.

"Abu," I said with a smile. "You are a very interesting person."

"It's part of my mystique," he said with mock modesty. "We

spiritual leaders are at your service."

"Thank you. Here's what I think, and would like you to do. The reason I asked you to come is that I believe these Homo sapiens are very primitive and probably superstitious, and that perhaps we can make them fearful and nervous when it comes time for the battle.

"What I think we should do is head for North Cove, and if, as I think, the savages anchor there for the night, I would like you and your shaman friends to act like evil spirits when it gets dark. If they put candles inside the skulls, hold them in the air at the end of their sticks while dancing around, the savages might think they really are evil spirits and become afraid. What do you think?"

"I'm evil," he said with a grin. "Spiritually evil." He laughed hideously like a bad spirit in a bad movie.

Then he turned to his friends. "Fellow evil spirits, let's party." Then they all began to jump up and down with their skulls on their sticks, all imitating Abu's hideous laugh.

"Satisfied?" he said to me as he motioned them to stop.

"Perfect," I said with a laugh.

"You are wonderful," said Alia to them.

"Who are these people?" asked the Administrator.

"Just some people Alia and I met up in the hills while doing research," I said.

"Yes," said Abu, "we're quite excellent citizens who perform serious community service, now just having a little fun at Danny's request."

The Administrator looked at me seriously. "Is that Abu Abu, Danny?"

"Yes," I answered and explained my reasons for him being here. "It could work. Don't you think it's worth a try?"

"I suppose so." He pointed to the Homo sapien skull Abu was

holding. "Is that the one you told me about?"

"Yes," said Alia. "Don't you think it looks just like Danny?"

Everybody around us laughed.

"Very funny," I said, and projected a thought to Alia, "not funny."

Her thought came back to me. "I'm in training to be a sit-down comedian."

"Now that's funny," I projected back. "Sort of. But I love you anyway."

"And I you, my mate."

Back to the business at hand. I asked Abu and his group to go to North Cove to get ready to go into their act. I then got into a baku tied up at the quay, and paddled out the short distance to Bogi.

"Do you have something we can do to help Danny? We have examined the ships and they are too big and solid for us to do any damage by ramming."

"Not only that," I said, "but even if you could their spears and arrows would make it extremely dangerous. But I do have an idea if the battle goes our way and they start retreating to their ships."

"What's that?

"Well, as you probably have realized, they can't take their big ships right up to the shore because of the beach and shallow water. However, each ship has some small landing boats that their men transfer into and row to the shore.

"These are small enough for ramming, but ramming them would be too risky if they are on their way to the beach because of their arrows and spears. Besides, the water would be to shallow for your big bodies as they get close to the beach.

"However, if we have beaten them on shore and they are retreating back to their ships in the landing boats, they will be vulnerable, undisciplined, and much less dangerous in their run to escape. Then once they get into deep enough water for you to operate you can ram them and knock their occupants into the water. The sharks, who by that time would have smelled blood and sensed the thrashing around, will finish them off."

Bogi smiled at me. "Danny, I know you area a funny Homo sapien, but I didn't expect you to be a fight planner. Your ideas are excellent."

"Thanks for the compliment, Bogi. I've never had any experience at this sort of thing, but I am good at an Earth game called chess, which is very much like the situation we are faced with. Besides, I've seen a lot of war movies."

"What's a war movie?"

"It's complicated. I'll explain later when this is all over."

"Okay, but don't forget. Be careful, Danny, and may the orca God be with you."

"Thanks, Bogi. I'll also take the dolphin God and the Earth God.

"As far as I'm concerned you can have all the Gods in the universe and even one, if there is only one. So long, friend." With that he turned, shook his dorsal fin and headed for the harbor gates. The other orcas followed him and the guards let them through with a wave.

I watched until they rounded the point and headed back to the quay, thinking of what good friends Bogi and I had become.

I smiled to myself. On Earth I had always wanted to be friends with orcas. On my kayak trips to Canada, where they congregated between Vancouver Island and the mainland, I had paddled among them. But although there were obviously aware of our presence because they would go out of their way to get within 10-20 yards of us, they never came closer or interacted. I admired them greatly.

"How about us dolphins?" said Alia's projected voice within me.

I concentrated real hard and shot back the thought, "Not even close. You guys are too nosy."

"Very funny," came her thought back.

"I learned from you," I said out loud as I pulled my baku up to the quay and tossed her a line. "If you grab this line and tie my boat up I may love you anyway."

"Oh yeah?"

"Yeah.

Just then a messenger arrived from North Cove. "They're there," he said, "and they are lowering their sails."

"Thank you," I said. "Please go back and tell everybody we are on our way with many more armed dolphins, and that they should mass on the beach, spears pointing toward the ships. Let's hope that there is no attack at least until we get there."

We arrived at North Cove, more than a thousand strong. There was just enough light so that the savages, who were standing at the rails of their anchored ships peering at the beach, could see us. We waved our spears in the air in a threatening manner. They did the same thing in reply. I was glad that the water close to the beach was so shallow that they couldn't bring their ships into bow and arrow range. Not that they didn't try. However, their arrows feel far short, and they ceased trying.

I asked that fires be built and maintained all night with guards so that we would be able to see if the savages were going to attack in the dark. Not that I expected them to. Night fighting was uncharacteristic of primitive peoples.

As soon as it was completely dark I asked Abu and his group to come out and do their stuff with the lighted candles in the skulls.

They did and it was great. It was very eerie to watch. If I had been a primitive I would have been scared shitless myself.

We supplied them with some Squid Squirt which we had brought with us for this very purpose, which made them better still. Although I am sure we were all nervous and more than a little frightened contemplating what the morning might bring, everyone also seemed to be having a good time watching the entertainment.

We hoped it was having the opposite effect on the savages. Maybe they would be so scared they would raise their sails in the morning and head back to where they came from. I didn't think so, but hoped I was wrong.

To find out how they really were reacting I asked for volunteers to swim out to one of the ships, holding their lighted skulls out of the water. Two of Abu's revelers volunteered and he went with them. Ten minutes later they came back with big grins on their faces, Abu with the widest smile of all.

"Danny, my friend," he said. "You should have seen them. It was great. Between our candle-lit skulls and some lights they had on board, presumably to ward off evil spirits of the night, we were able to get a pretty good look.

They were cringing at the sight of us. The closer we got the more they shrank back. Not a sign of a raised spear or bow and arrow. They were just plain scared."

"Good," I said, "and well done. I think we can be pretty sure they won't attack tonight. Any sign of them preparing to leave?"

"No, I'm afraid not.

"Well," I said. "I think we should all get some rest for tomorrow. Judging from the way they talked when I was on their ship, they want to take over Sea, in which case we will have to fight them tomorrow."

I told Ami my thoughts. He agreed and walked among our troops spreading the word. I asked for volunteers to keep the fires going in shifts all night, and suggested Abu do the same with his evil spirits; they should keep lit candles in their skulls as long as possible.

"Do they have to dance?" asked Alia.

"Only if the moment moves them," I answered. "Would you like to?"

"No," she smiled. "I think I'll stay with you to make sure you are not overcome by the evil spirits."

She looked warm and beautiful in the firelight, and in spite of what might await us in the morning I felt like the luckiest man on Sea, or anywhere in the universe for that matter. Oh, Gatekeepers, you don't know how good you have been to me. Or do you?

Then I laughed to myself as a thought struck me. I also owed my good fortune to Olga. If she hadn't given me that membership gift in the silly Intergalactic Society I would never have told the Gatekeepers where I wanted to go. I would never have come to Sea, never would have talked with dolphins and orcas, and, of course, never would have met and fallen in love with Alia.

"You never told me about Olga before," said Alia, somewhat petulantly.

"You're spying again."

"Did you love her?"

"Just a little temporary infatuation."

"I believe you. Because I want to."

"And because it's the truth."

"Yes."

We each picked up a torch, and looked around the beach and walked into the vegetation behind it to check things out. I noticed that many of the dolphins had spread mats on the ground, and also that there were many tent-like structures made out of brush that they had cut.

I also saw pairs of dolphins, mostly males and females, going into them. I realized that for some of these dolphins, not many I hoped, this might be the last night they would spend with their mates, or lovers, or whatever.

Alia read my thoughts and took my hand. "It's time for us, too," she said. "I'll be right back." She left and returned in a few minutes with a mat, two short poles and some cloth.

"My uncle got this for us," she said. "That's what makes him such a good Administrator," she smiled.

It was the makings of a tent. We set it up and before going inside I issued instructions to be called at the first sign of activity on the ships.

It was small and cozy inside. We put out our torches and crawled in. First we lay on our backs quietly, soaking up the joy of being together. Later we made love, not with abandon, but with a quiet, gentle sublime passion that melded our bodies into one.

When we were complete we lay on our sides in the darkness facing one another. "I see you in my mind," I said.

"And I see you in mine."

"I feel you in my body," I said.

"And I feel you in mine."

"I have never felt anything like this before."

"Nor have I," Alia said. "Do you know what this means?"

"That we are lifemates?"

"Truly."

"Yes," I said. "Truly."

I was never religious in my life on Earth, but at that moment I felt a spiritual bliss of the kind I had only read about in books.

A oneness with Alia... and with the universe.

No matter what might happen tomorrow, we were together tonight.

My lifemate and I.

Together....

For life.

"For life," she whispered.

And we fell asleep... together... our bodies and souls entwined.

We were awakened from a deep sleep by shouts around us. It was dawn, the dawn of who knows what kind of a new day. The shouts were loud and emotional.

"They're coming... they're getting ready... they're putting their bakus in the water."

We pushed the entrance of our makeshift tent aside and stood up outside and looked. Sure enough the savages were on their way to fight us. They were climbing down rope ladders into their landing boats, armed to the teeth with bows and arrows, spears, knives and swords.

I looked at Alia. "This is it. Please stay back in the bushes when the fighting starts. Please."

"No. I want to be at your side."

"But you've never handled a poison spear before. Besides, I'm in charge of our defense. I'm going to be moving around a lot. And I'm going to have to think, and think clearly. There's no way I will be able to do that if I'm worried about you out there in the middle of the fighting. So please promise me you'll stay back. You can help by tending to the wounded."

"I'll promise if you promise not to take any unnecessary chances."

"I promise. Remember, I'm a lover, not a fighter."

"I'll remember... always."

We held each other tightly for a long minute; then a final kiss.

There were tears in her eyes as she said, "Put on your dakti. Your external tinky is showing."

I laughed, reached into the tent, pulled out my sandals and dakti and put them both on.

"Don't worry," I said. "Bad things only happen to stand-up comedians on the stage... and this ain't no stage, baby."

"Just make sure you don't tell any bad jokes anyway."

"Impossible, my love. Remember your promise."

"I will. And remember yours. I love you, Danny."

"And I love you, Alia." There were tears streaming down her cheeks as I put a macho expression on my face, blew her a kiss, turned and made my way to the water's edge, holding back my own tears.

The savages were still loading their boats, so I figured we had at least five possibly ten minutes. I called the troops together for a final briefing about the tactic I had planned.

"You have never seen bows and arrows before," I said, "but you will soon. The most important thing to know about them is that they can kill from a distance. Some of you saw the arrows sticking out from the orca that was hit. Those arrows were sent off by their bows from a distance of probably at least 100 feet.

"Therefore, we don't want to be just standing on the beach when they approach it, waiting to be killed before we have a chance to defend ourselves. Therefore, when I motion to you, I want everybody off the beach and back in the bushes where they can't see us or shoot directly at us with their arrows. We want them to land and advance up the beach until they are close enough for us to use our spears and too close for them to effectively use their bows and arrows.

"At that point they will probably drop their bows and arrows and come toward us with their swords and spears. And remember that not only are our spears longer, but they are poisoned and theirs are not. So all we have to do is thrust our spears into them before they can do the same to us. The poison will stop them just like it stops the sharks. Does everyone understand?"

"How will we know when to engage them?" Someone asked.

"I'll give the signal," I said. I'll stand up and yell… 'Geronimo'. Then everyone charge at them with your spears extended in front of you as if they are sharks.

"Then hopefully, we will have hurt so many of them that they will give up the attack and retreat back to their ships.

"Any questions so far?"

There were none, so I continued. "Once they start falling back, follow them closely so they can't use their bows and arrows. Remember, as long as you have your spear, you have the reach on them. Just try not to let them push your spears aside to get at you."

"All clear?"

No one said anything, so I spoke again:

"One more thing. Since I am the only one who can talk with them, I will try to convince them not to come ashore by calling to them before they arrive at the beach. I'll step to the water's edge and you all mass behind me waving your spears. Perhaps when they see that they are outnumbered they will not attack and leave."

Abu stepped forward. "Danny, I have an idea."

"Yes?"

"How about me and my friends standing next to you with our skulls pointing at them? Perhaps that will help frighten them and help encourage them to leave."

"It's worth a try," I said. "Just be ready to run like hell for the bushes if they start stringing their arrows."

"You don't have to worry about that. We're shamans, not fighters."

I turned back to the troops. "As soon as the savages look like they're getting ready to string their bows I'll wave my arms and you get back into the bushes as fast as you can. Then let them come to us. Is everybody ready?"

There were loud yells of affirmation. The savages hadn't finished loading their boats so I kept talking to keep the tension from building too much.

"Remember," I said, "when you're waving your spears at them while they're on their way to the beach, try to look fierce. Think of them as sharks. Try to look as if you've been used to killing all your lives."

The dolphins looked around at each other smiling and practicing fierce killer looks. They made faces, trying to look malicious and hateful, which is pretty hard for a dolphin to do. Their attempts produced laughter among them, which helped to break the tension.

The tension was really broken when an obviously exaggerated feminine voice from the rear called, "Look at me. I'm a killer!"

We all laughed, I perhaps more than the others because I was also laughing at myself. Here I was, Daniel David DiVinci, who had never served in the military, was strongly non-violent, who quit the boy scouts after one week because he didn't like the regimentation, here I was giving military orders as if I had been doing it all my life, and doing it pretty well, I might add.

Was this militarism ingrained in the male psyche, or was my professed non-violence just a cover-up for aggression? Or had I simply seen to many war movies and television shows?

I didn't have time to think about it any more because the savages had pushed off from their ships and were on their way. Sixteen boats, loaded to their gunwales with hostile looking albinos, their spears pointing straight up in the air, their bows slung around their bodies. All were bare chested, except for one huge giant of a man standing in the rear of the largest boat. He wore a white vest. He looked like Klug.

When they got within hailing distance I raised an arm, palm out, then cupped my hands to my lips and shouted,

"Wait. We want to talk!"

The one in the white vest raised his hand, said something to his men, and they all stopped rowing. It was Klug. He peered at me, grinned and turned to the others. "Look, it Sharkshit man." He turned his head back to me and boomed,

"Huh, Sharkshit man. I try fuck myself, but no do. You smart shithole, so maybe this time we eat you."

"Not possible," I called. "We outnumber you. You can't win. Why don't you go back north where you came from?"

He laughed. "We warriors, you just dark meat. They tasty dolphins. Give up now and we no eat all you."

I motioned to Abu and his men to show their skulls and start dancing around, which they did to the frantic beat of a drummer they had brought with them. At first the savages looked frightened and started to cringe. But Klug stopped them.

"Look," he said. "They not real evil spirits, just dolphin meat. We no tell in dark but in day now we see. They taste like two day ago dolphins, maybe better."

He waved his sword in the air and motioned his men forward. "Row hard. It meat time!" he shouted.

The rowers moved their oars quickly while the other savages in each boat began to string their bows. I waved my arms in the air for our troops to run for the bushes, which we did.

Before we reached there the arrows were flying. A few dolphins were hit, but none seriously injured. If they fell down other dolphins rushed out to help them back into the vegetation. Those without weapons grabbed their spears.

The savages shot arrows into the bushes with little effect. The vegetation was thick and helped deflect and slow down their speed. A few more dolphins were hit by arrows which did get through the brush, but not many.

Peering through the gaps we could see the savages' landing boats touch the beach. They quickly jumped out, dragged the boats partially up on to the beach so they wouldn't float away, and stood there looking to where we were hidden. We kept perfectly still, looking out through the gaps in the bushes from which we would emerge when the time come.

Klug took a position in front of them and raised his sword high in the air. He was an imposing figure, and I hoped a good target.

"Ready, men?" He called.

"Ready," came a chorus back to him, along with spears pumped up and down.

"Want meat?" he yelled.

"Want meat," came the chorus back to him, along with a repeat action of the raising and lowering of spears.

"Meat. Go!" he yelled slashing his sword down through the air.

"Go!" they shouted as they began advancing slowly up the beach, the bowmen firing barrages of arrows toward the bushes, the rest of them pointing their spears straight ahead. We crouched and waited.

When they were about 30 yards from us Klug raised his sword in the air. They stopped. The bowmen lay their bows and arrows on the sand and drew their short swords out of their scabbards.

I passed the word along to our men to get ready to charge out between the gaps. As we moved into position the savages could see us through the openings. They looked to Klug for orders.

He raised his sword in the air and spoke. "Me see. You no run. Give up now We spare some. Too much eat anyway. Huh, huh, huh."

His men joined in the laughter, but not very enthusiastically.

"You, Sharkshit, what you say? You no say I fuck myself or when you still alive I take you puny grundig, chop in pieces, feed to sea gulls."

Was he trying to draw me out so he could attack me personally? Not a chance. I may have thought about being John Wayne at one time, but now I was Sitting Bull, and Sitting Bull sure as hell didn't lead the charge against General Custer. He organized it.

So putting myself in an organizing mode (or was it a cowardly one? Whatever?), I stepped behind a bush and yelled,

"This is your last chance Klug. Go back to your ships and we'll spare your lives."

He pushed his sword up and down in the air and yelled, "Fuck yourself, Sharkshit. Not possible. Huh, huh, huh."

Then he turned to his men. "You not laugh. No think funny?" They began to laugh, and when they stopped I yelled as loud as I could,

"Geronimo! Geronimo!"

The dolphins streamed out through the gaps in the bushes, spears in front of them, running straight at the savages. When the savages saw them coming, those with swords raised them, those with spears thrust them forward.

The dolphin spears were long with needle-like points so they puncture rather than stab. And puncture they did.

The shark poison had an instant and devastating effect on the savages. Within a second those who were punctured started screaming and writhing in pain. They threw their weapons on the sand. Some fell to the sand rolling around in pain; others ran back to the water, screaming all the way, dove in and splashed and thrashed around, hoping to relieve their agony that way.

It didn't take long for the sharks outside the cove to be attracted, and they streaked in to attack and feast on the savages in the water.

When the savages who were not punctured saw what was happening to their comrades, most panicked, dropped their weapons, scrambled back to their landing boats, piled into them, pushed off into what was now water pink with blood, and started rowing right in the midst of their fellow screaming comrades and the feasting sharks. Those who remained on the beach shortly fell victim to the dolphin's spears.

The rowing savages was the signal for the orcas to go to work. They glided in groups; a vanguard of orcas on the sides and rear to protect against the sharks, not that the sharks paid the slightest bit of attention to them, and two in the front to ram the boats. They head butted each boat, knocking its occupants into the water, where they were torn apart by the sharks.

Within twenty minutes all was quiet, except for some moans from the few savages still alive on the beach. Soon they, too, were quiet.

The water in the cove was even redder than before, with body parts floating on the surface — an arm here, a leg there, an occasional upper torso, some with heads, others without. The whole scene was a gruesome, horrific nightmare.

The beach wasn't much better. There were no body parts, but there were savages' bodies everywhere, many with hideous, tortured expressions on their faces resulting from the agony caused by the poison. The good guys had won, true enough, but the victory was bittersweet. All that pain and suffering.

There were very few dead dolphins, and about fifteen to twenty wounded ones. I did what I could to comfort and tend to them until medical help arrived, which came very quickly from prepared dolphin doctors emerging from behind the bushes. Some of Abu's medicine men, who had brought their kits with them, also helped.

Alia joined me and we worked together helping where we could. Neither of us had much to say, we were so overwhelmed by the death and suffering and blood, and all that had taken place just a short time before. The whole area had an aura of horror.

After a while we walked hand in hand to the water's edge where there were still a few unused landing boats with their bows up on the sand. Near one I spotted a giant of a savage body lying on its side, the end of a dolphin's spear sticking out from his white vest, which on close inspection looked like polar bear fir. It was the leader of the savages, Klug.

I pointed him out to Alia and explained who he was. In spite of the terrible scene around us, I couldn't suppress a pleasant feeling that we had beaten him and his horde. I only wished that the sharks could have eaten him. What a stroke of poetic justice that would have been.

We looked out into the cove. There were empty landing boats, partially filled with water, whose occupants had been knocked into the water by the orcas. There were overturned boats with their bottoms just above the surface, and shark fins cutting lazily through the water as if they were too full to move with any energy or speed, which they probably were.

Most of the orcas had left, but there were still a few further out near the savages' ships anchored in the deeper water.

Alia and I stared out at them.

"Danny," she said. "Do you think there are more where they came from, and that we may be attacked again in the future?"

"I'm afraid so," I said gloomily. "It may be a long time from now, but if they could make it here, there is no reason others couldn't also."

"That's awful to think of."

"Yes, it is." Then I had a positive thought.

"Do you realize, Alia, that these ships now belong to Sea, and that we now have a way to explore the rest of the world. All we have to do is learn to sail them. I know how to sail. I could teach —"

All of a sudden huge hands wrapped around my ankles and jerked hard so I fell to the sand! I looked up and saw a gigantic white figure rising up from the beach.

It was Klug. He had been playing possum, pretending to be dead. I guess he was smarter than I thought.

He let go of one of my ankles momentarily, and with his now free hand slammed Alia so that she went sprawling.

Then with that same hand he pulled the dolphin spear from the vest that covered his chest and set it down on the sand next to him.

He laughed, "Huh, huh, huh. Puny point no go through not puny bearskin."

Then he gruffly lifted me up and threw me into an empty landing boat nearby. I was stunned both by what was happening and by the physical shock of landing in the boat.

He picked up the spear with one hand and with the other the bow of the boat. He pushed it into the water and stepped inside.

"So," he said, staring down at me, "you dolphin meat surprise and win battle, but Klug win between us. You sit up and row, Sharkshit. Row to ship," he said. I did as he commanded.

He stood up in the bow, holding the dolphin spear in front of him. First he brandished it at me and then to some dolphins who had gathered on the beach, and lastly he quickly turned forward and made a feint toward a shark that had come over to investigate.

The shark fled.

"Danny! Danny!" came Alia's scream from the shore. She had gotten back up to her feet and was staring at us, eyes wide with fright.

A group of dolphins who had seen what was going on came up to her, handed her a spear, and all of them waded out into the water right behind us.

Klug saw them, pointed the tip of his spear at my throat, and yelled at them. "No come near meat, or I kill him."

They couldn't understand his words, but his actions and intent were obvious, so they held back.

"Row more, Sharkshit. Fast."

I scrambled into a more comfortable rowing position facing the bow and started pushing hard toward the ship he pointed to. Alia and the dolphins followed us at a discreet distance.

We had gone about half way there when all of a sudden a great shark head raised out of the water alongside us. Its mouth was open displaying row upon row of great white teeth. It was Big Teeth.

Klug immediately drew his sword, put it at my throat and swung the spear around to Big Teeth. The shark backed away.

"So, we meet again," Big Teeth said to me. "I told ya I'd get ya. You can count on it. Ya body may not be good ta eat, but dat little dangling thing between ya legs will make good desert. Ya worth waiting for."

"You're making a mistake," I said. This big white animal pointing his spear at you has a bigger one than mine, a much bigger one. Twice the size, at least. And it's not circumcised."

"Oh," said Big Teeth. "Very interesting."

"What you talk for?" said Klug. "Shut mouth, keep rowing, or I cut throat."

"Then you would have to row yourself," I said. "Then how

could you keep the dolphins and sharks away, and what about that big killer whale right behind you?"

It looked like Bogi. I recognized his tall dorsal fin. He raised his head out of the water, and I knew for sure it was Bogi.

"Hey, Danny," he said. "Don't worry. I'll help you."

Klug quickly jerked his head around, then just as quickly back to me and Big Teeth. Seeing how occupied he was with Big Teeth and Bogi, Alia and the dolphins came closer and around to the other side of the boat.

I flashed a falsely macho smile at Klug. "Hey," I said. "I think we've got you surrounded. Give up."

"No happen," he answered, putting the sword blade even closer to my throat and making a cutting motion so that everyone would get the idea that if they went for him I would be dead.

"Keep rowing," he bellowed. "Faster. To ship."

I nervously did as I was told, but noticed that Klug was beginning to look like he was feeling the pressure of the situation. His albino brows were furrowed and glistening with sweat, his spear was shaking a little, and so was his sword. That made me even more nervous and frightened than I had been. It would have been a hell of a thing to have my throat cut by accident just as I was on the verge of being rescued, I hoped.

And so two scared Homo sapiens kept heading for Klug's ship, surrounded by an entourage of dolphins, a shark, and an orca. I tried to visualize the sight in my mind as I rowed, and succeeded. I smiled, as apprehensive as I was.

"What you laugh for?" said Klug. "Not funny."

"No, not funny," I answered, and waited for something to happen. Nothing did. My friends wanted to keep me from harm, Big Teeth wanted to keep me for himself, and Klug wanted me to keep rowing. Being wanted is good, but the circumstances weren't.

We got closer and closer to the ship until I could clearly see the rope ladder hanging down. I suddenly realized what Klug was probably planning to do.

When we got there he would more than likely throw or drop the spear, cut my throat, and throw me into the water. In the ensuing confusion he would grab on to the ladder and scurry up on to his ship, where he would be safe from the dolphins, the orcas and Big Teeth. The shark, of course, would be occupied with eating me, and I would have eventually earned the name Klug had given to me: Sharkshit.

Not a pleasant thought. I knew that everything was up to me to do something to change the situation. But what? Before I could do anything, I had to distract Klug.

We were within ten yards of the ship now. Then a thought hit me. I remembered an old political slogan I didn't believe in but would try anyway.

So I stopped rowing.

"What you do?" roared Klug. "Keep rowing."

"No," I said.

"What you say?"

"I just say no."

"I kill you."

"You kill me now and you'll never reach your ship. The orca will ram and overturn you, the dolphins will stab you, and the shark will eat you. Any questions?"

He was clearly frustrated; his eyes darted around wildly. I didn't think it was possible, but his skin got even whiter. He looked over to the ladder to see if he could reach it by jumping. It was obvious he couldn't. He looked back at me.

"Row!" he commanded.

"I just said no."

He looked back at the ladder. This was my chance.

I let go of an oar with one hand and while he was looking at the ladder pushed the sword away from my throat. It cut my skin and drew a little blood but didn't penetrate.

With my other hand I lifted the oar from its groove, and with both hands holding it quickly swung at him, knocking him off balance.

He was furious as he regained his position. "You be shark meat now!" he shouted as he stepped toward me, lifted me into the air with his immense arms, held me up over his head, and with a roar of defiant laughter flung me high in the air toward the waiting open-mouthed Big Teeth.

My recollections of the next few moments are foggy, but I clearly remember as if in slow motion, flying through the air, seeing the dolphins repeatedly stabbing Klug, seeing Bogi's huge black and white body also in the air hurtling toward Big Teeth and landing on top of his open jaw a split second before I reached there, and at the same time banging into me, his immense bulk sending me flying once again.

But this time in a different direction — not into Big Teeth's jaws, but into the side of the boat. My momentum slammed me against it. My chest hit first, knocking the breath out of me. Then my head hit, and I gradually began to lose consciousness.

I felt myself dropping into the water, heard Alia screaming, "Danny! Danny!" And Bogi calling, "No! No! No!"

I was almost gone as my body entered the water and sank fast because the breath had been knocked out of me.

Everything began to slip into darkness as I sank toward the bottom. I could dimly hear Alia wailing in my mind, "Danny... Danny... my lifemate... my lifemate...."

I tried to answer her in my mind... Alia. I love you... My lifema —"

But I couldn't. Blackness overcame me.

Alia was gone.

Bogi was gone.

Feeling was gone.

Sea was gone.

All was gone.

It was the end.

Afterward

by Sam Melner

The Coast Guard found Danny bobbing in the water just ten miles outside San Francisco's Golden Gate Bridge.

He was conscious when they pulled him out. It was about five months after I had reported him missing and presumed drowned during the storm that had swept him overboard.

The newspapers reported that he was in excellent physical condition except for a bump on his head and a cut on his neck; and that since they found him completely naked and without identification papers, they could not identify him.

He either could not or would not talk, and appeared to be emotionally depressed.

The Coast Guard took pictures of him, called in the newspapers, asked that they be published and a description of him given, along with a request that anyone who might know him step forth.

Since he also had a beard, they had an artist do a rendering of his face without one. The papers published that one along with a photograph.

My wife, who reads the paper more thoroughly than I, spotted the story, read it and passed it to me.

The report stated that not only did the man refuse or was unable to speak, but that he appeared to be almost in a trance, and that at times, for no apparent reason, he would burst into tears.

He was now in San Francisco General Hospital under medical and psychiatric observation. The story went on to say that since he appeared to be in perfect health, if no one could identify or communicate with him he would be placed in a homeless shelter.

When I finished reading, I stared at the pictures. Marjorie was looking over my shoulder. "Doesn't that look like Danny?" she said.

I looked harder. "A little," I said, except that he's a lot thinner and has that awful expression on his face. Besides, Danny is dead."

She ignored my last sentence. "It sounds like they picked him up just about where you said he went overboard," she said. "Wouldn't it be funny if that really were Danny?"

"It would be more than funny. It would be impossible," I said.

My thoughts went back to that awful time. The huge waves, the roaring wind, my frantic searching for him; then the four days the Coast Guard ships and planes and helicopters scoured the area for him.

And the sickening guilt feelings I had. Why did I let him pull off his life jacket? Not that I could have done anything about it, stubborn bastard that he was. Danny was my best friend. I still missed him, and woke up many a night reliving that day.

Marjorie was less of a realist than I. Anything was possible in her mind. Even the impossible.

"Let's go to the hospital and see if it's him," she said.

"All right," I sighed with resignation. When she got an idea in her head it was very, very difficult to dislodge it. This time she stirred a deep hope within me that I barely allowed to climb into my consciousness. Could it possibly be Danny?

When we arrived at the hospital and informed the receptionist why we were there, we were escorted to a bed in a four person room. Danny had the one closest to the window and was staring out it.

I looked at him from the end of the bed. I was beginning to think the impossible was possible.

"Danny," I called softly.

He turned his head slowly toward me.

"Hello, Sam," he said barely above a whisper.

"My God!" I exclaimed. It really is you. You're alive!"

"Am I?" he answered.

"Hi, Danny," said Marjorie enthusiastically.

"Hello, Marjorie," he said dejectedly.

"Well," she said, "you can at least act as if you're glad to see me."

He smiled slightly and nodded his head.

"Would you like to come home with us?" I asked.

"Okay," he said.

It took us over an hour to take care of all the paperwork, but we finally arrived at our house.

We led him up the steps and inside. His gait reminded me of the many zombies I had seen in the movies of my youth — many of them with Danny. He sat down on the sofa and stared off into space while Marjorie and I went into the kitchen to prepare dinner.

We ate mostly in silence. Attempts to engage him in conversation were futile. I even tried telling a few of his own jokes. No smile. No comment.

After dinner, along with some decaffeinated coffee, we had Marjorie's homemade triple chocolate truffle cake, which he often insisted was the closest thing to paradise he had ever tasted. Not even that stirred him.

Eventually, we led him up to our spare room, where he plopped down on the bed, stared up at the ceiling and was asleep within minutes. We decided not to disturb him.

And thus began our efforts at rehabilitating Danny DiVinci.

He stayed with us for about the next four months as we did our best to get him back to the old Danny. After the first week we could actually get a volunteered statement out of him, not simply an answer to a question.

After another we could carry on a basic conversation with him.

By the third week he showed a few signs of returning to his old, flip, funny, sarcastic, ironic self. He was actually beginning to be fun being with, although most of the time he was serious.

Then one evening he turned especially serious. "Do you want to know what really happened to me?" he said.

I looked at him skeptically. "We assume it's what the doctors and shrinks at the hospital surmised," I said, "that you had a case of amnesia, were picked up by a passing boat and somehow and for some unknown reason were dropped back in the water in the same place. You never denied it. "No, I didn't. But that's not what happened. I remember everything quite well. Would you like to hear the true story?"

"Of course," we said together.

"Okay. But I want to tell you right up front that it's absolutely true. It's going to sound impossible, but it's not."

"Danny, my friend," I said, "it's almost impossible that you are here at all, so please tell us."

And he did.

We sat there enraptured for the next few hours while he spoke. When he was finished he asked, "Do you believe me?"

"I don't know," I answered, "but it's a hell of a good explanation for the past months."

"I believe you, Danny," said Marjorie. "I think it's a very wonderful and beautiful story."

"Thank you."

"Danny," I said, "if what you told us is true, and I think it may very well be, it would be valuable to scientific research. Why don't you write it all down?"

"You know I'm not very good at writing. I'm a talker and story teller."

"All right, tell it. I've got a tape recorder. You can just talk into it, and I'll transcribe and type it later. Start from the beginning and tell everything you remember. It will help to get it out of your system, too. It will be good therapy."

And that's exactly what he did over the next two months. As he kept getting further and further into his tale he became more and more like the old Danny.

He worked at it almost every day for at least a few hours. He also spent a lot of time in the public library, and often brought books home with him.

At first I didn't understand the reasons for his selections, but after listening to the tapes I do. I remember subjects such as Viking and other early sailing ships, how they were built and sailed, and navigated with the equipment of their times. There was a book about the primitive Amazon natives and their use of blow guns with poisonous darts, methods of making gun powder, the bows and arrows and spear throwers of primitive peoples, and endless titles on dolphins, whales and other sea mammals; histories of primitive man and evolution of species, geological evolution of the Earth, astronomy, and so fourth.

He also spent a lot of time in what appeared to be meditation. Often Marjorie and I would come home from work and find him in his room sitting in a straight backed chair with his eyes closed, one of the traditional positions for meditation.

But instead of the relaxed expression on his face one would expect in meditation, his facial muscles would be tense, as if he were concentrating very, very hard.

In retrospect we think he was trying to communicate with Alia across the vastness of the cosmos. Was he successful? We'll never know. He never talked about it, and out of respect for his privacy we never asked. Now I wish we had.

One weekend he flew to New York to visit his parents. We had sent all his belongings as well as his bank books to them after his disappearance. They had sent him the money he had in his account along with some of his belongings. This was his first visit to them.

He returned with the Intergalactic Directory and map that Olga had given him. He called the Society to see if they had a new edition and map with his star name and was disappointed to find out that the new editions wouldn't be published until next year, but that the new map was now available. He gave them his name and membership number and asked that it be sent by next day air.

When it arrived he spent hours in his room examining it. Then one evening he came running downstairs, spread it out on the dining room table and called us in to see it.

"Look," he said excitedly, pointing to a tiny star in a distant galaxy on the map. "This is it! This is my star. It's actually a sun you know. And Sea is one of planets orbiting it. It's not shown on the map, but it's there." He was enjoying himself enormously.

The next evening he took us out to dinner at one of our favorite seafood restaurants. When the waiter came for our drinks order, Danny said, "I'll have a Squid Squirt, please."

"I beg your pardon," was the reply.

"Just kidding," he said. "Make that champagne, and bring three glasses."

The waiter returned with the wine, filled our glasses, gave Danny a funny look and departed.

We all raised and clinked our glasses. "A toast," Danny said, "to all three of us and our future lives, to other lives on other planets, and to one in particular. To Sea...."

We all drank up.

When the waiter came to take our food order, Danny said, "I'll have the live baby eels on a bed of picked sea slugs with a side of comatose jelly fish."

"I beg your pardon."

"Just kidding," Danny said.

He was in unusually high spirits all through dinner, told stories and jokes just like the old Danny, even more so. In fact, he would-n't stop talking. I didn't think it was the alcohol — we hadn't drunk that much — and he wasn't on drugs as far as I knew. The next day I found out why.

When dinner was finished, he ordered some more champagne.

When it arrived and was poured he raised his glass. We also raised ours.

"Another toast," he said. "Here's to us, and to you two, my best friends on Earth. May all our dreams come true."

We clicked glasses and drank.

"I'm going on a little trip tomorrow," he announced cheerful-ly. "I don't know when I'll be back, but I want to thank you for everything you have done for me."

"You don't have to thank us, Danny," I said. "We're your friends, and we love you. We only wish you the best."

"I know," he said. "I know."

The next morning when we woke up he was gone. There was a note on his pillow.

"I'm off to see the wizards.

Love you both, always....

Danny"

We never saw or heard from him again.

The newspaper the following day carried a story about a man who rented an open outboard motor boat, drove it out under the Golden Gate Bridge, and was missing.

The empty boat was spotted by the pilot of a private plane who reported it to the Coast Guard.

The Coast Guard searched the sea for the next few days but to no avail. The occupant had disappeared, and he was presumed drowned.

The boat had been rented from a marina. The clerk at the marina had rented it to a man without asking for his driver's license because he gave him a $500.00 deposit. The man gave his name as Bogi Alia.

Marjorie and I believe Danny made it back to Sea.
We hope you do, too.

ISBN 155369553-4